CURSED WOLF

CREATURES OF THE OTHERWORLD

BROGAN THOMAS

CURSED WOLF

CREATURES OF THE OTHERWORLD

BROGAN THOMAS

For more information, address: info@broganthomas.com

Edited by S. Maia Grossman
Cover design by Melony Paradise of Paradise Cover Design

Paperback ISBN: 978-1-8381469-0-0
Hardback ISBN: 978-1-8381469-1-7

First edition August 2020

10 9 8 7 6 5 4 3 2 1

www.broganthomas.com

For my hubby

CHAPTER ONE

Head on my paws, I relax against the sun-dappled grass as the light filters through the trees above. The green light lays dancing patterns across me with the slight breeze. I love the sun on my fur. If I felt genuinely safe, I'm quite sure I would be lying on my back, legs akimbo, doing my best impression of a dead fly with the sun on my tummy.

Sad to say, I haven't felt safe in what feels like forever, and being outside is the best I can achieve.

My name is Forrest. On the bad days, I repeat my name hundreds of times to remind myself that I was a girl once. A girl with green eyes and red hair.

Shit, I have been a wolf longer than I ever was a girl.

"Forrest"—did I imagine her? Some days I wish I had. It would be so much easier to let Forrest go, but I'm stubborn.

God, I hate my life. I bloody hate living with the constant fear of doing the wrong thing. No matter what they do to me, I can't fight back. If I did, they would declare that I'm feral and use it as an excuse to kill me.

It's fucked up.

I do a little stretch, my claws digging into the soft ground, my bum in the air, and then settle back to my noseying. The comforting smell of churned soil surrounds me.

It's ridiculous that a bunch of shifters have the gall to treat me like a bad, unwanted dog. But what did I expect as someone stuck in wolf form?

I think maybe it's a real deep-dark fear that they all have, knowing this could happen to them. One day, shifting into their furry form, and bam, not being able to turn back. Feral, wrong, and needing to be put out of their misery. I guess I can understand why I freak them out.

Why they hate me.

I'm sure they don't realise that I'm me inside, hence the dog treatment. A feral shifter, the nightmare scenario where the animal takes over completely, is an uncommon phenomenon, and it's not something I suffer from—I am not feral. I am the same person I'd be in my human skin. I'm in full control of myself—I am just stuck, and I don't know how to transform back. No one knows how to change me back. My magic is defective, broken.

I huff out a breath. Not being able to communicate is bloody horrible and unbelievably frustrating. Isolation and growing up trapped as a wolf—especially a wolf treated like a literal dog— has been no easy task.

A ladybird lands on my paw. I sniff at it. *Hello, little bug…*I am so fucking lonely, but I would willingly embrace being an outcast if it would mean that they would just leave me alone. Sounds ridiculous, I know. I've learned over the years that my pack doesn't have to like me—hell, I've given up trying. I only wish they didn't take pleasure in hurting me.

The days keep coming, time keeps ticking, the world moves around me, and yet here I am, never changing.

I love this spot underneath the trees, where I remain unseen but can see everything. The Packhouse draws my gaze, the ostentatious monstrosity. Temple House—as it's also called— with its five hundred acres, is located in Singleton, Lancashire. It is an extremely old house my mother built in the 14th century.

Mum was old as shit before she died. Shifters can live thousands of years, and my mum was a hard woman from a different time. She was tough on me and not one to coddle a child. Her focus was on teaching me things to help me survive. It always felt to me as if she raised me out of duty instead of love. Maybe if we had had more time…

Even so, I miss her. I miss my mum so much.

When I was little, my mum was concerned with my safety. Which looking back is ironic, as my mum unknowingly bought my current tormentors into our pack initially to protect us. Magic is commonplace, with all manner of people in our world: shifters, demons, witches, vampires, and an abundance of Fae. But there's a divide among the races—creature versus creature, with pure humans struggling to survive.

As a shifter female, I was rare and coveted—our female birthrate is low. To keep me safe, my pack didn't allow me to go to school. I was home-schooled—or home drilled, as it had felt at times. My mum had not enjoyed teaching me. Her subjects were varied and probably, thinking back, not suitable for a child. But my education was thorough, and by the time I was seven, I could speak several languages and skirmish like a proper demon.

It was kind of tragic that by the time I was nine, I would be unable to ever speak again. My mum was dead and I was stuck in my wolf form.

I hear the cars long before I see them. I lift my head and watch as two black vehicles wind their way up the tree-lined drive.

Oh, here they are, right on time. The Sunday lunch guests. Well, one guest, with her plethora of bodyguards to keep her safe. Not that I see anyone in their right mind trying to kidnap Liz. Ha, if they did, they would give her back pronto.

Liz Richardson. I curl my lip with my contempt. If you spent time with the cow, you'd understand. She's a spoiled purebred wolf shifter with an attitude. Oh, she is all smiles and niceties when she wants something. But toward unimportant people—or in my case, animals—she definitely displays sociopathic tendencies.

Getting out of the car, Liz waves away her three hulking bodyguards as she answers her phone coming towards my hiding place with her mobile against her ear. Liz is dressed in a pretty pale blue summer dress today. The colour matches her eyes, and her brown hair is styled in a perfect bob.

Liz is, unfortunately, Harry's girl. Harry is my stepbrother slash pack member. Can you call someone your stepbrother when both sets of your parents are dead? I give a mental shrug. Anyway, at a year older than me, he was sent away to boarding school when our parents died—perhaps to protect him from the feral wolf shifter at home, to make sure that what I had wasn't catching.

I don't know how many years passed—it is not like I have access to a calendar. Every day feels like a week and every month a year. I've lived a thousand lifetimes in my fur. I grew up fast; I had to. But when Harry came back, my life improved massively with his input. Hugely. I owe a lot to Harry's benevolence. I think I was going insane before Harry came back home to live with the pack.

Shit, I don't want to go back to those years—I would rather die. It still leaves me shaking when I recall them. For a long time, it was—

I shudder, close my eyes, and take an unsteady breath.

I will get to the point: they don't hurt me as much with Harry around. He is my unintentional shield and their conscience.

I open my eyes. Liz is still on the phone, and she's sauntering towards me. Shockingly I can hear a man on the other end. *Ewww, gross*—he is talking absolute filth to her. Oh, and spoiler alert, it isn't Harry on the phone. This is a real problem, as today, from what I have overheard, is the day Harry and Liz are supposed to announce that they're officially mating.

What is Liz doing...oh my God, is she cheating on Harry? Why on earth would she do that?

I scowl and wrinkle my snout with disgust as Liz finishes the call with a giggle. A little growl spills out without my permission, rumbling up from my chest. If I had hands, I would be slapping them against my muzzle about now to muffle that growl. What the heck was that! What was I thinking?

Liz freezes, and her eyes widen.

Her panicked gaze searches the garden and surrounding trees. She catches my eye, and I find myself trapped in her venomous blue glare.

Now would be a good time for the ground to swallow me up. I lower myself further down on my belly, trying desperately to make myself smaller. Liz's expression changes to a confident, cocky sneer. She flashes her teeth at me in a warning.

"Oh, this is cute. Are you spying, dog?" Liz surreptitiously looks around again, and then she smooths her blue dress and picks imaginary lint off the skirt. I have no doubt she's making sure we're alone. "What are you doing out here? Shouldn't you be in a cage somewhere?" She lets out an evil, over-the-top Cruella laugh and starts to strut toward where I'm huddling. "Bet you hate it, don't you, dog? Are you jealous that I'm visiting my mate? That I'm having lunch with your pack? Hell, you're not allowed to grace the floor in my presence. Does it upset you that I'm living my best life while you're rotting away inside? How does it feel, dog, to know that when I join your pack, your days are numbered?" Liz narrows her eyes, stepping off the driveway and into the trees. She saunters closer to me, and the foliage rustles under her ridiculous high heels.

"What you heard just now is none of your business, not that *you* can do anything." She sniffs and rolls her shoulders back. Crossing her arms underneath her breasts, she drops her voice to a whisper. "Between us, dog, the bitten shifter I'm fucking is far more fun than boring Harry." Liz regards the house with a smirk. "To get this estate, I'd mate a troll. Everything that was yours is mine now, dog. So keep out of my way and I might ignore you." She lets out another creepy laugh and glares at me again.

Huh. I tilt my head. I am sort of amazed at her impressive arsenal of nasty looks—Liz can contort her face into so many expressions.

"Fuck it, who am I kidding?" She suddenly screams as though someone's torn off her arm.

I flinch in shock and flatten my ears at the shrill sound. I can barely hear the pounding of feet over her shrilling as the bodyguards come running.

Oh, shit.

I try my best not to panic. I wiggle back into the protection of the trees. Squirming like a worm, I inch slowly back on my belly. *Nothing to see here, scary bodyguards.* I've made a colossal mistake—why did I growl at her? I know better than to be seen, I know better than to react. I know better than to draw attention to myself, especially with this evil woman. Stupid.

As the bodyguards get closer, Liz flaps her arms about dramatically. She then holds her hands to her chest like she's clutching a set of pearls. All the while, she is *still* screaming. Her three guards surround her protectively, and one of them literally picks her up and places her behind his bulk as he searches for the danger.

"It growled at me!" she whimpers feebly. If I weren't so pissed, I'd be rolling my eyes. But my eyes are firmly focused on the bodyguards and the three swords pointed at me. Yes, swords! The three guards have silver swords. Fuckers.

It's a little bit of overkill.

I tremble. I can smell the fear wafting off me. God, I hate being stabbed. I refuse to whine in terror.

I'm still clinging desperately to my tattered pride and sanity.

"What is that doing out? I thought they killed it years ago," one of them grumbles.

"Shame, what a waste, a broken female shifter. She could have been exceptional. Her mother was a beauty."

The huge guy who's blocking Liz from my imaginary threat and my previous fear-inducing growl huffs out a laugh and puts his sword away. He shakes his head. "You were chatting with her a minute ago. Don't think I didn't see you," he reprimands, wagging his finger in Liz's face. Liz grinds her teeth, and her eyes follow his finger as if she wants to bite it off. "You know she doesn't understand what you're saying. This little wolf is too far gone. But she's not dangerous. Otherwise, there's no way the council would allow you to visit." He turns his back on me. "If she were dangerous, she would have done something when you played 'football' with her a few weeks ago." He points the same meaty finger towards the house and propels Liz in that direction. "Get inside! This shit is getting old."

Liz pulls a face and digs her heels into the ground, stopping her forward momentum. I guess she hasn't finished with me yet.

"Football?" the grumbly one repeats incredulously. He too puts away his weapon, and he tilts his head to the side in question.

"Yeah, Liz thought she could kick the poor wolf like a ball." All three of the guys turn and stare at Liz.

"That's not very nice, Liz," the grumbly one chides, shaking his head in disbelief. She shrugs, glaring, probably pissed that someone knows what she did.

The relief I feel at no longer being under their scrutiny is almost cathartic.

I wiggle back a little more. *Please ignore me, please ignore me,* I chant with each wiggle.

"You need to kill it!" Liz swings back, pointing at me, a snarl on her face. I freeze. *Uh-oh, oh shit.* "Give me a sword. Give me a bloody sword. If you're not going to kill it, I will!" The bodyguard closest to me still has his sword in his hand, and Liz attempts to grab it. She manages to get a good hold on his arm. She braces her feet and pulls the sword towards herself with an unladylike grunt.

"Whoa, what are you doing?" says the guard, his eyes wide with panic. They are probably matching my own.

Grabbing Liz not-so-gently by the shoulders, the huge guy turns her away from me again. Holding her elbows, he pins her arms to her sides. Liz struggles and snarls. "Are you nuts!" he shouts. "You could have cut yourself! What is wrong with you?" He shakes her a little. "A small nick and you'd be in a world of pain. You don't mess about with silver!" He's right—enough silver in the system of most creatures and it is fatal.

In shifters, silver stops the shift. As shifters, when we change forms, the magic repairs us at a cellular level. It's the whole part-and-parcel of the magic and the entire reason we live so long. So a small amount of silver in a shifter's system and we're sitting ducks. If you can't shift, you don't heal—or, as I have found out over the years, you heal human-slow.

I use the distraction to slip away.

Shit, that was a close one. God, Liz is such a psycho. I shake off my fear as I run, dodging between the tightly packed trees. Pain shoots up my spine as my lame back legs protest the fast movement. I grit my teeth. The stiff limbs drag slightly behind me, not quite in sync. I follow the line of the driveway, and I slip around to the other side of the house.

Why is she so horrible?

If Liz thinks she can cheat on Harry with a bitten wolf and get away with it—well, she bloody well can't!

What I can do, though, I have no idea—but Harry can't mate with her. Liz will break his heart. Shifters mate for life—when you mate, you form a bond. It's a beautiful, sacred thing. Better I fix this now rather than have Harry find out later.

I need a plan.

I need Liz's phone.

CHAPTER TWO

I have a rough plan that involves sneaking into the Packhouse, a house I haven't been inside for years.

The back door is open—if that isn't a good omen, I don't know what is—and I creep inside. My nostrils flare as I catch the cloying, multilayered scent of the pack. It makes me shiver, and my hackles rise. The polished wood floor creeks. I freeze. My gaze darts about. My heart is pounding so hard, I wouldn't be surprised if it left my chest and splatted onto the ceiling.

What the hell am I doing…My mouth fills with sour saliva, and I clamp my muzzle closed. God, I hope I don't puke. It would be simple, easy, to turn around, go back outside with my tail between my legs and forget I ever thought of doing this. This is a stupid idea.

Stupid stupid stupid.

I've got this crazy notion rattling around in my head, to go out in a blaze of glory. The Bon Jovi song fills my head, and I silently hum along. Motivated, I quickly pad down the wide hallway, the beat in my head. I sneak into the dining room. I manage to get myself safely behind the dining room curtains without further freaking out.

The dense, old-fashioned red and gold curtains hang in front of a beautiful square bay window. I know from other sneaky endeavours as a child that they hide me and my scent well.

I take the opportunity to rub myself along the fabric in a vain hope that my fleas will jump off and disperse around the house, infesting the pack. Yeah, I have fleas. Plain old non-magical ones that drive me mad with the itching. My body is full of scrapes and sores. A particularly painful one at the back of my neck continually throbs. I can smell the infection as the pus oozes into my surrounding fur—I can't reach the spot. I'm falling to pieces. At least my coat isn't matted. The manky dirty, flea-ridden fur sheds without issue.

As I wait, I berate myself. Why on earth did I growl? I will be punished later. By the time lunch is over, Liz will have convinced the pack that I took a chunk out of her or something equally dramatic. It's irrelevant that Liz wanted to go all stabby on me. That growl could be the one thing that tips them over the edge. I swallow. I am the idiot who put myself in that situation in the first place. Now I'm going one step further. Here I am hiding in the dining room, trying my best to put the final nail in my coffin. And I call Liz a psycho…

I blow out a breath. I care about Harry. Harry matters to me; his happiness matters. If I can keep Harry from making a mistake with Liz, irrespective of what happens to me, it will be worth it…

God, I am absolutely nuts! I've finally lost it. I have to be honest with myself: if I do this, there's a big chance that they're going to kill me.

I lie down. My back legs make it too painful for me to stand for extended periods. I try to swallow the lump in my throat. The truth is painful to admit—but I can't live like this anymore. I'm barely surviving. I might as well die for something.

If I'm going to do this, I am going to own this shit.

I focus on the times when Harry intervened on my behalf. Maybe he doesn't remember his interference, but I do. What he did matters to me.

What type of person would I be if I rewarded his kindness by turning my back on him? Horrible people shouldn't get away with doing bad things just because they can. If good people don't do anything, then that makes them as bad. I know that's probably a very naïve way of thinking about things. You've got to remember, I'm not worldly.

I'm a memory of a girl.

I first met Harry when I was six years old and Harry, his two older, nastier brothers Vincent and Jason, and my new stepfather Dave came to live with my mum and me. When my mum became pregnant with Grace, our little sister, our pack of two suddenly became a pack of seven. My eyes fill with tears. *Grace—*

"So, no babies yet?" The clunking of Liz's heels on the wooden floor follows her snide question as she enters the dining room. I freeze—I didn't even hear them coming. Sloppy. "Being a human mate"—Liz sniffs, the distaste evident in her voice—"you would think you'd be trying. You don't want to miss the boat. You humans die so easily. Or has Vincent decided to wait for a pureblood female to be available? Let's be honest, your children would be next to useless—no offence—apart from the slight strength increase and a few more years added to a pathetic lifespan. They can't even shift. I see no point in anyone breeding with you." *What a cow.* Liz is talking to Beth. Beth intelligently remains silent.

I mentally grumble.

Liz is such a hypocrite—it's okay for her to have a bitten lover. Bitten shifters—turned human's who are always male—don't shift.

Like I said before, female wolf shifters are very rare. Female shifters are treasured, as only one in a thousand shifters are born female. Male shifters like Vincent have no choice but to mate with other races, as no one wants to live alone. Vincent is fortunate to have Beth as his mate.

15

"It looks good on you, by the way—the extra weight."
Ugg, Liz is such a liar. Beth is gorgeous. I like Beth. When
Vincent is out, she leaves the television on in the kitchen so
that I can watch it through the window. She also plays
music loudly so I can hear from the garden.

My thoughts drift to my estranged biological brother,
John. I wonder if he has a mate and any children. John is a
super-shifter, a hellhound—"hellhound" is a name given to
all fire shifters, gifted with magic. The ability is rare, and
only a few male shifters get to that level of power. My
brother is a total badass. He's the hero type you send in to
save the world. Shifters have long lifespans and are difficult
to kill, but shifters do die and all that's left of my bloodline
today is John and myself. Yeah, go John. No pressure—our
bloodline now rests on his shoulders. It isn't like I am going
to be of any use. I won't be popping out any babies.

I glance down at my dirty paws and sigh.

While I've been reflecting and not paying attention—again,
highlighting that I'm not in the right frame of mind—I have
missed the rest of the pack's arrival. They have already taken their
seats around the dining table. The clink of plates, the soft murmur
of conversation, and the smell of food drifts underneath the curtain.

The smell makes my stomach cramp. I am always so
hungry and God, it smells good. I take a deep breath in and
briefly close my eyes in appreciation. *Mmmm.* I learned a
trick many years ago: when I smelled delicious food, I'd
close my eyes and imagine I'm eating it—the taste, the

texture in my mouth. I don't even know if my imaginary food tastes the same as food in real life. I'm sure mine is way better. I nod my furry head with conviction.

Come on, Forrest, get a grip. I take a steadying breath, trying my best not to disturb the curtain with my muzzle. I peek through a gap. I need to see where everyone is sitting.

Okay, Harry is seated next to Liz, and he's sitting with his back to me. His blond hair brushes the collar of his smart blue shirt. He needs a haircut. On Harry's right is Jason. Vincent is opposite Liz with Beth.

Vincent. My stomach tightens. He is the oldest of the brothers. He is my torturer, my tormentor, and will be the man who ultimately murders me. The monster has been killing parts of me slowly for years. He was initially assigned by my mother to protect me. Vincent and Jason were supposed to be my bodyguards. I huff. Instead, when my circumstances changed, they became my prison guards and self-appointed abusers. They're both tall and bulky, with dark hair and eyes. Jason's eyes are almost black. He is so creepy. The dread I experience when they're near is like a living thing.

I can't do this if I look at them or think about them—I will lose my nerve. I take another shaky breath and focus on the job at hand. I wrangle the butterflies in my tummy. They feel like they're going to climb out of my throat and take flight.

Luck is with me, as Liz is sitting in front of my hiding spot. The phone is sitting at the end of the table next to her fork. My whole focus of attention switches to the phone and planning my next move.

So it takes me a while to tune in to the conversation, and I wish in a way I hadn't. The members of the caring, sharing pack are all talking about killing me.

Yay, fun times.

Liz places her hand on Harry's arm and pats it. "I've chosen you to be my mate. I could have chosen anybody. But I chose you, Harry. I've said that I will live with your pack—join your family, as the humans quaintly say. We're going to be mated, and our future children will not be growing up in a home with a feral wolf. Harry, it's getting ridiculous." She fake-shudders and pouts annoyingly. "Every time I visit, the savage attacks me! It is dangerous and should be put to sleep." Huh, "put to sleep." *Really? Why not say what you mean, Liz. Dead.* Not that she has anyone to disagree with her, apart from Harry and a silent, wide-eyed Beth. "I am sure we can convince the brother to let it go. He doesn't care about it, anyway. With enough evidence, the council will sign off on it." I am surprised she doesn't say, "It's either the dog or me." Liz sadly smiles. Wow, not only does she have an arsenal of horrible looks, but it seems as if she has a catalogue of impressive fake smiles as well. "You are selfish and cruel. Insisting on keeping that thing alive when it would be much better—" Harry is shaking his head, and I guess he's about to reply when Liz's phone rings.

Oh my.

My muscles tighten in readiness. I know it's the filthy talker—it's the same ringtone.

I make my move.

I have seconds to somehow get to the phone.

Between one breath and the next, I spring from behind the curtains.

All I can hear is my panting and my heart pounding. With more focus then I have given anything else in my life, I home in on the handset.

I need to get this right. This might be the last thing I ever do, and I need to make it count. I ignore the pain in my back legs. I just need to…My hand lands on the phone, and I press the screen to answer. With another swipe of my finger, the phone is miraculously on the loudspeaker.

"Liz babe, when are you coming back to bed. I need you…" I smile with satisfaction as the male voice echoes around the room. *Ooops, no talking yourself out of that one, Liz.* Bingo, *I got the cow,* boom, *take that, Liz. Eat your heart out, Liz Richardson.*

Everyone but Harry is ignoring the phone. I wince. Poor Harry.

They are all staring at me. *Uh-oh.* Vincent has an evil look in his narrowed eyes.

Uh-oh. Oh no.

I wobble. My legs shake as I back away from the table. My hands lift in the age-old sign of peace. I didn't touch Liz, just the phone.

HANDS. Oh my God. I let out a squeak of fright.

Oh my God!

I glance down at the tiny hands, so pale they seem transparent. My *hands*. They are no longer paws!

CHAPTER THREE

The whole table erupts into shouting. Everybody is trying to speak at once. Shit shit shit. I freak out.

I run. Adrenaline floods my veins as I make a wobbly run for the door—a wobbly naked dash. I am so not hanging about.

I think I am in shock. No. No, I know I am in shock. Did they kill me? I bounce off the wall as I run into the hall. I almost fall, but my momentum keeps me upright. I huff out a pain-filled breath. Ow. Nope, still alive.

The shouting from the dining room is getting worse, and the three bodyguards—yes, the ones with the swords!—are rushing to the dining room from the kitchen nearby.

I keep going. Please don't see me, please don't see me. They start shouting at me to stop. Oh crap, they have seen me!

I do the most sensible thing I've done today. On instinct, on the way past the hallway table, I grab the house phone. I bounce into the toilet door and manage to get the door open. I fling myself into the tiny bathroom, slam the solid oak door behind me, and hit the lock.

Wow, who knew I had that in me?

My whole body is shaking, and my heart is pounding. I gasp. God, I can't breathe.

Running on two legs is not fun—how the hell do people balance?

My wobbly legs give out, and I slide down the closed door onto the cold, tiled floor. I shiver. I never thought I'd miss my fur...I feel so bloody cold. I pull my knees to my chest and grip the phone.

The door shudders behind me. I squeak in fright and almost drop the landline. Someone wants in here desperately. Shit shit shit. Thank God the shuddering door is solid oak and not made from a lighter wood.

I have no option but to ring my brother John. I hope he will come now—now that I'm human again. I do my best to focus and dial.

How many times have I imagined this moment...

I mentally cross everything that he still has the same mobile number. One by one, the digits pop into my head. It takes over a dozen attempts to get the right sequence, as the banging on the door is seriously disconcerting and my fingers are like useless noodles.

The phone rings, it rings and rings.

Please pick up. Please pick up.

"What! Why are you ringing from this number?" comes a gruff, angry voice.

I open my mouth to speak, and nothing bloody comes out. I want to say John's name. But I can't. Oh my God, I can't talk! My hand not holding the phone flies to my throat and my heart skips a beat.

Finally, frustratingly, I say "J—" But it's more like a puff of breath rather than a letter or word. No no no. I whine in frustration.

"Forrest? Forrest, is that you?" His tone of voice changes, gentles. Somehow he knows. My brother knows! I manage another soft whine. "I am on my way. I will be with you in just…in under an hour. Are you safe? Is the pack with you? Why haven't they called me? Shit, never mind." His soft tone of voice disappears. "What the fuck is that noise!" The banging on the bathroom door must have registered. "Is someone trying to hurt you? I am on my way. Stay on the phone. Do not shift back. Do you hear me? Do not shift back!" There's a muffled shout, like he is half-covering the phone. "Owen, get one of them on your phone now! Forrest is back. Yes, now, damn it." He comes back to me. "Hey princess, are you in your room? Somewhere safe? I am bringing Doctor Ross. Everything is going to be okay—"

I pull the phone away from my ear and squint at it incredulously.

Everything is going to be okay? Really? I have scary bodyguards…or is it the pack banging on the door at my back? Their screams echo in the hallway. I swallow back tears.

My brother is coming…

The pack wants me dead.

My brother is coming…

I feel lightheaded. I whine, and my bottom lip trembles.

The same estranged brother that I haven't seen since I shifted. John dropped me off like an unwanted puppy, and off he went to save the world without a backward glance, leaving me with monsters.

Am I safe? No, I am not bloody safe. I've never been safe, and I doubt it will ever be okay. I clamp my lips closed and hold in a sob that wants to wrench itself from my throat. I hug my knees.

The noise level in the hall drops, and finally I can make out individual voices.

"She rang John. Fuck! The hounds are on the way."

"Are you sure that's Forrest? Didn't she have ginger hair?"

"Fuck's sake, get away from that door! You will scare her and then John will rip your throats out. Get the fuck away."

This is all too much.

"Go sort your female out. Liz is no longer welcome at this time. We will deal with this problem first. Thank you for your assistance, but this is no longer your concern as you aren't members of this pack." I shudder at Vincent's smooth voice. I think he's speaking to Liz's bodyguards.

Is Vincent getting everyone away so that he can come in here and kill me? Surely he can't, now that John is on his way? Visions of Vincent crashing through the door with a silver sword make me shudder. I bite my arm to stop myself from crying out.

"Liz, don't say a word, we're leaving," says the gruff voice of the big bodyguard. "The only job you had to do was land a well-connected mate. Produce the next generation. You can't even do that properly without fucking it up. Wait until we get home—you will be lucky to leave your room. Father will be selling your ass to the highest bidder. You better hope that we don't find that guy who called you…" His angry voice fades away.

There's shuffling, stomping, and finally, blessed silence. I think everyone has left.

"It is okay, urm…Forrest. You don't have to come out. Liz—"

Everyone but Harry.

There's rustling as if he's running his hand through his blond hair. I can picture it, as I've seen him do that hundreds of times. He lets out a puff of air. "Liz left. It's over. She was cheating. I can't…I can't trust her anymore. The phone call, you did that. You did that for me. God, it hurts. I feel sick. I am sure other shifters wouldn't care, but I'd rather be alone than that." The door squeaks—he must be leaning against it. I let out a whine, and I bang my head against the closed door in frustration. I can't talk. I can't console him.

After a few minutes, I wiggle about, trying to get comfortable. My bottom is hurting. The floor is hard, and my bum is bony. It's going numb, like the rest of me.

Glancing around the room, I spot the mirror above the sink. It feels like it's miles away from my slumped position on the floor.

But I get the most overwhelming urge. I need to see.

I don't know how I manage to get off the floor. The phone falls, forgotten.

I wobble on my feet. I brace myself against the narrow walls. My useless toes scrabble, trying to get a grip on the tiles. I lunge and grab hold of the sink. I hold on to it. Lift my head and look.

Hello Skeletor...My face is gaunt, and my features are way too big for my face. My eyes are huge and wide with shock. My left eye is an unnatural gold, and my right eye is almost gold apart from a sliver of green pooling at the bottom of my iris. The green sits at the bottom of my eye unevenly, practically taken over by the gold. But it is green. The green I didn't imagine in my head. The green I dreamed of.

I touch my forehead to the mirror.

Oh, and my hair, it's not red. No, it's a shocking shade of pink. I huff out a breath. I am a skull with hair, fucking pink hair and freaky eyes. Fuck my life.

Harry is continuing to talk to me from the door, and John is still talking on the phone. But it's all white noise. I am so overwhelmed. Even in my human form, I am not normal.

My skin is so pale it's translucent, the blue of my veins standing out. The black of my dog collar stands out on my pale neck. I don't understand how it shifted with me—it must be the magic in the collar. The rest of me, my body...I am supposed to be an adult, but my tiny childlike frame is hideous.

I let out a silent sob that hurts my chest. I am repulsive.

CHAPTER FOUR

I am sitting on the closed toilet seat. I have used the available hand towels as padding underneath my bony bum—not that that is much use. My skeletal body aches.

It feels like hours since I called John. The phone is still on the floor by the door, abandoned. I can't make myself get up and grab it to check if he's still on the line. I can no longer hear him from where I am perched.

The constant pain from my long-ago shattered pelvis has gone, and my skinny legs show no signs of the poorly healed trauma. I'm shaking, and the toilet seat is squeaking in protest.

I don't know if all this is a dream; it doesn't feel real.

Emotionally I feel like an autumn leaf: dead but still

clinging desperately to the branch and dreading the next gust of wind.

When the knock on the door comes, I start, burning my leg on the radiator next to me. I let out a little hiss between my teeth. Bloody hell, this still isn't a dream.

"Forrest, it's me, your brother. Can you open the door for me, please."

I peer at the door and nibble on my bottom lip. I take a deep breath and pull myself to my feet, using the wall and the toilet as leverage. I find it challenging to place my feet onto the floor. They want to curl inwards instead of staying flat.

Ha, it's a bloody miracle, and it's thanks to a shitload of adrenaline that I managed to get this useless bag of bones into the bathroom in the first place.

I'm pathetic.

I grit my teeth and use the wall to steady myself. I decide that I have little choice but to chuck myself at the door and hope for the best.

Oof. I hit the door with a thump. Once I am steady and in no danger of falling, I attempt a little bit of modesty. I pull the horrendous pink hair forward to conceal as much of my body as I can. Weirdly, the hair is mega thick and long—it reaches halfway down my thighs.

My fingers fumble with the lock, and it takes a few attempts to get the door open. The heavy door swings open with an ominous creak.

I nervously peek up through my hair at the huge man in

the doorway. I probably resemble a pink Cousin Itt from the Addams family. John, my brother, is broader and taller than the door frame—he dwarfs me. John has to hunch over slightly to see into the small bathroom. He towers over me, frowning as his green eyes quickly take me in. He doesn't look impressed. I have a massive urge to close the door and lock it.

"You didn't bother to get her any clothes?" John asks, directing his question behind him.

"Well…urm, I can grab something of mine—Forrest hasn't got anything," Harry answers quietly. "I am sorry. I didn't think."

There's the sound of movement in the hallway. My brother moves slightly to the side of the door, and a man appears next to him. He grunts and slips a backpack from his shoulder. Unzipping the bag, he hands my brother some clothing.

John steps towards me but then freezes in place. Total horror crosses his face. I flinch. Without my seeing him move, he has Harry by the throat, pinned to the hallway wall.

Shit! What did I do?

"You put a fucking dog collar on my sister!" John growls menacingly into Harry's face.

"Not me—Vincent," Harry sputters, going red and desperately clawing at the big hand around his throat.

I freak out.

My fight-or-flight must have kicked in, as I am trembling with the adrenaline rushing through me.

Heart pounding, I can't get enough air into my lungs. I take a step back.

I'm going the wrong way. I should be trying to stop my brother from hurting Harry. What am I doing? But I can't stop. I can't even stand up properly. I'm too weak. This body is too alien. Knowing all that still doesn't stop me from feeling disgusted with myself. I am a coward.

Even worse, I scramble to close the door. The shifter with the backpack blocks me. "John, now is not the time— you're frightening your sister," he says. John's head snaps around, and he drops his hold on Harry. Harry takes big gulps of air. His face is red, and he's shaking.

I'm so sorry, Harry. This is all my fault. God, I'm surprised he didn't wet himself—that scared the crap out of me. A hellhound grabs hold of your throat like that, I would sure pee a little.

"I will be talking to Vincent later," John says, shoving Harry back into the wall. Harry nods, dropping his eyes. "Now fuck off." Harry visibly deflates. He nods, keeping his eyes fixed on the floor submissively. *Please don't go!* I mentally scream as I watch Harry shuffle down the hallway. He disappears from my line of sight.

I dimly notice the other two hulking shifters, who must have arrived with John and the Backpack Hound, and they're all staring at my neck.

I jolt with the sudden realisation; I want to scream at them, *Bloody hell, still naked here, guys!* I weakly tug at the bathroom door. The hellhound's foot is in the way.

John steps back in my direction, a soft smile on his face...it looks wrong. It's that kind of smile that a predator gives its prey just before he starts eating.

Shit, he's scary.

I need to trust him. But he's scary.

He is my brother...but he left me here to rot.

My conflicting thoughts make me feel as if my head is going to pop off.

"It is okay, Forrest. It's okay." He holds both hands up to me in supplication. I flinch. "I'm sorry, sweetheart, that I lost my temper. I will try my best not to do that again. I am sorry. I want to help you get into these clothes, okay? They're going to be a little big on you, but we will make them work, right?" John's voice is soft. The backpack-shifter hands him the clothing that he dropped while attacking Harry. John holds up his hand, the one that isn't holding the clothing, towards me. I warily eye it. "Is that okay?"

I want to shake my head no.

I know I can't do any of this by myself. There's no way I will leave this house alive without his help.

I reluctantly nod.

John puts the black jumper over my head, and then, like he's dressing a child, threads his hand through the sleeve. Taking hold of my wrist, John gently guides my hand out. He repeats the process with my other arm. He then kneels in front of me and helps me with the black jogging bottoms. The clothing is ridiculously huge.

"Okay, let's get you to your bedroom. Doctor Ross can meet us and check you over." John turns and strides away down the hallway, expecting everybody to follow. I take a wobbling step forward and find myself tipping to the right. Before I can fall, the Backpack Hound scoops me up in his arms. I tense and let out a horrified squeak of surprise.

"Oh, hush now, Forrest, you're okay, I promise I'm not gonna hurt you. I promise that I'm not gonna let anyone else hurt you either—that includes you. You're gonna hurt yourself if I let you walk. So let me help you, at least until you get your legs figured out again," he says in a low, soft tone. He surprises another squeak out of me by gently stroking my hair away from my face. His humongous hands pull the mass of hair around so that it's in front of me. It pools in my lap like candyfloss. "Hush…this is hard, isn't it? Everything that is happening is some scary shit. Please …please let me help you." His steady grey eyes are weirdly comforting; they stand out against his dark hair and skin tone. His whole expression is kind, and I believe him. "I don't know what you've been through…I know you can't talk about it. Heck, you do all of your talking with those big frightened gold eyes. Sometimes, it's better to bury the bad things until you're strong enough to deal with them, so that you can keep moving forward one step at a time to make sure your demons can't keep up. You understand?" I blink at him. "Okay?" I take a big breath, release it, and nod. Miraculously I let myself relax, and I lean into his massive chest as he lumbers down the hallway with me tucked safely in his arms.

We follow in the wake of my brother. Within minutes, we're at my bedroom door. It's kind of surreal as I haven't seen this room in, well, forever.

CHAPTER FIVE

I sit on the bed and glance around my old bedroom; I can't remember it being so big. It smells of dust and forgotten memories.

Everything is exactly how I left it: books on the shelves, an abandoned notepad on the table next to the bed. I was never allowed to put up posters. My mum was convinced that they would mark the walls. But if I had, they would still be here.

The room is like a time capsule.

I glimpse a silver photo frame alone on a shelf, surrounded by a thick layer of dust. It's a photo of my mum, my baby sister Grace, and me. If I could walk, I would pick it up, maybe hold it close to my chest, pull it to my nose and never stop staring at it. God, I miss them so much.

For my sanity, I force myself to look away.

Everything in here feels like someone else's life, another girl's life; it doesn't belong to me anymore.

Doctor Ross doesn't look like what I imagined. He's dressed in black fatigues like the other hellhounds, and there is no white coat in sight. With his big build, bald head, and intelligent blue eyes, he looks like a soldier.

He isn't messing around, with his extensive array of medical equipment. It's like he has brought a whole hospital with him. I have no idea why we're doing this here. This is crazy. If they're attempting to make me feel comfortable in familiar surroundings, they're doing a piss-poor job. We would be better off in the garden or far, far away from this accursed house.

The collar is removed immediately from my neck. Doctor Ross examines it, and he dictates his findings into some sort of magical video-camera-and-fancy-tablet combo. John has to leave the room for a few minutes to get control of himself when they realise that the collar is an electric shock one.

How do you stop a wolf from running away? You snap their pelvis like a Polo mint. Then you put a magical collar on them that knocks them out if they crawl too far. The fancy collar is also voice-activated and can be electrified as punishment if they don't come to call like a good doggy—yeap, fun times.

Doc R uses a complicated-looking scanner to take my vitals. He waves the thing at me and it automatically processes my height, weight, heartbeat, blood pressure, and body fat. Samples of my blood and saliva are taken and added to the data. Huh, it even produces a little chart of me on the screen. It flashes red, and my eyes widen as it beeps an urgent tone. That doesn't sound good. Doc R frowns at the screen and taps the device until it's silenced. He then examines my eyes. He uses a small penlight scanner that flashes various lights, making me dizzy. He's so close to me that our noses almost touch. Luckily his breath is minty.

My head pounds and my eyes hurt.

"Have your eyes always been this colour?" he asks me. I shake my head no.

"Forrest's eyes were the same colour green as my own. Her hair was red, and if I correctly remember, she was around the same height as she is now. Maybe an inch or two shorter before she shifted," John replies on my behalf.

"That is interesting. What age was your first shift?" Doc R asks. I start to hold up my fingers to answer him, but frustratingly I can't seem to get the digits to work, so again John explains for me.

"She was nine."

"Nine years old...that is extremely young. I've never heard anybody shifting before sixteen." Doc R turns away and adds everything to the tablet. "How long has it been since she first shifted?"

Well, that's the question of the day, isn't it? How long have I been stuck as a wolf? I observe John, terrified of his answer.

I hold my breath.

John clears his throat and rubs the back of his neck. We make eye contact. His eyes are sad. "It's been over fourteen years."

The room goes a little black, and I see black spots in front of my eyes. I am glad to be sitting down; otherwise, I think I'd be falling on my bum.

Fourteen years.

Fourteen.

"Breathe, Forrest. You're okay."

I gasp in a breath and rapidly blink. I focus on the kind grey eyes that are looking back at me with concern.

The Backpack Hound is holding my face in his hands. When did that happen? I nod. I am okay. I am okay. All I can do is nod. I take another shaky breath.

Fourteen years as a wolf. Shit shit shit.

The kind hellhound nods back at me, gives me a small smile, stands from his squat, and steps away.

Both Doc R and John gaze at me with concern.

"Forrest, are you all right to continue?" I nod at the doctor—bloody hell, stop nodding, you look like a bobblehead, your head is going to pop off. I instead give him a shaky thumbs-up. "Well, hopefully I can give you a little bit of control so you know what is happening to you. Okay?" He places the fancy tablet in my hands. Even though it's lightweight, I can't hold it up. I prop the tablet on my lap; it digs into my thigh.

The text swims slightly in front of my eyes as I try to focus on the words. It takes a few seconds for my brain to adjust. The data, the words, make zero sense.

"You are emaciated. I'm unsure why that is, at the moment. We will have to talk about your diet, as you're missing essential vitamins and minerals. I have never seen these kinds of dangerous results in a shifter." He looks at me sternly, and I find myself physically leaning away from him. Not my fault. "It is very concerning. If you hadn't shifted today, I calculate that you wouldn't have lasted much longer. The results sho—"

"What?" John barks. I flinch, and the tablet tumbles onto the bed. "I don't understand why. What do you mean, she 'wouldn't have lasted much longer'? Forrest? What the hell have you been doing to yourself!" John's whole face morphs as he bares his teeth. His rage, directed at me, fills the room. I sit frozen on the bed as the massive hellhound barrels towards me; a deep growl resonates in his chest. My lips disappear between my teeth, and I bite down hard to stop the whine that's bubbling up in my throat. It's better to be silent. I avert my eyes. I shove the tablet further away, and I attempt to make myself smaller. I hunch in on myself, using my hair as a shield. I avert my face close my eyes and prepare for the pain.

When nothing happens, I peek through my hair, and the Backpack Hound is standing directly in front of me, rigid, blocking John. I blow out a breath. Wide-eyed, I take in the situation. Is he…is he protecting me?

"I made a promise. What are you planning to do, John?" he admonishes.

"I wasn't going to hurt her," John snarls. He turns and stomps back across the room, his fists clenched at his sides, his shoulders tight and a muscle ticking in his jaw. "I'm too fucking busy to deal with this shit—if she wants to kill herself, she can crack on."

The Backpack Hound silently moves back to his position against the wall as if nothing happened.

Bloody hell, what…why is John angry with me? He left me here with them. It was John who didn't come back…as if I had a choice in what I ate?

Betrayed. That's what I feel, which is ludicrous. For there to be betrayal, there has to be trust, and I don't trust John.

I study my trembling hands. Wow, pack doesn't mean anything to my brother. I don't mean anything. What was John going to do if the other hellhound hadn't stood in front of me? Hit me? I was right not to trust him. I puff out a breath. I don't feel the need to scream or shout my case. Not that I can…I curl inward, a familiar feeling of inadequacy piling up inside of me. John is never going to believe me over them, so if I could talk, there would be no point—it would be a waste of words. I tense to ward off the full-body shakes and lift my chin.

Doc R, looking pained, clears his throat. "Well, it is something we will have to make a priority. From now on you will be heavily monitored, to find the cause." He drops another stern look at me. "Theoretically, being stuck in your wolf form should not have affected your growth rate." He leans over and retrieves the tablet. I flinch away, and the doctor grimaces. He steps back, clears his throat, and continues, "Your height, according to previous estimates on your medical charts as a child, should be at least six-foot. Unfortunately, as you can see in the data—" Doc R points to the screen—"you are five-foot-two, and approximately three stone underweight. Your build is also a concern—you would be small for a human, and as a shifter, it's unheard-of to be so petite." He shakes his head in disappointment. "With weight gain your overall body aesthetic can be enhanced. We can't do anything to improve your bone structure and height. It is permanent damage—at twenty-three, there is no fixing that any further." He pokes the screen again. My eyes cross. I don't bother to focus on the data. "Your eye- and hair-colour is a side effect of long-term magical damage," Doc R continues. "Shifters are not meant to be in animal form for so long. There should be a balance within us—no shifter can stay in animal form indefinitely, or the other way around, and not shift—which is even worse. To have lasted fourteen years and not lost yourself is impressive." Doc R taps the tablet again. "I am sure we will work it out as we go along. The good news is, we can improve your body weight with a controlled diet. Your natural healing will help. Unfortunately, your eyes will remain as they are, an amber-gold colour with the slight sectoral heterochromia." He points to my right eye. "Although I think your eyes are quite beautiful," Doc R says with a smile. "Your skin will improve with daylight exposure and a better-balanced diet. Your hair pigment has gone—again, a similar reaction to that of your eyes." He tilts his head to the side. "I am surprised it is pink and not white." He looks at John and then back at me. John is standing as far away as he can get. He must hate me.

"What I do recommend is hospitalisation for a few weeks." Doc R holds up a hand as if he expects me to object. "Just to get you healthy, walking, and talking. You need specialised help. Let's get you back to normal, okay?" He smiles.

I dare to peek at John, and he stiffly nods. So I nod also.

I am up for anything to get me out of this bloody house.

Fuck my life. I don't even look like a shifter. I look like an unhealthy human. It couldn't be that I was just stuck in wolf form for fourteen years. Oh no, when fate, that fickle bitch, finally allows me to change back to my human form, I'm an even bigger freak! I'm never going to blend into shifter society looking like this.

Rage and hopelessness fill me. My vision goes hazy.

I feel sick, my mouth is dry, and there's a lump in my throat that I can't swallow.

I close my eyes and simply breathe.

Shit, listen to me moaning. I need a slap. I need to get a grip on myself. I can handle this calmly. The rage can't have me. I am human-shaped—forget the height thing, forget the hair and the eyes. I am me: every cloud and all that crap.

Today I promised myself that I was going to own this shit. It's a billy bonus that I'm alive and that I'm getting away from this house and the pack. I'm getting out of this shithole, and I'm never coming back.

I should be dancing with joy, not whining like a baby.

I open my eyes. Doc R and John are whispering in the corner of the room. The Backpack Hound—whose name I still don't know, as John has yet to introduce us—is looking around my room, quietly sniffing. I tip my head to the side, curious. What is he doing?

"John, the only scent of Forrest is from today," he says quietly. Oh wow, he is a smart one. "If this is her room, why can't I smell her?"

As a unit, all three shifters turn and stare at me. Wow, they're synchronised. An old Take That song plays in my head. I wonder, can they do it again to music? I want to cackle maniacally.

Well, gentlemen, I want to say, it's because this hasn't been my room for fourteen years, obviously.

CHAPTER SIX

We are going on a bizarre treasure hunt, like a bunch of scary pirates. Everyone is now fascinated and focused on finding out where I sleep. I'm back in Backpack Hound's arms, and like a helpful interactive treasure map, I point the way to my room.

I can hear John's teeth grind harder and more loudly as we leave the house and go further into the grounds. Come on, I want to say. You don't have to be Einstein to realise it's shit. Hello, magical dog collar.

I am kind of amused in a manic, sick sort of way at how upset they all are when we arrive, crammed into the small, dark garage. The garage is set away from the main house.

It's a modern metal one, which makes it extra cold in winter and extra toasty in summer. It was purchased just for me.

I think what is causing all the drama is the main feature of the room: the silver cage that sits in the middle of the concrete floor, with the creepy drain in the centre.

Even in my human form, I can smell my scent in the air. It permeates the building—ahh, home sweet home.

"Get Vincent," my brother says quietly. "Get Vincent here now." One of his guys disappears, and we are left looking silently at the cage. Well, they're staring; I've seen this shit before.

My Chauffeur Hound—formerly known as Backpack Hound—is standing in the corner with me still in his arms. He's standing as far away as he can from the cage. He is holding me a little more tightly to his chest and is unconsciously running his fingers through my hair. It feels nice, the hand in my hair. Everything else hurts. Being held hurts. I am bony, and every bone feels like it's touching every other bone and somehow grinding together. It isn't a pleasant feeling, but I try my best to ignore it.

My brother is standing like a statue. I never thought I'd say that someone is radiating fury, but John is. He's pissed. Boy, is he pissed.

Oh, oh…My eyes widen.

Wait a minute…I blink. Yes, John's hands are on fire. Blue flames dance across his skin. Oh crap, John is radiating not just emotionally...my brother is on fire like, literally.

Wow. The warm garage is even getting hotter. The lack of air makes me yawn.

Wary I peer up at the hellhound holding me. Shit, I hope he isn't suddenly going to burst into flames.

I tense in the hellhound's arms as Vincent is shoved unceremoniously into the garage five minutes later. The guy who went to fetch him wipes his hands on his fatigues with blatant disgust and steps back outside, blocking the exit. Seeing Vincent here in the place where he regularly used to hurt me...I can't stop the trickle of fear.

I don't want to be in here with Vincent. I don't want to be here at all.

I screw my eyes shut and count silently down from ten.

Be brave. I'm pretty much shitting myself.

Be brave. There's not a thing I can do about any of this.

Be brave. I'm along for the ride.

The worst is behind me and I can do this, I can control myself. The worst is behind me, and my world has changed. They see me again. I'm a girl again.

Don't look back; keep moving forward. Surely Vincent can't hurt me while the hellhounds are here? That bone-deep fear I have lived with forever slowly changes into something a little more manageable.

Be brave. I can do this. I open my eyes.

No one is speaking.

The overhead strip-light buzzes in the silence, and the heat from John's magic makes the sheet metal pop and clang.

The thick dust-filled cobwebs hanging from the roof trusses sway. The minutes tick away.

John eyes the cage. Vincent nervously watches John. It's the first time I have seen Vincent nervous. A bead of sweat runs down the side of his face.

Well, this is awkward.

Doc R steps forward and inspects the cage. He's too big to enter the actual enclosure, and he's careful not to graze the silver bars. Crouching, he pays particular attention to the stained floor. The magical camera he used in my examination is recording. It bobs about in the air, following his movements.

I peek back at John as he struggles for control over his fire magic. His body shakes with the effort, and his eyes are closed. The blue flames weirdly drip from his hands onto the concrete at his feet—the flames hiss and spark. I've never seen my brother struggle with his fire magic before. Not that I know John anymore, we're strangers, but his lack of control is frightening.

The doctor turns from his inspection and switches his full attention to Vincent. I think Doc R understands that John isn't quite ready to deal with him, so he takes control of the situation.

"Why the cage?" he asks conversationally. Vincent shrugs.

My Chauffeur Hound tenses the muscles in his arms, and they bulge. He lets out a growl. It vibrates around me. The hair at the back of my neck stands up. It's a bloody scary growl. Before I can clamp my lips against the sound, a small whine escapes. With a jerk, he immediately stops growling. He gently pats my head as if to say, "There, there," and starts the hair thing again.

"Why?" Doc R asks again, his tone polite.

Vincent huffs, shrugs again, and then he surprisingly answers. "It was feral. John dumped us with a fucking feral wolf." He shakes his head. "No, you can't even call that thing a wolf—it's just a dirty dog. My father, my sister, were killed because of it, and he decided to dump it here. For us to look after, to keep it safe? Fuck that. You think I was gonna let it stay in the house?" Vincent huffs out a laugh, sniffs, and wipes a hand across his sweaty face. He turns his full attention to John, demonstrating how stupid he is or revealing to everyone that he has a death wish. "Be glad that it's alive. Thank me." He points to the flaming floor in front of John's feet. "Get on your fucking knees and thank me!" Vincent's voice echoes around the garage. His voice drops ominously. "'Cause not a day has gone past that I don't want to put my hands around its throat and strangle the life out of it." Vincent swings around and points at me, his dark eyes furious. "That fucking bitch killed my pack."

Well, that escalated quickly.

I sniff. As if we all didn't know who Vincent was talking about—no need to point. I try to disappear into Chauffeur Hound's bulk. For those few moments, while Vincent's hate-filled attention is on me, the hellhound turns me slightly away so Vincent can't see me, and more importantly, so I can't see him. I have never been more grateful. I pat Chauffeur Hound's chest, and when he glances down, I attempt a small wobbly smile. The big hellhound frowns.

The silence in the garage is deafening.

Prompted by the hellhound's frown, it slowly registers, what Vincent is insinuating. I mentally replay the conversation. The dawning horror of what he said starts to sink in. Vincent thinks I killed my mum? Does he think I'm the reason Grace died? What the fuck. Is that the reason why Vincent and Jason hate me? The reason for everything? I rub my chest. I open my mouth to explain, to shout at him that it was his precious father Dave who was ultimately responsible for their deaths. My pack is dead because Dave fucked up.

It was not me. It bloody wasn't me.

I swear on my own life I didn't do anything wrong. I followed the rules.

But the words don't come.

Instead, a raw, soulful whine leaves my lips.

Frustration and fear swirl around in my chest, cramping my tummy and tightening my throat so I can't take a full breath. Oh God, my brother doesn't believe him, does he? Is that why he left me without a backward glance? Is that why he was angry?

A horrible thought bounces around in my head. What happens if I'm wrong? What if I made everything up, and everything that happened was my fault? Perhaps my version of events didn't happen the way I remembered?

Doc R ignores Vincent's outburst and after a few minutes, calmly asks, "Has she always been in this cage? In this garage?" He looks about in disgust, toeing the cage with his boot. "Where are the claw marks?" Vincent looks blankly back at the doctor. Vincent is breathing harder, flexing his fingers. "Have you seen a feral shifter, Vincent? I have. It is such a sad and frightening thing to see. The rage…" Doc R shakes his head and brings his arm to his mouth to demonstrate his next words, snapping his teeth. "A feral would be quite happy to chew its leg off or rip its mate to pieces to escape confinement. A feral would make short work of this cage. It would smash itself against the bars, even though they are silver, without care—and do you know what?" He points at the floor. "Because this cage isn't bolted down, it would take not even a minute for a feral to get out."

Doc R steps into Vincent's personal space. He leans forward, his nose almost brushing Vincent's. In a quiet tone that sends a shiver down my spine, he asks, "Why did you cage her? A nine-year-old child? A female shifter in need of care. You said she was feral? Where is the proof?" Pointing at the cage angrily, he raises his voice, losing his calm. "Where are the claw marks? How long did you cage her? When did you put a frightened little girl unable to shift out of her wolf form. In. A. Cage!"

Vincent quickly backs away from the angry doctor.

The corner of his lip and eye twitch sporadically. "About ten years." He rubs his hand across his mouth. "I had it in that cage for about ten years. Until Harry came home from school, the kid…the kid, he urm, he got upset—"

"Ten years?" Doc R repeats incredulously, throwing up his arms into the air. "What is wrong with you?" The doctor turns away from Vincent, and he looks imploringly at my brother. "John, are you listening to this?" Doc R rubs the back of his bald head with frustration. John remains unresponsive.

I let out a sigh that's more exhaustion than frustration, much to my chagrin. Do I have to be here?

"Look, it came back," Vincent says with a snarl. "My pack didn't! I knew it was at fault. Grace died; my two-year-old little sister died. My dad died, and his mate died. You talk about female shifters—what about Grace! Why the fuck didn't the real killer, the real reason my pack died, get punished?" Vincent puffs out his chest while I try to make myself smaller. "I punished the dog, something that you fucks didn't have the balls to do. So don't start this shit." He thumps his chest. "I am not ashamed. I did what I had to do."

"I sent Forrest home so that she could be with the pack," says John. Finally, he starts to address the elephant in the room. I listen intently, my body tense with fear. Is this where he agrees that Vincent is right? Will John ask Chauffeur Hound to put me back into the cage? I peek up at the hellhound through my lashes, trying to disguise my growing horror. Will he obey?

God, I don't want to be here!

"I had no idea you'd do something as evil as this. I knew your father was rotten. I didn't realise that the rot went so deep and into his sons. My mother was adamant that you could be trusted; she was blind." I notice that the flame in his hand is now entirely in John's control. It dances across his palm, changing colours among red, orange, yellow, and blue. It's mesmerising. "I returned a traumatised child to a nest of vipers, and I didn't even visit. Except for the odd phone, call I left you to it." The flame continues its dance. "I was too busy with my vengeance, hunting down the perpetrators, to even sit down and tell you the whole story of what happened. The truth about your father and what he did." The flame jumps to his other hand. "At the time, I thought it would be better that you didn't know. That it was healthier for the pack to not dwell on things you couldn't change. I also didn't want the pack name tainted, my mother's memory tarnished." As John continues, Vincent flings his arms into the air with frustration. His head is shaking vehemently in denial. "Forrest was a child—where in that stupid fucking head of yours did you imagine a nine-year-old girl could be responsible? Is that your bullshit fucking excuse?" The tightness in my chest loosens, and I take a full breath. "I was wrong in not giving you the full story. I made a massive error in judgment. I'm going to make it right. Your pack and the whole of shifter society is going to know the truth by the end of the day. I shouldn't have kept it a secret for so long."

Apart from the flame in his hands, John hasn't moved a muscle; his eyes remain closed. I have a feeling that if John looked at Vincent right now, he would probably burn him to a crisp.

John opens his eyes. "Have you seen her, Vincent, have you had a chance to see what you have done? Look in her eyes and tell me you see a monster. Then do the same while looking in the mirror. You, your pack...you are so fucking done."

Vincent looks away, unable to meet John's gaze. He's still shaking his head in denial, his hands clenched into fists. I don't think whatever John tells him will be enough. His hatred for me is too deeply ingrained.

John turns his head and examines me. "I find out about all this, and what we have discovered so far is just the tip of the iceberg, isn't it, Forrest? The tip of what you had to suffer." His head drops to his chest, and he runs his hand across the back of his neck.

Wow, was that an apology? I'm left more confused than vindicated.

Vincent looks away with a snarl. His whole body jerks when his eyes catch the half-full bag in the far corner, near the hose pipe on the wall. He surreptitiously tries to block the bag with his body. A small sound escapes me. No one else is watching.

John turns to leave the garage, his head lowered. As he passes us, I cringe away as he squeezes Chauffeur Hound's shoulder. The hound grunts an acknowledgement.

Vincent dabs at his forehead. His knees sag in relief.

"John," Chauffeur Hound says, intervening in John's exit. "What is in that sack in the corner?" The smart hound hasn't missed Vincent's movement at all.

"What sack...what the fuck..." John turns. He clips Vincent's shoulder on the way past, pushing him intentionally against the silver cage. Vincent lets out a hiss of pain and the smell of burnt skin wafts into the air.

John stands in front of the bag; he kicks it so he can read the label. I look away, burying my head against the hound's shoulder. I have no idea why I feel embarrassed and ashamed, but I do, and my chest hurts again.

"'Working Dog Mix.'" John reads the label out loud. "Dog food? What the hell is this..." It takes just a second for everything in his head to click. "You fed my sister fucking dry dog food!"

All hell breaks loose.

* * *

John, urm, burnt the garage down. Full-on magical meltdown —he completely lost his shit. You would have thought he'd been offered a handful of dog food for dinner by his reaction.

On a positive note, at least Doc R now knows about my diet. Mmmm, dog food, crunchy and nutritious.

We all managed to scarper out before he went boom. Nobody was hurt, except for maybe John's pride at his loss of control.

I wasn't sad to see the garage burn.

If I could, I would have asked for Chauffeur Hound to break out the celebratory marshmallows so I could toast them on the flames. Maybe do a happy dance with the joy of never having to see that particular cage again. Never be forced to sleep underneath that roof. But my hound carries me into the house, mumbling something about silver particles.

Huh, silver and marshmallows might not be that tasty after all.

CHAPTER SEVEN

The atmosphere in this lovely sitting room is seriously uncomfortable; the cheery yellow room with delicate furniture is full of silent, angry shifters. With the energy coming off each of them, you could boil a kettle. No one is sitting down apart from me, and it's unnerving. It's as if I'm still in my wolf form, forever looking up at the angry people towering over me.

I'm all trussed up in a chair in this cosy room, waiting for the show-and-tell part of the evening to start. My Nanny Hound—formerly known as Chauffeur Hound—has tucked me into the chair with a soft fluffy throw and about ten squishy cushions. At least I feel the most physically comfortable I've been since I shifted. My tummy is full for the first time in what feels like forever. I hum. I'd have been happy to eat a scabby rat—any form of protein would have been perfectly fine to me. I ate chicken noodle soup, it was served in a bowl, and it was delicious. My imaginary food dinners...yeah, total bullshit.

I have plans, big aspirations for when all this crap is over and I'm free. I'm going to hunt myself some real chocolate cake, a whole cake to myself, as soon as possible.

John hasn't explained anything about why I'm sitting here. I'm presuming that he wants me here for some meeting or big Scooby-Doo reveal. Doc R wanted me to go straight to the shifter private hospital, but John overruled him. I don't like John very much at the moment. Even if I could speak and ask to leave, I have a feeling I'd still be ignored. My opinion doesn't matter. It's better to fight the battles that you can win and sit out the ones that you can't.

All I want to do is get out of this bloody house.

The whole pack is here, luckily on the other side of the room. I don't want to sit around in the same room as Vincent and Jason. Why would I? I'm sitting here like a target is painted on my forehead. Useless and vulnerable. I can't speak or run. I wouldn't even be able to bash someone over the head with a cushion. So fighting is out, and if it all kicks off? I'm going to hide under my cover like a boss. God, that thought pricks at my pride.

Two members of the shifter council have also graced us with their presence. I have no idea why they're here. We haven't been introduced—hell, no one has been introduced to me. I keep catching them casting me strange calculating looks, looks that I have no idea how to interpret. If they leave me alone, I'll leave them alone.

But if they come after me, I'll fuck them up. I rein in my growl and force myself not to glare at them, glare at everyone. I fidget in the chair. My strange thoughts and rage are unnerving. Yeah, I might be a tad angry and seriously unbalanced. The frustration, anxiety, and fear thrumming through my head at the moment is troublesome. Troublesome? I huff. Understatement of the century, and it's freaking me out.

Heck, I'm either so frightened I can't function, or so angry I want to burn the world.

The lost human part of me doesn't know whether to crawl away and hide, or worse, start screaming. Any minute now, I feel as if my anger is going to bubble up and I am going to snap. Break apart, and nothing is going to be left but an angry, bitter person.

My sanity is fraying.

To keep my sanity intact, I need to pack my shit up, as the hound suggested hours ago. To bury everything deep, I desperately jam the memories further and further down until they no longer exist. Pack them into boxes.

Boxes in my head that echo with my screams.

I shiver and pull the cover to my chin. It smells clean.

It's impossible to bury the memories if the two evil bastards that contributed to them are standing across the room.

I want out of this house.

I focus on the other people in the room. My brother has called in more hellhounds as backup. As well as the original three, another six have arrived. Ten hellhounds, including John. I tilt my head to the side in thought. I watch the two hounds stationed across the room, the only hounds that I can currently see from my seated position.

Hellhounds have twice the strength of standard shifters even without using their fire magic. The hounds in this room could probably start and finish a war. Natural walking weapons. It's puzzling to me that the massive shifters also feel the need to display impressive amounts of silver. I bet they carry double that with the silver I can't see. I'm surprised the hellhounds don't jingle and clink when they walk. It's all a little bit of overkill. What are they all doing here?

Nanny Hound answers my silent question.

"They are here to keep John under control. He is worried that he will either set fire to the house or kill the pack. It's a precaution, plus he hates the paperwork that killing always brings."

All I got from that was, John needs nine guys to stop him. Nine super-shifters...God, he's a total scary bastard. Why can't he control his magic? It makes what the hellhound behind me did, putting himself between John and me, more impressive. He promised to keep me safe, and he did.

John, who has been talking to the two council members, now steps into the middle of the room. Gaining everyone's attention, he holds up his hand to ask for silence.

John starts to talk. He drones on, giving a full report on what he has discovered so far. I let John's words flow over me. I sit and play with a loose thread on the fluffy cover. I focus on the thread and the movement of my fingers.

I am back to feeling like I'm not here, like this whole time, I have been dreaming.

Instead, I think about the past. Harry helped to get me out of the cage, although I still found myself in there for regular punishment. At least I wasn't in there permanently. I had the chance to breathe fresh air, see the sky, feel the sun and the rain on my fur—the grass on my paws and the dirt in my claws.

In the early years, I convinced myself that someone, namely my brother, would come and rescue me. But it never happened, and John, he never came. It took my shifting back and making a desperate phone call for John to come. Ultimately I saved myself.

I can't quite believe that it took my getting angry with Liz, my protectiveness over Harry, to force the shift back into my human form. Oh my God, when I think about it, Liz's wayward vagina helped me! I pull up the soft cover to hide my amusement. When nothing else could, it stepped up to the challenge. Go vulva magic. I bet Liz now wishes that she had stabbed me when she had the opportunity.

I focus again on John when he starts talking about the history of what happened with our pack and their deaths. He has full details, including surveillance footage—it's all pieced together like a factual police report. He goes through it in a monotone, as if he isn't talking about his mother and sisters. John has the facts, but he didn't live it, and he didn't see with his own eyes what happened.

I nudge open the imaginary box in my head and let myself remember.

CHAPTER EIGHT

Fourteen years ago

Manchester Airport is busy. I arrive at the terminal and immediately want to find a corner and hide. People are everywhere, humans and creatures. The check-in lines are full. People with baggage trolleys get in the way of people with small suitcases on wheels. One lady runs over my toes and a man going the other way elbows me in the temple. *Oww!* I let out a growl that rumbles around in my chest. *Stop that, Forrest,* I think to myself.

I scamper past all the check-in desks, getting out of the way of the crazy, and find the blue seats where I am supposed to wait. With the people checking in and then going straight through to security, these seats are empty. I can see a clock on the flight information board, and the yellow digital clock flicks the numbers slowly.

Today has been crazy. My mum woke me up so early—middle-of-the-night early—and I automatically got dressed, like a firefighter getting ready for a call-out. I was so fast. Ever since I can remember, we have always had a plan, an emergency drill. Being a shifter is extremely dangerous when you are female—kidnapping is rife, and my mum is harsh with the whole reality of it. I have never been in any doubt that there's a target on my back. I have been taught from a young age to blend in and disappear, to go to certain busy places and wait.

The chair starts to get uncomfortable. Two hours pass and then three. I wiggle to ease the discomfort, too worried to move and traipse about in case my mum comes. She would be mad at me if I moved.

Come on, Mum, I chant in my head, bouncing on the seat.

After the fourth hour and no sightings of my mum, it's time to call in the cavalry. I'm going to ring my older brother, and by older, I mean mega old. I could ring my stepbrothers Vincent and Jason, but I don't trust them. Jason gives me the creeps. My mum adamantly declared that they were my bodyguards.

I huff. Bodyguards—what a joke. They're rubbish! If they were any good, I wouldn't be sitting here on my own.

It's now time to find a phone. I stand.

I know the scent-masker magic works for only so long, but I am hoping it's still keeping me covered. I am a wolf shifter. We do the whole wolf thing in our twenties—full furry wolf; it's incredible. My brother John is extraordinary; he can turn a single body-part wolf while keeping his human form. So he can turn his teeth or his claws. So cool, to think you'd never need a pair of scissors to open anything, ever. Just, bam, a claw and open-sesame. Not very hygienic if you're opening food, but way cool. I am so doing that when I'm older. I giggle to myself as I imagine what I could open.

I make my way towards the check-in desks, looking for some kind of phone. I should have had a spare mobile in my go-bag instead of having to hunt for a landline. But it was safer, Mum said, if I had nothing to trace me. Deciding to do the whole "I've lost my family please may I use your phone to ring my brother" routine at the information help desk, I head in that direction.

A scent hits me, and I freeze. *Demon.*

I try not to panic. So far, I have done everything by the book. I swallow down my nerves and take a deep breath. I have the scent masker on, and the airport stinks of thousands of creatures. Demons are poor trackers, and if I can blend in and use a phone and keep safe, get hold of John, then there's no reason why John can't help me find our pack. I keep moving slowly between the people. I am glad that I am still quite short. Shifters can grow huge, but at nine, I am still a tad over five-foot.

Instead of looking frantically around for the demon that I am smelling, I focus on walking straight ahead. The trick is to do the opposite of what you want to do. At the moment, I want to run and cry, grab the closest adult, and beg them to sort things out. But my mum didn't raise an idiot. She'd kill me if I did something so stupid, so I suck it up. I am going to do everything to keep myself safe and then I will find Grace, my mum, and my stepdad Dave.

I dodge a carry-on suitcase being pulled by an angry-looking human and spot a mobile phone in his jeans' back pocket. Perfect. I speed up, bump him, and stuff his phone up my sleeve.

My first thought is to get to the toilet, but to leave the busy part of the airport wouldn't be smart. I stand to the side and pull out the phone. It's password protected, but it's a simple Android handset. I hold the power button down for ten seconds, and then I hold the power button and volume-down button at the same time to factory-reset the phone. Bingo. After following the instructions on the screen, I'm now able to make a call without needing to input the password on the phone. I dial my brother's number. It rings. I glance around nervously.

"What!" My brother sounds grumpy.

"John, hey, it's Forrest—"

"Forrest, whose phone are you using?" Trust him to ask an unimportant question.

I roll my eyes. "John, that's not important. I ne—"

He interrupts again, a growl in his voice he speaks in his lecturing tone. "Forrest, you know this number is for emergencies. You can't ring me if Mum doesn't let you watch something on TV or she won't buy you some shit. I am too busy to—"

"John." I stop him mid-rant. The demon is close; I can smell him even more strongly now. The hair on the back of my neck is rising and I huff a little with panic. "John, will you listen to me—this is a bloody emergency," I whisper-shout at him, trying to cover my mouth and the phone with my hand. "I am at Manchester Airport, Terminal One, on my own. Mum, Grace, and dickhead Dave are missing. Mum woke me with a drill last night. I've been waiting over four hours at our meeting point at the airport. John, I smell a demon."

"Why didn't you start with that! I am on my way, but it's going to take me over an hour. I am going to see if anyone is closer. Give me a sec, stay on the phone." I can hear him shouting in the background. I glance around. Everybody is moving, and no one is looking at me. I turn my back to the airport concourse and lean my head on the wall. I feel so tired. So tired and so frightened.

"I have Owen, a hound who is twenty minutes away. I am going to ring you back and then you're gonna stay on this phone till he gets to you. You hear me, Forrest?"

"Yes, okay." I nod even though he can't see me.

"Okay, hang up. I'm ringing you back right now."

I end the call.

Immediately the phone starts to ring. I press to answer, and the phone is no longer in my hand.

I look up, and a scruffy human I have never seen before has hold of the phone. He puts it to his ear. "The little redhead can't speak at the moment." He drops the mobile to the floor and kicks it. It spins away, disappearing into the crowd.

Why did I turn my back? I want to smack my forehead in dejection. I have zero time to berate myself.

This guy is a human and I've got skills. I might be little, but I am fierce. He grabs hold of my upper arms. Instead of trying to pull away from him, I step into his body. I can't throw him or kick him; it would cause way too much attention. So instead, I drop to the floor. As he follows me down, trying to keep his hold on me, the position he is now in is blocking me from view. So I punch him between his legs. He lets go of me immediately with a squeak, cupping himself. As I stand up, I neatly throat-punch him.

Striding away, I shout, "That man is choking or having a heart attack. I think he needs help." A lady in a bright yellow jumper turns and takes in the situation.

"Oh my God, poor fella. Help, is there a doctor?"

Another lady with massive boobs in a cat jumper rushes to aid, her glorious chest bouncing in her excitement to help. "You poor man, I'll stay with you until help arrives, someone call an ambulance…"

I scurry away. Tilting my head, I check the airport clock. Damn it, I still have seventeen minutes before my brother's hound comes. Where is that damn demon? His potent scent, a sweetish sulphurous stink, surrounds me—it makes my nose itch.

I turn left, and another human slithers in front of me. He looks just as scruffy as the last guy, and he has a nasty smirk on his face.

Decisions, decisions—do I go through him or do I change direction? Before I can do anything, I'm yanked into a muscled chest. The scent of demon wraps chokingly around me.

"Now, Forrest, do not be doing anything stupid." The demon leans in close; his lips brush the shell of my ear as he creepily whispers. I shudder. "You want to see your pack, do you not? If you run or cause a scene, I will not hesitate to kill your mother. Do you understand me?" His whispery voice is harsh but with a very refined English accent. His cruel hands dig into my shoulders and the back of my neck. I nod, squeezing the top of my thighs. I worry I am going to embarrass myself and pee.

I don't feel brave or smart at this moment. I am a little girl who wants her mum.

Dimly I think about the hound that will be here in less than ten minutes. I need to cooperate, and we need to leave now—if the hound gets here and stops the demon from taking me, my mum will die. I can't let that happen. I need to keep calm and go with him. Hopefully the hound will arrive, see us leaving, and follow.

"I have been hunting you for such a long time, little Forrest. I've accepted an awful lot of money to procure you. A female shapeshifter, a rare little wolf, and what a pack line. So impressive. You're such a pretty little thing, with all that red hair." He runs his fingers through my hair, making me shiver with disgust. I fight the urge to slap his hand away.

"Did you know your pack line has produced the most females of any other?" the demon says as he starts to herd me towards the exit. "Your mother is a DNA jackpot ticket—the ultimate female shifter prize. Six children and five of them were female, two being twin girls, totally unheard of. So impressive, and your brother is a hellhound, as was your father. It's fascinating, such a worthy hunt. Such a shame your older sisters and father were murdered. Oh, I wish I could keep you, you'd make a fine contribution to my collection when you're older." He chuckles darkly, patting me on my head. "Although I have a courtesan picked out, and she is even rarer than you and such a beauty." He sighs. "My harem always needs new, nubile concubines—alas, they die so easily."

Are all demons this posh and pervy? I have no idea what a concubine is, but I get from the way he's whispering, it's not a good thing to be. As he's talking, he steers me outside—the scruffy guy follows behind us.

I know the rules about strangers, more so the rules about demons. But this demon has my mum and my little sister Grace. I will do anything for them, including sacrificing myself.

CHAPTER NINE

Fourteen years ago

We head towards a black range rover. Scruffy Number Two runs in front of us and opens the rear passenger door of the car with a bow—what a weirdo. I am shoved into the back seat of the vehicle, and the demon follows me inside. I take my first good look at him, and he's old. He looks about thirty in human years. I bet he isn't older than my mum. I know my mum will kick his ass for taking me, and my brother will light it on fire when he gets here.

The demon has black hair, long on the top and short on the sides. It falls into his blue-grey eyes. I think he's going for a boyish boyband look, not that it's working. He has high cheekbones and a delicate nose, and his lips appear big and puffy, especially the bottom one. His chin is strong. From what I remember of him behind me, he's tall. Although he isn't huge like a shifter, he's taller than a human. Mum would say he was elegant, elf-like. My brother would say weak, like prey. If I get the opportunity, I am going to kick his ass.

"Unfortunately I am the middleman for this transaction— you have been sold to a council member for an extortionate price. When you're more mature, once your body changes, you will drive him wild." The demon bops me on the nose. I blink at him. "I would have thoroughly enjoyed parading you in front of all the shifters. So exciting that a council member has bought you—who knows your fate. I have a feeling you will be in my care for some time. Then your owner will come in on a proverbial white horse and rescue you—that's why all this is just so much fun." He taps his fingers on the seat between us.

"I made a bargain to collect you. Your owner said nothing about keeping our bargain a secret." The demon chuckles and winks at me. "I might not be able to keep you, but I can sure mess things up a little bit. I do so hate happy-ever-afters. So you will remember, young Forrest, that everything from now on is your owner's fault and nothing to do with me. Don't be taken in by his handsome face, that's a good girl." He pats my cheek. I glare at him. I wish he would stop touching me. A council member bought me? I don't understand what he means. It's something that I'll have to deal with later and talk to my mum about. I'm a shifter, not a Mars Bar. This demon is weird.

I lift my chin and look him directly in the eye to show that I mean business. "My mum and my sister, you'll let them go, now that I am in the car with you. Ring your men, and please let my pack go." I know he said nothing of the sort, but maybe I can shame him into letting them go—it's worth a shot. He might want just me. If that's the case, I can make it easy for him to do the right thing. "I did what you asked—now let them go."

He tilts his head to the side, looking at me like I am stupid. His hand comes up, and he taps his fingers to his mouth. Once, twice, squishing his puffy lips.

"No," is his reply. I open my mouth to argue, but the look in his eyes stops me. Instead, I turn and gaze out the window. His blue-grey eyes have turned black, totally, freakily black. A primal shiver runs down my back, and I do my best to suppress the total and utter horror. I realise that I won't be kicking demon ass today.

The truth is, my *mum* would struggle to hurt him. He isn't just a demon—he is a first-level demon. I know with sudden clarity that we are all as good as dead.

I perch on the edge of the seat, spine straight, and focus outside the car, keeping my eyes wide to stop my fear from leaking down my face. I don't want to cry; I don't want to show any weakness. It would be a win to him. I might be nine, but I am stubborn, and however long I have to live, I will do so with my head held high. Being brave isn't about not being frightened; it is about being shit-scared but still doing the scary thing anyway. The right thing. If I can protect my pack, I will.

Be brave.

"Are you not wondering how I found you?" No, I don't want to know how I messed up. I watch the demon out of the corner of my eye. "My men tracked you to the hotel, but we lost you. You put a scent masker on, what a smart little wolf you are. It made me want to find you all the more. Your mother was equally tricky. Puff, she was gone"—he wiggles his fingers—"completely disappeared. But your stepfather, Dave...my my, he was too easy." The demon tuts. "With half his DNA, it is no wonder Grace is not good enough for my collection." I turn my head to look at him. "What a horrid, snivelling creature Dave is." He chuckles. "I didn't even touch him"—he shrugs, shows me his palms, and wiggles his fingers, pouting—"he was squealing like a pig. His life, his daughter's life for your mother's. For you." He raises an eyebrow, doing a fake sad face. "Such a wealth of information, so quick to tell me where he was going to meet your mother. So quick to tell me your protocols and how to find you—he even called off your bodyguards. That's why you were on your own." He shakes his head mockingly. His eyes are sparkling and finally back to their original colour. "I cannot quite believe your mother chose such a weak mate, especially after your father. That's why you are going to be safer in my care, my dear Forrest. These imbecilic wolves don't deserve you." He pokes my leg.

I want to shout at him that it isn't true, that he's lying. I know demons are said to twist things. But if I am honest, really honest, it sounds like he's telling the truth. I don't call my stepdad "dickhead Dave" for nothing.

"Now there's you, a nine-year-old child on her own with the enemy, no snivelling, no crying, only a proud little chin held high and a single demand to release your pack. You could rule the world with that attitude, young Forrest...yes, you're very intriguing. I think I shall keep you." He nods and quickly leans forward, tapping the end my nose again. His bright smile makes me want to puke.

I am dragged into a warehouse building, Scruffy One and Two holding me between them. Scruffy One is squeezing my upper arm painfully, probably in revenge for the punch to the balls and throat. The demon is strutting in front of us.

"A pack reunion—how wonderful." I can't see around him— something for which I will be eternally grateful. Blood, sweat, and a strange cloying musty scent I can't identify fills my nose. Combined with the stench of demons and humans, the whole place smells like I've stepped into Hell.

I gag. Some inbuilt alert in my head is going nuts, and my instincts are screaming at me to run.

"Now, now, gentlemen, not something we should do to our lovely guest. Pull your trousers up, that's a good chap." The demon chuckles and shakes his head in amusement, wagging a finger at me as he turns. "Look, Forrest, at what your naughtiness has done. Your poor mother had to entertain all my men while you were running around the airport. What a bad little girl you are." He steps away, and for the first time, I see my mum.

She is on her hands and knees on the dirty concrete floor. Blood on her face, her lip is split, and there's blood between her legs. I don't understand why she hasn't got any clothes on. Perhaps she's going to shift into her wolf form to heal? That's the only reason I can think of why she would be naked. Tears fill my eyes. I can hear my little sister crying.

I scan around frantically for Grace. She's fighting with her dad, trying desperately to get to our mum. She wiggles out of her coat, leaving it behind in his grasp, and runs across the building at a speed only a toddler can do. Nobody stops her as she throws herself into my mum's arms. If I weren't being held back, I would be doing the same. I watch my mum hug Grace to her chest, and I can hear her saying to Grace how much she loves her.

My mum looks up and meets my eyes. She gives me a tearful but determined smile. "I love you so very much, Forrest. Sticking to our plan...I'm so proud of you—you have been such a courageous girl. I need you to be brave for a little bit longer. Can you do that for me?" I nod. The tears I was valiantly holding in now trickle down my face. I hiccup a sob. "I am so sorry I couldn't keep you both safe," my mum says. The desolation in her eyes almost breaks me.

She nods meaningfully.

I know what my mum wants me to do. My heart pounds in my ears, and it's difficult to breathe with the lump in my throat.

My hoodie has plastic toggles at the end of the cords that tighten the hood. The toggles are cone-shaped and are the perfect place to hide a potion ball.

"I love you too," I whisper. The lump in my throat makes it difficult to speak.

Everything after that happens so fast. Yet at the same time, it feels like a lifetime passes as I watch my mum take Grace's face in her hands. She smiles down at Grace and wipes the tears from her chubby face with her thumbs. Mum gently strokes Grace's blonde hair—a perfect match for her own—out of her eyes. She leans down and kisses my baby sister gently on the forehead.

From one breath to the next, my mum sharply twists Grace's head to the side, breaking her neck.

My baby sister slumps, dead, into my mum's arms.

The howl of anguish from my mum is chilling as she clutches Grace to her chest with trembling hands. With a look of such sadness in my direction, my mum's fingers on her right hand shift to claws, and with a quick clean motion, Mum slashes her own throat open.

The two men let go of me, rushing towards my mum and Grace.

Sometimes the last move you have is to extract yourself from the hands of your enemy permanently. With a sob, determined,

I place the toggle with the poisonous potion ball in my mouth, and I bite down.

Onto a finger.

The demon has shoved his finger into my mouth.

With his free hand, he smacks the back of my head; the poisonous potion ball hits the floor, smashing. Useless.

"Naughty puppy!" the demon scolds. He keeps his finger in my mouth, and his other hand snakes around my throat. He pulls me to his chest, preventing me from moving. He shakes me a little in frustration. "Well, I didn't see that coming," he quietly says. Then more loudly, he snarls at the demons and humans in the room. "You must have broken her, you fucking idiots! Dave." He turns his anger towards my stepdad and pulls me around to face him. His finger is still in my mouth and digs into my cheek. "I am down two females. What have you to say?"

Dave, my stepdad, is on his knees, hugging Grace's coat. He shakes his head from side to side in shock, his eyes never leaving the crumpled bodies.

My mum never looked at Dave once, I think numbly. She never told him she loved him.

My suspicions are confirmed when Dave says, "You were only supposed to take Forrest. Not my little girl. We had a deal for you to take Forrest, but not my Grace, not my Grace." He rocks forward and back, stroking the coat in his hands. His expression is one of agony.

This is all Dave's fault—my mum, my sister, it's all his fault.

Dave finally lifts his eyes from the little pink jacket. "We had a deal!" he screams.

I feel the demon shrug. "I didn't kill them." He waves a hand at Dave. "Someone shut him up. Kill the useless fuck, he is getting on my nerves."

I wobble in the demon's arms. My knees go weak as the men surround Dave. His yelling is abruptly silenced with a wet-sounding gurgle.

Everything hits me at once. I failed. I've failed my mum. She would be so angry with me.

Something inside me snaps, and my body starts to shake.

I don't want to be here anymore.

I don't want to be here anymore, repeats over and over in my head.

Magic floods my body, and I embrace the feeling. I fall into my magic.

I escape into the darkness.

"Oh, for fuck's sake," I hear the demon shout, and then nothing.

CHAPTER TEN

I catch John's voice as he continues his report, pulling me from the horrors of my past. I bury them again inside my head in a box marked *Do not fucking touch*.

I run my hand shakily through my hair, trying to tamp down my anxiety over the horrific memories. On my other hand, my finger is swollen and red. I have been wrapping the thread of the cover around it, cutting off the circulation. I stare at the digit in fascination.

"Forrest shifted extremely early, as you can see. Although she was only nine, she impressively managed to kill two humans and a lower-level demon before they contained her by knocking her unconscious." I lift my head, and as John talks, a 3D video of the CCTV clip plays. My mouth pops open in shock as I watch.

I watch myself attack three of the bad guys. I killed them, or my subconscious piloting my wolf killed them, which should have been disturbing. But those men hurt my mum and I managed to get a small amount of justice.

I had no idea I did that. To escape, I folded into myself and let the wolf take over. That first shift was a total blank to me, due to the whole trauma. I assumed I'd been knocked unconscious. Looking at the evidence, I have to admit to myself that I might have gone feral for a while.

I am a killer, a murderer. The angry part of me rejoices, thrilled. I want to bounce in my seat with inappropriate excitement—what a badass.

"Did she bite that demon's…" one of the hellhounds says behind me, abject horror in his voice.

Oh yeah, yes I did. In my head, Billie Eilish's song "Bad Guy" plays. Huh, this is fantastic for my confidence—to see that wolf-me hadn't started out so meek, so pathetic.

"Yeah, fucking hell, looks like it."

I glance behind at the hellhounds. One of them gives me a supportive nod, while the other unconsciously shields himself. I snort. Nanny Hound gives me a little nudge to turn back around. I am such a badass I scare even hellhounds. I hum.

John continues talking about the evidence collected and the details on the demon who acted as a broker. He also explains I was held for a further week and details the rescue.

Everything around that time is hazy. I was in an awful place not only physically, but in my head. I was a mess.

John skims the room, making sure he has everyone's attention. Then he turns his focus on the pack. For the first time this evening since I sat down in this chair, I make myself look at them. I've been avoiding them. They frighten the shit out of me.

Seeing and hearing the evidence must have been extremely hard, to see irrefutable proof that Dave, their father, had been a coward. Captured by a demon, he had given away the locations of three female pack members, two being vulnerable children. The rarity of shifter females also makes the crime particularly heinous.

Vincent especially had built up his father to be the ultimate hero. Over the years, he made the Dave of his memory into someone he never was.

Beth is sobbing in Harry's arms. Jason is standing motionless, his face blank. Vincent, not bothering to comfort his mate, steps forward, his arms open wide in challenge.

"Is this a joke? So that's what you were hiding, John? Your bitch of a mother snapped Grace's neck like a twig." He clicks his fingers. I wince at the sound and the imagery that flashes into my head. "She was what, over a thousand years old, couldn't handle a bit of rough sex, so she goes and tops herself," Vincent snarls, "You heard my father—he made a deal to protect Grace. That crazy bitch didn't need to kill her. I can see as clear as day what you're doing here.

Dragging my father's name down to protect that thing?" He points at me, and I can't help flinching. I wish he'd stop doing that. "Are you fucking kidding me? All this manipulative crap today, knowing what that crazy bitch did, makes me wish I'd hurt her dog of a daughter more. You want me to cry with guilt?" Vincent's hate-filled brown eyes are on mine, his finger is still pointing at me. "Get fucked. If you leave it in the same room alone with me, I will finish the job I should have done years ago. You gave up the right when you dumped it at my door." Vincent spits at the floor. His angry eyes never leave mine. He lifts his lip, showing me his teeth, and sneers at me. Nanny Hound growls behind me. I feel him move a step closer.

John lets out a dark-sounding chuckle. "Forrest's door, Vincent. Not your door."

"What?" Vincent's head goes back a little in shock at John's quiet answer, and his pointing arm drops.

"The house, the grounds, the money is all Forrest's. It has always been in Forrest's name. Everything belonged to our mother, not the pack. Passed down to her sole surviving daughter."

Vincent grinds his teeth a little, and what looks like a flame lights John's eyes, making them glow red. The hellhounds behind me move a little with discomfort, readying themselves to jump in and stop John if he loses control.

"Let me be clear. If you or anyone calls my sister *it* one more time, I am going to kill you, and I am going to do it extremely slowly." He makes eye contact with each member of the pack. None of them can meet his eye, let alone hold his gaze. Beth buries her face in Harry's chest. "Now, Jason, have you got anything to add?" John asks the usually silent, creepy shifter.

Jason looks at me, his dark eyes unemotional. The dead expression in his eyes screams *retribution*. I drop my gaze and fuss with the cover; I pull it higher and tuck it under my chin. I don't want to be in this room. Why can't they do this without me? Jason will not lose his composure and yell like Vincent even though Jason is Vincent's puppet, his shadow. Jason is always in full control. Sadistic control.

As expected, he shakes his head *no*.

"Now, unless you make a derogatory comment about my sister, none of you are going to die tonight. What you are going to do is leave. You are no longer welcome in this house." Vincent starts to protest but John waves away his comments. John's voice drops. "I will kill you all if you don't shut the fuck up." A puff of smoke comes out of his mouth— similar to hot breath on a cold day. I blow out a little—nope, the room is warm. It's John's fire magic; he is running that hot. "You have thirty minutes to pack your shit. Take a bag with essentials only—one bag. The pack accounts are frozen, so don't bother taking your cars, either. You're hereby banished from our society for crimes against a purebred female shifter. Everyone in agreement…"

The two council members now step forward. They had been so quiet, I had forgotten about them. Which is stupid—

you should never ignore the council. The taller of the two men, a golden-blond cat shifter, nods. "As a council witness, I agree."

"As a council member, I feel the sentence is too lenient. I would not be opposed to a death sentence. But as that is my personal opinion, I will witness today, and I am also in agreement," the smaller of the two men says; I think he's a bear shifter. He glares at the pack. John nods his thanks.

"Harry, stay behind. Beth, if you want to discuss your options, you can do that with me now. You do not have to stay with your mate. As you are human, I have the resources to help you. Banishment means a tough life, one you are not equipped for."

Beth gives a little nod. Still standing in Harry's arms, she says quietly, "Vinny has continued to lie to me." Looking at her mate, she calmly continues, "You told me so many horrible things about Forrest that are untrue. I know from this meeting today that they never happened." She points at the floor where Vincent had been standing. "Just now I had to listen to you equate and trivialise rape as a bit of rough sex." Beth shakes her head, her hazel eyes accusing, full of disappointment. "What is wrong with you, Vincent? If I was in that situation, would you expect me to lie back and think of England?" Her voice cracks and she starts to cry again. "I have spent eight years in this house, and I have watched your cruelty. I did nothing, nothing." Beth pokes her own chest. "I could have done more, I should have done more. I alone am responsible for my non-action. I will never forgive myself, and I will never forgive you, Vincent. May I?" she asks John, nodding in my direction. John waves his arm, giving permission. Beth moves out of Harry's arms, turns, and takes a few small steps towards me. Her eyes and nose are red from crying. "Forrest, I am sorry." Another tear rolls down her cheek, and her lips tremble. I untangle my hand from underneath the cover, and with my thumb and forefinger, I make a wobbly OK sign. Beth lets out a little sob-laugh. "Okay," she whispers back.

"You're leaving me?" Vincent says in disbelief, his face flushing red. Beth looks at him and rapidly blinks. Nervously she backs away. Once she steps back into Harry's arms, she nods. "Un-fucking-believable." Growling, Vincent turns away, his shoulders and arms tense. His hands curl into fists. If the hounds weren't in the room, I do not doubt that he would be hitting the wall or me, his favourite punching bag. I can feel his anger, smell his rage.

My eyes flick from Vincent to Beth with concern. I am worried about Beth's safety. Yet, like the coward I am, I find myself sinking into the chair in an attempt to make myself smaller.

"Hounds, please escort these rogue shifters. Rogues, you have twenty-six minutes remaining," says John dismissively.

Vincent, with the help of a hound shoving him from behind, staggers towards the door. A visible vein throbs in his neck, and as he passes my chair, his body tenses. I huddle underneath the fluffy cover; I try my best to become invisible. Vincent bares his teeth at me.

Between one breath and the next, he roars and lunges at me. Everything slows…

I whine in fear.

My hands tangle in the cover. I can't get them out. Oh my God, I can't get them out in time, I'm unable to protect my face. I cringe and slam my eyes shut tightly.

Warm liquid splatters my face and neck.

I take a shaky breath. The sweet metallic scent of blood fills my nose.

No pain.

I slowly open my eyes.

I blink, my eyelashes heavy.

Nanny Hound is standing over me; Vincent is standing over me.

A knife is buried in Vincent's neck. Vincent's eyes are wide open. He gasps.

My eyes widen and my thoughts scramble. Frozen, I listen to Vincent gurgle and choke; his breathing turns into a wheeze.

I pant. I can't get enough air into my lungs.

John prowls into my sightline. He casually moves up beside Vincent. His head tilts to the side and he takes in the situation.

John smiles.

I'm glad that nightmare-inducing smile isn't aimed at me.

Dimly in the background, I can hear Beth screaming, but

I'm hyper-focused on the scene in front of me. I dare not move my eyes. It's like everything is silent around us, as if the entire world has shrunk down to a small bubble that encapsulates us.

John grabs hold of Vincent's arm and holds the bleeding shifter up when his legs threaten to buckle. "You didn't think I'd let you live did you, Vincent?" John whispers, that same smile on his lips; his eyes dance with sick amusement. I can't breathe.

Nanny Hound lets go of the blade. I sit frozen; I dare not move. It's macabre, seeing it sticking out of Vincent's neck. Blood weeps from the wound.

Vincent's blood is cooling on my face, my lips, dripping from my eyelashes.

"I wanted to watch you lose everything. See the acknowledgement of your utter failure. Before I took your miserable fucking life." John flicks the blade; Vincent groans. "What kind of self-respecting shifter gets off on hurting little girls? You thought that we'd be impressed?" He laughs nastily. "Thank you for making it easy for me." Another terrible wheeze comes out of Vincent. I think he is choking on blood. John lets go of his arm and roughly grabs the back of Vincent's shirt. He kicks Vincent's legs out from under him, and my stepbrother falls to his knees. John leans down to speak into Vincent's ear. "Look at that—dying on your knees as a rogue, while Forrest sits above you like a queen." John tilts Vincent's head up, using his hair. Vincent's brown eyes are glazed over, and blood dribbles from his lips. I shudder.

John braces his knee on Vincent's side, and slowly, deliberately, he pulls the blade from Vincent's neck. John lets go of his shirt, and Vincent falls onto his side with a thump. Vincent kicks and fails—his breath rattles.

Finally, his body stills in the centre of a growing red puddle. Silence.

I stare numbly at the monster dead at my feet. The pool of his blood. It's inconceivable to me that Vincent is dead.

I was so sure Vincent would have been the one to kill me. *What the fuck just happened...*

The bubble bursts and all the ambient sounds rush back to hit me at once, too loud for my nerves—Beth is wailing, her shocked cries filling the room.

"Great, I get the bloody extra paperwork," Nanny Hound mumbles. With a flick of his wrist he produces a cloth. He leans over me and proceeds to casually wipe the blood from my face. I give him an incredulous look, and he winks at me.

Jason, held between two hounds, is dragged out the door. The scary creepy shifter doesn't make a sound.

Harry, shifting his weight from foot to foot anxiously, watches as John steps over his dead brother, avoiding the growing puddle of blood on the floor. John prowls towards him and starts speaking. It's as if what happened to Vincent was nothing but an everyday, trivial thing. Perhaps to John, it was. God, he's scary.

John's voice drifts across the room. "Harry, even though you are banished and classed as a rogue, I am sure Forrest will not want to see you suffer. We will chat privately about my sister being caged and starved as you looked on." John has his back to me, but I can see Harry's terrified, pale face.

If Harry is guilty of that, then John bloody is too. Hypocritical bastard. I won't let John hurt him. The coward in me disappears, and I growl. John glances over his shoulder at me, and I narrow my eyes at him. He smirks, shakes his head, and turns back to Harry. "I am mindful that you are only twenty-four. I will allow you your belongings, including your car. You have till tomorrow to leave." Harry, in relief, closes his eyes and sighs; he nods his thanks. Hopefully he will be able to avoid my brother. John turns away from him in an apparent dismissal and starts to talk to Beth.

Harry shuffles towards me; his eyes flick around the room. Ignoring his dead brother, he slowly squats so we're eye-level. Nanny Hound gives him a small warning growl.

"Hi, Forrest. Wow, your hair is pink—that's kind of cool. I can't believe you shifted back. I am so proud of you. I also can't believe you went for the demon's crown jewels…" He shudders. "I think you freaked out every guy in the room." He chuckles, and then his smile falls from his face as he says nervously, "Once you get yourself healthy…we could maybe…urm, I dunno, go have a coffee, hot chocolate or something, chat about stuff? You're still my little sister, Forrest. I hope you know that." He rubs a hand across his face, and his eyes drop. "He was never the same after Dad and Grace died. Vincent was always difficult, and I wouldn't say he was a nice person, but growing up, he was good to me..."

Harry is hurting; I lean forward and wrap my arms around his neck in a hug. I almost make him fall over with the suddenness of the movement.

Oh, who am I kidding—he doesn't move a millimetre. I am so tiny. I nod and Harry pulls away. "Okay, well...urm...I will see you soon." He gives me a sad smile and hurries out of the room.

THE HOSPITAL

The shifter hospital is more like a medical-themed boutique hotel than a human hospital that you see on the television. I guess it's quite rare for shifters to require medical intervention, hence this fancy-schmancy hospital. If there are any other patients, I don't meet them. It's just me and a handful of rotating specialists that fly in from around the world.

I'm rapidly passed from one specialist to the next, like a shifter game of You're It.

Coincidentally, I didn't see any of these *specialists* when I was trapped in wolf form. From being left to rot to, now everyone is concerned about my health? Yeah, it's a bit of a head-fuck.

I'm a pro now at hiding behind a mask—my guise is "sweet and innocent." It matches the tiny pink-haired human I see in the mirror perfectly. Outwardly I'm small, weak, and female, the underdog. Why not use that assumption to my advantage? Huh, "innocence"—survival sucked up my innocence like the dry ground sucks up the rain. Now I play the victim to keep from being one. I'm a survivor.

Since John dropped me off here over a week ago, he hasn't been back to see me. John is under a lot of pressure—you know, saving the world—the world is way more important than his sister. Protecting everyone else is what John does; it would be selfish of me to think I'm above that.

At least the years stuck as a wolf taught me infinite patience, and I need that skill in abundance to deal with this shit-show. All this medical stuff is a joke. The doctors don't tell *me* anything—my medical file is the property of the shifter council.

I keep any questions I have to myself—what you don't know doesn't hurt you and all that. My mind thrums with the need to be left alone, and I long for normality. The only reason I stay and I'm not running for the hills is that my primal instinct screams at me to set aside my fears and accept help, and to use this as an opportunity to get stronger. It's the smart thing to do.

Hiding my anger is a challenge, and stopping the bitterness from leaking out is a constant struggle. I have to swallow it down; it makes me feel physically sick.

I'm sitting on a chair in a luxurious examination room. Jodie, my nurse, is sitting next to me. Her gentle brown eyes are warm and reassuring, and her pretty face is relaxed. Jodie, who is a talented witch, has wormed her way into becoming my friend. To kick off our friendship, Jodie snuck me a hair-removal potion ball on my first night. When helping me shower, she was horrified at my healthy armpit hair. Urm…who knew? I think I could have pulled a knife on her and not gotten as much of a reaction as a little bit of hair did. I smirk at the memory. Jodie told me I was hairy as a kitten and promptly educated me on all things *woman*, which I promptly forgot—to be honest, the whole lecture confused the hell out of me. According to Jodie, the hair removal potion is fantastic, a must-have as it even does facial hair. I had no idea women got lip and chin hair until Jodie explained it to me, in detail. Oh, and my eyebrows look nice, I guess. So unless I take a reversal ball for the spell, I will be *bad*–body-hair–free forever.

Not only is Jodie a witch and a nurse, she's also my speech therapist. A triple threat, and so far a thoughtful, talented lady. I'm not sure if I can trust her, nor do I know ultimately whose side she's on, but Jodie fascinates me. Witches are extremely impressive, and from what I can gather, they're not fighters. But with the ability to create the most incredible magic, they don't need to be. With Jodie and her coven keeping me amused with different ingenious potion balls, I have a new love of everything to do with witch magic.

Jodie's brown hair is styled into two fancy French plaits on either side of her head. My own hair is in a low, loose plait. I have been getting to grips with it after Jodie smuggled in a human hairstylist to cut my thigh-length hair into a more manageable mid-back length. The hairdresser went nuts about the light pink colour; he loved it.

My natural red hasn't hinted at a return, and I can't even change the colour either—shifters don't dye their hair. We can, I guess, but I think it's a total waste of time. You see, as part of the magic of shifting, artificial hair colour disappears when we return to our human form—same with makeup and even regular tattoos. Everything regenerates through the change—that's why shifters live for so long.

Jodie's pink scrubs rustle as she gives me a double thumbs-up, and her full mouth curves into a toothy grin. I wrinkle my nose at her antics and swing my attention back to this afternoon's doctor, Doctor Gregory; he's a cat shifter. Tablet in hand, he reads my notes with an unnerving gleam in his eye. Dr G lifts his eyes from the device and smiles at me.

I don't smile back.

Instead, I watch him warily. I don't want to be rude to the nice doctor, but he specialises in shifter gynaecology. I mouth the words "vagina doctor," followed by a full-body shudder and a lip curl. Jodie's smile gets bigger. I clutch my hands in front of me and lean slightly forward in the chair—protecting said vagina.

It's his turn today to poke and prod me. Yay…the urge to tell him to bog off is huge. It has been only eight days and I'm all tested out. I feel as if my body isn't my own. In wolf or human form, I belong to everyone but myself.

I shelve my unhelpful feelings, sit up and anchor my spine, lift my chin, and try to at least look like the adult I'm pretending to be. Out of the corner of my eye, I see Jodie nod her approval. I take that as validation I did the right thing. God, it's harder than I thought it would be to behave like a normal, balanced person.

I don't know the rules.

I've taken it upon myself to emulate the people around me in the hope that I will at least appear to know what I'm doing. All this is hard to comprehend, and I can't help feeling like a kid who has woken up from a bad dream and fourteen years have passed.

"So, Forrest," Doctor Gregory says, placing his tablet with a clack on the glass coffee table. He leans forward, resting his forearms on his pinstriped thighs; he isn't shy about scrutinising me. "The council is concerned that your reproductive system may have been compromised by your previous living situation. We can't introduce you to potential mates if you aren't viable." Oh, and there it is…this shit can't be ethical. I fight to keep my face blank. The anguish I feel wells up in my chest and threatens to register on my face, to knock off my mask. "This afternoon, we're going to discuss your heat cycles. Can you remember if you have had your first estrus?"

I drop my head so fast my neck twinges with pain, and I can no longer meet his eyes. I know he's a doctor, but do I have to talk about this? I don't trust him, and I certainly don't trust the council. I wrap my arms around myself.

Usually, a female Canidae shifter will have her first estrus, or heat, after the first animal shift, between the ages of eighteen and twenty-five. Shifters don't menstruate monthly like humans. Twice a year, we go into estrus. Estrus can last from two to four weeks, and only during that time we can conceive. One regular shift into animal form after the heat cycle and the unused material from the lining of the uterus is gone. The magic replaces cells so the body doesn't need to, so female shifters don't have periods—unless for some reason they can't shift.

I swallow the sour bile that fills my mouth. I wiggle in my chair and tuck my hands underneath my thighs to stop them from shaking. I struggle to keep my breathing even; bloody hell, I need to wolf-up. I can answer a simple question.

I shifted early, and I had my first estrus prematurely.

Tell him.

I take a big unsteady breath. The lemon cleaner they use on the floor makes my nose itch. The clock on the wall ticks, each second louder than the last. I rock slightly forward and back as I try to form the words. I am acting like an overly dramatic weirdo.

I clear my throat, and slowly, like I've been practising, say, "At…about…ten." My rough voice grates. I swallow. My mouth is now bone-dry.

Stuck in my wolf form, I had to suffer through five traumatic heat cycles and the bleeding afterwards as I couldn't shift. It was a blessing and a relief when they stopped. I guess my body was too fucked up, too run-down with malnutrition. I swallow the lump in my throat, and I keep my eyes down.

My lips tremble, and to stop them, I pinch them shut with my teeth.

A memory gnaws at the edges of my consciousness. It must be a bad one—I can tell by the way it gets harder to breathe. I jam it back in its box with all the others.

Dr G is speaking, but I can't hear him above my madly beating heart. I move my hands and grip the edge of the chair; the leather is slick under my damp palms. I hold myself in place. I need to stop the rocking.

The lump in my throat is now blocking my airway, and I can no longer take a full breath.

What the hell is wrong with me?

A noise from outside startles me and the memory slams into me like a physical punch to the face. Flashes of imagery flood my senses, and I'm back in the cage:

Am I dying? Cramping pain. Star-shaped droplets of blood hit the concrete.

"You disgusting, dirty dog!" Cold water from the yellow hose blasts between my back legs.

Cold so cold. I want my mummy.

Blood mixes with the water, swirling, swirling down the drain.

No. No. No.

Long-buried shame tightens my throat. I come back to myself, and something digs into my spine. It takes me a few seconds to gain awareness and to work out that I'm wedged between the black leather exam bed and the wall. I'm curled underneath the bed, and I hug my knees to my chest. *I can't breathe. I can't breathe.* Black spots appear behind my eyes. I rapidly blink, attempting to clear my vision.

Then he's here, a big black wolf.

The exam bed shudders above as he creeps closer to me on his belly. He mournfully whines at me, his warm, soulful grey eyes full of concern—Nanny Hound. I bury my hands in his fur and place my forehead against his.

What have I done? What did I do?

Nanny Hound puffs out a breath and the hair sticking to my sweaty forehead flutters. He does it again; he breathes in and out, and I make myself breathe along with him. In and out.

I'm okay; I'm okay.

Once my heartbeat has settled and I'm no longer shaking. Nanny Hound wiggles backwards. He takes hold of my jumper in his teeth and pulls me out with him.

Well, this is embarrassing.

Ashamed, I blink up at the shocked doctor and nurse. My chair has tipped over; otherwise, the room looks the same.

Tears shine in Jodie's brown eyes, and a worried line has appeared between her brows. I mouth the words *I'm sorry.*

Jodie straightens her scrubs. She wrinkles her nose and frowns at me. "I didn't hear you. You need to try that again like we have been practising." I roll my eyes toward the ceiling, already feeling better with this switch to our regular routine.

"I'm s…s…sorry," I rasp out obediently. Jodie gives me a bright smile, drops to her knees, and wraps me in a comforting hug.

"One step at a time," she whispers, squeezing me.

After a cup of tea, I manage to give a hesitant and distracted Doctor Gregory the information he needs. He concludes his session without a physical exam. That decision is mainly due to the angry hellhound that refuses to leave my side. Nanny Hound—whose name I finally found out is Owen—is seriously my hero.

The uncomfortable doctor also let slip that there should be no issues with my ability to produce children; my weight gain should resolve my heat cycle and any fertility problems. Yay, the council will be pleased—cue eyeroll.

CHAPTER TWELVE

I'm sitting cross-legged on the bed in my cell. Hospital room. With my new diet, I have put on enough weight so that it doesn't hurt to be human—especially the pointy bits like my knees, elbows, and bottom. With more flesh on them, my bones don't ache or crunch against each other, and I no longer look like a female version of Skeletor. I still look childlike, but I have hope. My strength has rapidly improved, and I take every opportunity not only to stand up and make myself walk but also to stretch and make myself more flexible.

My body is adapting, and everything is less alien. I've still not gotten used to the whole not-having-fur. I'm always cold, but all in all, I'm physically doing okay.

Except my voice. Talking is more complicated than anticipated. At first, the doctors were puzzled over why I'm unable to speak. Many tests were done, and while there's damage to my vocal cords—they are shot to shit—it doesn't account for my unwillingness to speak. The problem is written off as a mental health issue. Emotional trauma. All those years I spent locked inside my head with my inner voice screaming, I would have given anything to speak. Now I find using my voice disconcerting. Hearing my voice is extremely strange and I avoid talking out loud. I am not used to expressing myself vocally with strangers. Like a wind-up toy, I force myself to speak when required. Otherwise, I'll never get out of here.

This afternoon, the doctors—the council— want me to work on my shifting; they want me to shift back into my wolf form.

I'm shitting myself.

I worry that I won't be able to turn back, or even worse, I'll get stuck in my wolf form again. The fear is a living thing inside me, eating me up. No matter what the doctors say, I'm not reassured, but I'm aware that it's something that I have to do.

I've got to wolf-up—pun intended.

I'm sure not waiting for a gaggle of doctors to stare at my naked human form, adding pressure to an already stressful situation. I've decided to shift on my own in my room.

I know, I know, I'm crazy.

I should wait or at least ask Owen for help. But the anticipation is freaking me out, and I need to get this shit over with. I puff out a nervous breath, wet my lips, hop off the bed, and square my shoulders. I glance about uneasily and remove my clothes. I don't know if it would be better for me to be on my hands and knees. But standing here feels right.

I take a fortifying breath.

I scrunch my eyes closed and think of my wolf, my fur, my paws. I start to tingle all over. I embrace the feeling. It's surprisingly invigorating, and between one breath and the next, I am in my wolf form.

I feel like I've come home.

I do a little stretch. *Oh my God, look at that!* I wiggle my bum in disbelief and my tail moves. *Wow, look at that!* I marvel at my once-lame back legs, which are now strong and sure underneath me. *No pain!* My muzzle opens, and my tongue lolls out in a happy grin. I twist in a sharp circle and gape at my strong legs. I flop to the floor, stunned. I squirm onto my back and wiggle each paw above me.

Wow. The magic fixed me…shit, the magic fixed me! I knew it would have done, but seeing is believing and I feel stunned, overwhelmed, and light-headed.

Dimly in the back of my head, I think that I'd better turn back; otherwise, I might stay as I am. Hell, it would be much easier to keep in wolf form. Simple. Unless they chuck me in another cage. I do a full-body shudder. Even thinking about it frightens the crap out of me. I can't tempt fate. I scramble to my feet.

Sighing, I again close my eyes, and I imagine my human self. My pale hands and toes, and astonishingly I think of my pink hair.

God, the relief I feel when I stand on my two human feet. I grin and fist-pump. I did it! I did it! I'm a proper shifter. I promptly burst into tears.

That's how Nanny Hound finds me—a naked, snotty mess.

"Forrest, are you alright? Did you…did you shift?" My lips tremble, and I nod. "Are they happy tears?" I wobble my head weirdly, nodding and shaking my head at the same time. Hell, I'm not sure. "You shouldn't have done that alone…do you want some cake?"

"What's wrong?" Jodie says as she comes into the room. She steps around Owen and eyes me up and down. I stand hunched and snivelling. I don't bother to cover myself.

"Forrest shifted into her wolf and is feeling—"

"Why is she naked?"

"Shifters shift naked. Clothing doesn't shift."

"Oh, I have a potion for that." Jodie rubs her hands together with a grin.

* * *

An hour later and I'm in the dining room, nestled at a table in the corner, my back to the wall. I'm next to the window, which overlooks the courtyard garden. When I arrived, they thoughtfully put me in a downstairs bedroom with access to the same courtyard.

The double doors to the kitchen swing open and Karen, a skinny blonde human nutritionist, shuffles across the room.

Karen gives me a nervous smile as she holds a plate of chicken, peas, and mashed potato in a white-fisted grip. I hum in approval—it has gravy.

Karen has been hired to sort out my dietary requirements. The poor lady is so frightened of me; her distress wafts around her, filling my nose, making me want to sneeze. I wiggle in my chair and attempt a reassuring smile. The human's eyes dilate and go round. Her fear floods my senses.

I sag in my seat, pout, and glance down at the table as Karen's whole body starts to shake; a pea rolls off the plate onto the floor. I wrinkle my nose at the pea, sadly wishing it goodbye. They don't like it if I eat things off the floor. So the poor pea has to stay where it lands.

Karen places the plate in front of me with a clunk and quickly backs away. "Okay, F-Forrest, try to eat as much as you can." I mouth the words "thank you" at the trembling Karen.

I smile again, this time at the plate. I practice on the chicken and this time try to show fewer teeth. Everything at the moment is practice. I will have to add my smiles to the never-ending list, and maybe practice in the mirror.

Clumsily I take hold of my utensil. I still find it hard to hold my fork; my hands are going to be useless for a while. I grimace as I struggle to rotate the fork. I make a fist and stab down, effectively spearing the chicken. The human squeaks and scampers away out of the room. I hunch my shoulders and cringe.

For fuck's sake, why did I do that?

Owen, who is silently sitting opposite me, lets out a snort. I peek up at him. His eyes are crinkled in the corners and his lips twitch—he's fighting back laughter. I pull a face in the direction Karen ran. I didn't mean to frighten her.

He nods at my meal. "Don't worry about it; eat up." I don't need telling twice. Hell, at least I'm trying to use the fork. It would be much quicker and easier to use my hands—again, not allowed.

I lift the speared chicken, almost going cross-eyed as I watch it, until I stuff the whole chunk into my mouth. I go in for another piece.

The hairs lift on the back of my neck.

The room is unnaturally quiet, and I glance up; the few people that are around are staring at me. What are they looking at?

I pull the plate towards me as I chew.

Owen lets out a little cough. "Forrest." I meet his eyes; he's frowning at me. I must have done something wrong again—when he pulls that face, it's a good indication.

Oops, I'm growling. I stop, huff out a breath. My eyes dart about, doing a double-check to make sure that nobody is looking at my food. "Don't worry; I've got your back, no one is gonna take your lunch." I nod a thank you, trusting him, and continue eating. A happy hum replaces my growl.

With my stab technique, I finish eating within minutes. Not pretty but effective.

Owen excuses himself from the table. When he returns

from the kitchen, the most fantastic thing happens: my empty plate is exchanged for a slab of chocolate cake.

Chocolate cake! I beam a smile at Owen.

I honest to God can hear angels singing; this is a heavenly cake, and I am positive the cake has a glow around it. I take a bite. My eyes roll into the back of my head.

I decide from this moment on chocolate cake: Owen and myself, we're best friends.

CHAPTER THIRTEEN

The meaty fist hits me directly in my face. Blood fills my mouth, and I snarl "You're not even trying," Owen grumbles, the arsehole, his eyes narrow the sweat is dripping off his forehead.

"I so am trying!" I bare my bloody teeth at him, and he chuckles.

"Again. This time block my strike!" He comes at me again; he feints a punch to the left. Which I catch, and I block his blow to the right. But I miss his left hand, which catches me in the stomach. I *oof* out a breath and a pained groan.

Owen steps away and circles me. He's so light on his feet for such a big guy. "Come on; fighting should come naturally to you. You're a shifter. Block me, hit me. You're fighting like a human."

I growl.

I quickly dart away as he dives towards me, and I hit him on the jaw with my closed fist, finally making contact. My hand crunches. Owen stumbles backwards, and for a moment, I allow myself a little bit of pride. I made contact with his face. Go me.

My taped right hand throbs; I think his face broke my knuckle. Damn it, I should have used my palm to hit him.

Owen hits me again. "Stop getting ahead of yourself— one hit and the fight isn't over." He narrows his eyes at me; his voice is laced with frustration. "Where are the combinations that we've been practising? The strongest part of your body is your legs, where are your kicks? Come on, Forrest, you can do better than this." Owen taps me on the shoulder with his left fist; I brace myself so I don't fall over. "Today, with me, you get it easy. It won't always be the case. Our life isn't rainbows and kittens. Even sparring, you've gotta fight hard." We go at it again.

I wobble slightly on my feet. Shit, I'm tired. But I force myself to focus. I watch his eyes, and I wait for an indication of what Owen's going to do next. I block his left and then block his right fist, which is heading again for my stomach. Owen tries to sweep my legs from underneath me, and I jump away. I go to punch him in the face with my left hand, and while he's blocking that move, I aim a palm-strike at his throat with my right. He blocks both. Owen doesn't see my left shin coming as I kick him in the side, knocking him sideways. I follow that up with an elbow to his temple. Owen goes down on his knees.

I grin. Owen's big fist hits me in the chest, and I find myself flat on the mat, unable to breathe.

I gawk up at the ceiling, gasping. It takes me a few minutes to learn how to take a full breath. Owen is sitting next to me. I roll my eyes to the side and glance at him. His dark skin is glistening, and he looks completely unruffled. Ha, I'm not glistening—I'm sure I look like I feel: a disgusting, sweaty mess.

"You did better," he says, eyes sparkling. "You need to shift to heal that hand." He nods at my now-swelling right hand. I grunt out my acknowledgement. "I will see you later tonight... movie night?" I can't move my head to nod; I wiggle my finger in confirmation. "Great, I want to introduce you to *Iron Man*," Owen says over his shoulder as he leaves. I scrunch my eyes closed. Even my hair is hurting.

I think I did better today.

It has been three weeks since I was finally away from the hospital of horrors, and I'm living with the hellhounds in an apartment building owned by John. It used to be a hotel on the seafront, but when it fell into disrepair a few years ago, John bought it and had it converted.

It now has sixteen self-contained apartments. It also has a modern gym with a pool. It's a lovely building. I have one of the penthouse apartments, which has a fantastic private rooftop garden.

The building is tall, so it isn't overlooked; the roof garden is perfect; and it has the most fantastic sea views on one side and a view of the city and the ocean amusement park on the other. That side of the building is crazy busy.

I often find myself sitting huddled outside and watching the world go by, the excited screams from the amusement park a steady piece of soothing background music. It's a confirmation that life exists outside my new prison walls.

The building is magically shielded; the ward stops the uninvited or people with ill intent from entering the building. The magic warns people away, and it can even zap them unconscious. If you look up, you can see the glittering gold of the ward like a dome around the whole building. It's beautiful.

If you think about it, who in their right mind would want to attack somewhere that hellhounds live? You would have to be a complete crazy person with some kind of death wish. I am in the safest place imaginable.

The best way to describe my apartment is "modern bland." I spend most of my time on the roof, bugging Owen, or like now—a sweaty mess splattered on the gym floor.

This afternoon, I've decided that while Owen is off doing what he does while not watching me, I am sneaking out.

I want to do something on my own, venture out and buy some clothes. Everything John has kindly gotten for me is a bit naff. I am sure some department-store personal shopper out there had a wonderful time picking out all the pretty outfits. Not that I am not grateful for everything—I am. John has been thoughtful in arranging my fancy clothing. But I can't shake the urge to shop for myself and find my style.

I will probably order stuff online in the future, once I get to grips with using tech again. I need only a few things, as I want to wait until my weight has stabilised. I am still underweight but no longer skeletal. Gentle curves have replaced skin and bone, filling out my once-emaciated frame. Parts of me almost jiggle! I look like a woman instead of a child. Delicate and ultra-feminine, the outside clashes with the person I am inside, and my visage is an outright contradiction of what I imagined myself to look like, with no trace of the statuesque shifter I dreamed I would be.

At least my skinny arms have slightly more definition, and I've got good lean muscles developing.

I also want to explore the city without having my hellhound buddies escorting me. The urge to explore: to find out if there is more to the world than I have experienced so far.

I want the freedom to choose.

I spent fourteen years not only being a prisoner to my pack but also a prisoner to my wolf. I have a lot of things I want to do, and a lot of time to make up for; my life will not include hiding behind bodyguards or the dictates of the bloody council. If I don't aim to gain a semblance of freedom in some form, I'm frightened that I will never learn to live. It's easy to allow others to dictate my life. But how can I grow if my dreams aren't planted in the dirt? How can I grow if I have no human experiences and no mistakes?

The security risk to my person, I think, is low.

Nanny Hound will still lecture me when he finds out that I left the building on my own. But in my defence, I haven't been working only on the walking-and-talking stuff; I have spent the last few weeks fight-training, with Owen and the other hellhounds. The fight training has massively helped improve my coordination and fitness. I might not be that good yet, nor at the standard I was as a kid. But I can handle myself. My mum insisted on fighting skills, so from the age of three, I learned the human fighting forms Krav Maga, Muay Thai, and the demon style *Fbeed znvrhnjv.*

Owen knows I'm not a pushover, and I'm certainly not a regular Princess break-a-nail-and-cry female shifter. Hell, he has spent weeks punching me in the face and throwing me around the gym. I'm a tough cookie. So I'm sneaking out.

* * *

I've finished my shopping, and although I haven't bought much, I feel a real sense of achievement, shopping for myself. I guess it's a milestone. I meander down a side street away from the main shopping area. I allow my shopping bags to bounce off my leg and swing as I wander. My eyes dart to each new thing, and my blood thrums with excitement.

I grind to a screeching halt.

Creatures grumble as they swerve around my motionless form...oops, I almost caused a pileup on the busy pavement.

My brain has zero hope of scrounging up apologies, as my whole focus is on the glorious sight before me. My mouth fills with saliva and my face hits the window, and it squeaks as my nostrils squish against the glass. I can almost hear the angelic choir in the background. Eyes wide, I stare without blinking at the sight before me—oh my God, so many cakes! Homemade cakes.

The bell over the door jingles as I stumble inside. *Mmm, cake.* My nostrils flare with the scent of sugar, chocolate, and coffee. I've found a gem of a café; it's fantastic, small, and quirky.

My eyes swing from cake to cake, then back again. I feel dizzy and overwhelmed at the choice.

I take a deep breath, which frankly doesn't help.

I might have a cake problem.

I swallow my saliva and slowly back away from the display.

At the side of the cake counter is a colourful handwritten chalk menu, and prominently placed next to it is a board that says, "Pending food and drink." What is "pending food"? I shuffle towards the board. God, I hope reading will distract me from going into a cake frenzy. I'm at serious risk of pouncing on the counter display.

The sign on the board states: *If any person (creature or human) cannot afford to eat or drink, please pick an item(s) that someone has kindly bought in advance.*

I run my fingertips across the words reverently, and my heart misses a beat—it sobers me. I blow out a breath and the white receipts attached to the board flutter in the slight breeze.

Gosh, that is absolutely beautiful.

I know what it's like to go hungry; my circumstances have changed, but so many people are not as fortunate. This concept is beautiful, kind and thoughtful; it gives me hope that there's not just evil in the world. That kindness exists too.

After I order, I quietly point to the pending board and hand over a wedge of cash that I had left over from my shopping trip. The lady at the till blinks at me a few times in shock, her blue eyes filling with tears. I give her a shy smile, grab my order, and totter away, my cheeks undoubtedly radiating pink.

I juggle my shopping bags and glance about for a place to sit. Dotted about are ten small tables with bright, mismatched chairs. I spot a comfortable chair positioned so my back would be against the wall. I will not only see the whole café and the door, but I should also be able to see halfway down the street. I hum. It's a perfect position for people-watching. With an amused huff, I wonder if anyone else will leave a nose print on the window while I'm here.

I settle into my chair with a contented sigh, the clatter of dishes and clink of spoons a gentle background hum. I sip my hot chocolate and nibble on a fantastic slab of chocolate cake. Okay, so I am shoving great mouthfuls of cake into my mouth. But I pretend I am eating like a lady, even if I have to remind myself to chew. It's gooey chocolatey goodness. I will never go another day if I can help it without a slice of chocolate cake, nom nom.

The café's walls are clad halfway up with wainscoting, painted a pale green. On one side of the room is a whole wall full of books. My fingers itch to run across their spines. Tipping my head back, I glance up to study the ceiling, where a pink-blossomed tree branch spans the ceiling with dangling fairy lights. I love the unique, bright splash of colour.

This place is amazing.

Modern life is fascinating; the humans around me are so focused on their phones. Even humans sitting with other humans are staring and poking at their mobiles, occasionally murmuring to each other without their eyes straying from their devices. People no longer engage with each other; it's such a strange development. Crap, I guess I must look like a complete psycho sitting here, staring at everyone, without a phone in my hand.

I am sure the predators are well fed.

I bet hunting humans has never been so easy. Not that I'm advocating hunting humans! Pure humans are an endangered species. Mixed-race humans are a lot more common. It's rare to find a human nowadays without a drop of DNA from some creature. In evolutionary terms, it makes sense for humans to breed to make themselves stronger, healthier, and to ensure that they live longer.

According to Owen, there are thousands of humans that petition every year to be turned into vampires; everybody wants to be a vampire nowadays. I don't think many humans want to be shifters—the conversion rate is low, and only a small percentage of males survive.

I have a council-issued mobile, which is switched off and in a junk drawer. No way I'm giving the council information or carrying that thing around with me to be tracked. Today I bought my own phone to join the modern world.

I am not the only one people-watching; there's a young wolf shifter sitting a few tables away from me. He seems equally fascinated and has not stopped staring at me. I look at him and raise my eyebrow as if to say, *what are you looking at?* I saw someone do this in a film and thought it was cool, so I've been practising. He takes the eyebrow-raise as an invitation and gets up; his chair scrapes on the floor. My pulse rate increases—shit, I don't want to talk to him! I frantically rub my mouth to make sure I don't have cake on my face. He swaggers past me, over to the door, and leaves. *Huh.* I puff out a breath in relief, although I didn't mean to scare him off. I'm glad he didn't approach me.

I drag the paper menu across the table and study it, humming. I contemplate buying another slice, and I wonder if I can purchase a whole cake to take home.

The bell above the door jingles. My eyes flick up, and I freeze.

My mouth drops open. "H-Harry," I stutter in disbelief.

CHAPTER FOURTEEN

"How's it going, Short Stuff?" Harry strolls over to my table, a fixed smile on his lips that doesn't quite reach his blue eyes. "Can I join, and do you want anything?" He nods, indicating both the empty chair and my clean plate. Speechless, I rapidly nod my head. I can't believe he's here—wow, this is kind of surreal. My eyes feel like they're popping out of my head as I obediently poke at the menu. I bounce on my chair and grin goofily at him. How did he find me?

"So you're finally out of the hospital, then." Harry returns with another slice of cake for me and a coffee for himself. The plate clatters as it hits the table, and Harry slumps down in the chair opposite. He folds his arms across his chest and spreads his ripped-jean–clad legs wide. It's a proper wannabe-alpha pose. I barely refrain from sniggering at him, but I don't want to be rude—he's adorable. His left leg bounces slightly.

"Everyone is going nuts wanting to know about *you*, the *new* female shifter." Harry sniffs and scrubs his nose with the back of his hand. I wrinkle my nose and swallow the cake in my mouth. A new shifter? Huh, do they think I appeared overnight as a fully-formed adult? Harry's left leg continues to bounce. "Not much of a talker? Yeah, heard that too. Are you…are you alone? I can't believe you're out in the city alone. Where are your bodyguards?" He looks about as if they're going to jump out of the woodwork and attack him. I part my lips to answer, but frustratingly my throat locks up. "I heard you have hellhounds watching you?" I nod and take a sip of my hot chocolate. I hope the warm liquid will convince my vocal cords to work. "Spending time with all those hellhounds must be fun, huh?" Harry wiggles his eyebrows.

Eww, gross. Why would Harry say that? This isn't a conversation I want with him, he's my brother. I shudder. I vigorously shake my head, and if I let them, my eyes would roll back into my head and disappear without a trace. Maybe even get stuck back there. I'm not blind—I've noticed the handsome, buff hellhounds. But they are John's men, and they treat me with the utmost professional courtesy. Harry's words are disrespectful. I love Owen, he's my rock, but the thought of romantic feelings for him—for anyone at the moment, especially the hellhounds—would be wrong.

I'm not ready to have a romantic relationship—shit, I'm barely adjusting to the confusing world around me. In my head, I feel like I could be a hundred...hell, a thousand. But in this body, as a human, I feel overwhelmed and utterly lost.

"I'm sure the council has a mate picked out for you. I was chosen for Liz..." Harry's eyes light up, and he puffs out his chest proudly. He then flinches, pulls a face, and visibly deflates. Harry scans the café, avoiding my concerned eyes. "Yeah, that turned out great...cheating bitch. Now I've gotta watch while she fucks every bitten human that moves. As far as I know, she's been with half the shifters in the country...dirty bitch."

My eyes widen, and I gasp. I've never heard Harry rant like this before.

Harry sneers and holds up his hands, mockingly. "Please don't start talking about, 'time is a great healer' and all that shit...oh, I forgot, you don't speak."

The angry, bitter energy that comes off him in waves makes me uncomfortable. I open and close my mouth like a goldfish, and I squirm in my chair. I wonder if it would help if I smiled—should I smile again?

I have no idea what to do.

"Well, if you're not going to ask...if you're interested in me...I'll tell you about my shit-show." Harry points at his chest and narrows his eyes. He sniffs again, and his leg continues to bounce.

What I've failed to notice until now is that Harry looks like shit. His dark blond hair is greasy, and he has scraped it back into a dodgy-looking ponytail. Unshaven, his facial hair has grown in a bit patchy. Harry looks like he needs a good wash.

I have not seen Harry since that last day at the house. I always meant to see him; he's important to me. But circumstances and with everything that has happened, it was difficult and then impossible. I should have tried harder; I feel ashamed.

God, I am a shit person.

"After Vince got dusted, Jace split, so that left me the bad penny of society. Everyone is gossiping about my pack, my dad. I'm now known as the rogue who couldn't satisfy his mate." Harry lets out a self-deprecating laugh. "Oh, and I can't forget I'm the rogue whose father killed his mate, and daughter."

My eyes prickle with tears. I knew it. I knew Harry would have found it hard to adjust to his new rogue status, the death of Vincent, and the thing with Liz. I should have tried harder. I presumed wrongly that John would have stepped in.

I'm stupid.

Harry is hurting, and he has no one on his side. I twist my fingers in my lap. I deserve his ire; I'm selfish. I hunch my shoulders, and a small, sad sound escapes me.

"Don't pretend you give a shit. I've been sofa-surfing for weeks. Oh, don't worry, I'm not asking to stay with you and the hellhounds in your fancy-ass apartments." I open and close my mouth again, but none of the words on the tip of my tongue feel significant when compared to Harry's pain. "But if you can help me out with a few quid?" His leg stops bouncing, and his gaze becomes intense. "A deposit for a place? I'll pay you back when I'm up and running." He tips back, lifts his hips, and removes his phone from his back pocket. With a few stabs at it, he leans across the table and shows me the screen. It's an ad for a studio. "Forrest, I need a place to live. Being a rogue…it isn't safe. I've lost count the number of times I've had the shit kicked out of me." Harry sighs and sits back in his chair, leaving his phone on the table.

Sighing, Harry rubs his hand across his face and scratches his patchy beard. The noise makes me want to cringe. "Don't worry if you can't help. It's only me." He widens his eyes and pushes out his bottom lip.

I drop my eyes and stare at his phone, contemplating. I own property around the city, and a few are safe houses not linked to my mum's estate. Harry doesn't need to stay in a grotty bedsit.

I go through my shopping bags and hunt out the box with the new pay-as-you-go phone that the girl in the store had kindly set up for me.

Harry bristles as he watches me.

"So the packhouse is on the market? I looked online..." He whistles. "That's a lot of money…you are keeping most of the land, though? That's sick—it's a great place to run as a wolf." 'Sick'? I glance up from my new phone, and I guess my face shows my confusion at the word, as Harry misconstrues my look. He angles his chin down and pulls a sad face. "You know it's for sale, yeah? I know you girls are all about the mating and the pup-making. Must have been John that put it up? Shame, that." He sniffs, crossing his arms again.

Harry is wrong; I put the place up for sale. I loathe that house.

After a few blunders, I manage to open my email. Using one finger, I haltingly type an email to arrange everything. I'm satisfied when I get an immediate reply; they can have the place cleaned and stocked within a few hours.

I nab Harry's mobile from the table, open his messages, and type in the address and door code for his new home. I hold the phone back out to Harry, and with a sniff, he snatches the phone out of my hand.

"Woah, you're joking—I can't afford this place, it's well out of my budget," Harry sputters. He narrows his eyes when I smile. I nod and tap my chest, Harry growls. To explain adequately, I show him my phone and the emails. "It's your place? Motherfucker, check you out, poor little rich girl, someone has fallen on her feet. If I had known about this, I wouldn't have been slumming it." He snarls, tapping the corner of his phone on the table. He stops and points it at me. "I have a request—can you tell your people to make sure the fridge is stocked with beer? Oh, and I don't suppose it has sky sports? For the football?" I nod. I can do that, no problem.

I give him a hesitant smile, relieved that I can do something to help him and hopefully redeem myself.

"Thanks…hey, in all seriousness, you shouldn't be out on your own. I thought with the hellhounds as bodyguards they'd be better, more experienced at keeping a female like you in check. Shifters don't allow females to walk about alone. Only slags like Liz slip their bodyguards. You don't want to get a rep as a troublemaker. Hell, you're already odd-looking. Any other issues and you'll never get a decent mate." I blink, absorbing his hurtful words. Did he mean to be so rude? "I can walk you home. Don't worry, little sis, I got your back." With a toothy grin, Harry pulls out a knife and slaps it down on the table.

What the fuck…my gaze skitters about the café nervously. Thank God no one has noticed the big-ass knife sitting in front of us.

I raise my eyebrows as Harry flips the blade into his hand and digs the tip into the table. I gawk, horrified, as he inscribes the letters *L…I…Z* into the surface.

What the hell is he doing?

I'm not normal, yet it wouldn't cross my mind to deface someone else's property.

Instinctively I smack his hand, dislodging the knife, and I glare at him. Harry shrugs and smirks. He rubs the marks with his palm, knocking the curled shavings onto the floor.

"This place is owned by humans—who gives a fuck if I scratch the table?" More like *gouge.* I think indignantly. I care. I like this café. Whoever designed the décor did so with care and attention to detail. I don't want to see the place defaced because Harry is in a mood. I can't sit and watch that.

"What a sad existence you have, from being feral to being a human-loving goody-two-shoes. Don't worry: I won't mess up my new digs. In fact, here, take the blade." Harry flicks the knife, spinning it across the table. "You'll need protection. If you won't be a good female and keep your bodyguards close, you should at least learn to protect yourself, not that it will help. Fucking hell, Forrest, you can't even talk...it's fucking weird."

My heart shudders and drops into my stomach. I want to be understanding and show compassion for Harry and his feelings, but it's hard. I still don't know the right balance between my emotions, and Harry is making me bloody cross. My nostrils flare with my growing indignation, and I stuff the last of the cake into my mouth and chomp. I better go now; otherwise, my mask will come off, and I am liable to grab hold of Harry's greasy man-ponytail and smash his face into the table.

I rub my face on my shoulder and blow out a breath and remind myself sternly that Harry saved me. This is Harry. He has earned my respect. Harry isn't a bad person, he's hurting and what he's saying contradicts conversations I've overheard in the past.

I need to explain myself. I'm nothing like Liz, and I'm nothing like the poor repressed female shifters either. I don't want to be sequestered and bred, owned, while my male counterparts do whatever the fuck they like. My purpose in life is not to be a mate, a pup-maker, or to conform to unfair standards set by the council. His words make me feel sick.

I carefully place the new phone back in its box and grab my shopping.

"Oh, Forrest, don't be like that. I'm only telling you the truth. I can still stay in the fancy house, yeah?" I give Harry a stiff nod. He scrambles for his phone, and I stomp away, heading for the door. "Do you want my digits?" he yells at my back.

It takes everything in me not to raise my hand above my head and give him the finger.

CHAPTER FIFTEEN

I decide I should get myself off home. I'm safer being on my own. When I say *safer*, I mean for others—me wanting to smash someone's face in can't be healthy behaviour. I'm not a nice person, and leaving like I did was childish. Everything was so much simpler when I was stuck as a wolf.

I stomp through Market Square, and things go from bad to worse.

I certainly didn't count on being accosted by two beefy wolf shifters. One shifter swaggers in front of me, and the other one comes up behind. For a split second, I can practically taste my fear; it floods my mouth, bitter underneath my tongue. Freeze-or-flight is my natural response to danger, but I don't see a way out of the alternative this time. The ever-present rage that simmers inside of me sweetly sings. The two shifters are trying to box me in, and I let them.

"Hello, female, why are you alone? Where are your bodyguards?" *Oh, for fuck's sake.* I close my eyes and clench my fists around the bag handles—the plastic one in my right hand rustles. I forcibly blow a breath through my nose in exasperation. Honestly, what the fuck is wrong with these idiots? I move slightly so I can keep an eye on both of them.

Both men are suited and booted, wearing black suits that look expensive. Even with fancy clothes, they look like a couple of meatheads.

Meathead One, with his shiny bald head and goatee, doesn't wait for me to answer. He instead pulls his phone from his pocket and pokes at the screen with his meaty finger. I rhythmically tap my fingers on my thigh with annoyance. The nerve of this guy, his arrogance, presuming I'm happy to stand here patiently waiting while he makes a phone call.

It riles me, and my rage bubbles.

Meanwhile, Meathead Two is staring at me like he is in wolf form and I have a juicy steak tied to my tits. He has brown hair and eyes, with a face only his mum could love.

Maybe the hellhounds or John sent these guys?

"Boss, yeah, we found the female we scented…yeah, she is on her own…yes, sir, we're bringing her in now." He jams his phone back into his pocket. "Now, girly, you are coming with us. We have been following your scent for hours."

Oh, okay, an interesting development. These two meatheads are random wolves that have decided to grab me off the street because they smelled me. That's messed up.

"Our boss would like a word with you. He is… urm… concerned for your safety." Sure he is. I clench my teeth to stop myself from growling.

Meathead One reaches towards me to take my shopping bags. I release my hold and let him take them out of my hands. Happy for him to hold them for me—for this.

"Come now. We have wasted enough time tracking you." He also gives me a smarmy, lecherous look.

What is wrong with the shifters today? Treating me like I'm not a person—it's as if I am just a walking uterus.

I am sick of this sexist shifter shit. I'm sick of being frightened, sick of behaving like I'm meek. Well, I am about to give them a lesson in leaving Forrest Hesketh the fuck alone. My overwhelming rage has buried any trace of fear, and I can no longer control my expression. My sweet mask cracks and a crazy, hungry smile crosses my face. I've got a whole lot of rage and aggression inside me, and this situation is perfect.

I let my rage out to play.

I take one of Jodie's *don't see me now* potion balls from my pocket and flick it to the ground. It breaks on the floor at my feet, unnoticed by the wolves. God, I love witch magic, and that little ball will keep us invisible to prying eyes.

I sneakily enter a fighting side-stance. The trick to this is not to telegraph my move, so I transfer my weight onto my back foot and roll the heel of my front foot across the floor. I lift my toes to turn my whole body sideways onto the ball of my foot. I point my hip towards Meathead One, who is helpfully standing at a perfect distance for this move. I lift my arms to protect my face and for balance. I spin, twisting my whole body away, and as I turn, I pivot on my back foot. I peer over my opposite shoulder at Meathead One in my peripheral vision. Spinning quickly, I jump to gain added height, and my leg shoots out at a forty-five-degree angle. I point my toes to compress my tendon, and I smack him hard with the back of my heel.

I slam him with so much force in the back of his bald head, his body crumples. The whole move takes a matter of seconds, a perfect spinning-jump heel kick. I hum.

Meathead Two blinks in shock at Meathead One's unconscious body surrounded by my shopping bags. He looks at me, his brown eyes wide with disbelief, and his mouth hangs open. "What the fuck," he whispers.

My rage purrs, and with a manic smile, I launch myself at him. He recovers rapidly, and I duck as he tries to punch me in the face. I step under his guard and towards him. He helpfully leans forward, and I use my leg as a distraction. As he goes to block the kick, I thrust my palm out, hitting him under his jaw with a palm-heel strike. I then use my elbow to hit him in the face, catching his nose; I follow that up with a punch to the throat.

Blood splatters from his nose and lip.

He makes a strange gurgling sound and drops to his knees. With a smile and a little wave at him, I bring my right leg up in a sidekick and slam him on the head.

"Night-night," I mouth.

I glance about, checking that the potion ball is doing its job. Perfect, no one is looking at us. I grin. I turn both wolves onto their sides in recovery position. I have no idea if that will help, but I feel magnanimous. I also flick sleep-potion balls at the pair; I don't want them following me.

Oh, I need to do something before I go. I liberate the mobile from Meathead One's jacket pocket and hit redial.

"Are you on your way?" a male voice asks gruffly.

"Nope," I say, popping the *p*. There's silence for a few beats.

"Hello, little wolf, it is a pleasure to hear from you. May I enquire why, and more notably, how are you calling?" the male voice purrs down the phone at me; I pull the phone away from my ear and frown at it. Bossman is slimy.

"Your meatheads are in Market Square. Please send someone to scrape them up from the pavement," I reply to Mr Slimy, my voice annoyingly rough and husky from disuse. In this instance, it's handy that speaking on the phone is so much easier for me than speaking face-to-face.

"Are they alive? What hap—" I end the call and drop the

phone next to the downed wolves. I gather my shopping; I feel lighter. Almost skipping, I turn once again for home.

I get back to zero fuss. Owen gives me a nod and asks me if I got him anything. Then he tells me he will meet me in the gym in ten to work off the cake I ate. The sneaky hellhound must have followed me. Huh, he didn't interfere, so I guess I will take that as a win.

The illusion of freedom.

CHAPTER SIXTEEN

It has been a few weeks, and I'm back at the cake café waiting for Harry to join me. I have a big mug of tea and a slice of carrot cake...urm, well, an empty plate that once held carrot cake. The plate now looks like it has been in the dishwasher, as it's so clean. If anyone insinuates that I licked the plate, I will adamantly deny it—mmm, crumbs.

A few days ago, a contrite Harry got in touch. He was full of excitement over his new place and the accounting job that he managed to bag. Harry asked if we could meet.

I'm thrilled that he wants to spend time with me.

Unfortunately, to my chagrin, my usual table is taken. So I am sitting at a table next to the toilets. It's not ideal, but it's the only free table that didn't leave me with my back to the door.

After a few minutes, Harry joins me, and as he sits, he wrinkles his nose. "Not the best table, Forrest." He indicates with his head the toilets behind me, as if I missed them. I shrug. "So kicked any more shifter ass recently?" he says with a grin—oh yeah, he thinks he's hilarious. I roll my eyes.

"So have you heard about the vampires finding that girl?" He settles into his chair, eyes alight with fervour. Harry is a big gossip and has a fountain of information on all things creature—the guy loves to talk. "They say she got bitten by a cat shifter and she got all poorly-like. The vamps found her living in a garage." It takes all my self-control not to flinch. Garages and me... we aren't friends. "Homeless, only seventeen, the word is that she made it, that she turned. Can you imagine that? A bitten human female. I wonder if she will be infertile. If it can happen to her, imagine how many other women can make the change?" He nods, his face lit up with zeal. I glare at him. "Don't worry, Forrest, I won't hurt your precious humans. I'm not going to bite anyone. I don't want any more grief with the council." Harry mock-shudders and slurps his coffee in thought. "Vamps still have her—there's going to be war if they don't turn her over."

If Grace were alive, she would be sixteen. Maybe I can find someone to help her? I make a mental note to find out if Owen knows anything about the girl's situation.

Harry appears different today; I can't put my finger on it until I realise it's because he looks clean. He is wearing smart pants and a shirt, his hair is short, and he has shaved that awful beard. I hum, pleased to see he is back to normal.

The bell above the door jingles and out of the corner of my eye, I spot a walking nightmare.

Oh, my bloody God, no other than Liz Richardson is swinging her hips towards us, a ridiculous sashay that gets every man's attention. My first instinct is to drop my eyes and focus on my mug and pray she struts past. But I can't give her that satisfaction—I'm no longer a frightened, starved wolf. So I lift my chin and hold eye contact. *Please grab a silver sword now that I can fight back, you stupid cow.* Liz snarls, showing me her teeth, and I huff out a laugh. What the hell was that? Huh, it's not just her walk that's ridiculous. I chuckle.

Oh my, Harry is here! I mentally slap myself and squirm in my chair, aware that this could end badly. Poor Harry.

Liz reaches our table. A choking cloud of perfume follows in her wake. I frown as I watch with growing confusion as Liz places one hand on the back of Harry's chair and the other on his jaw. She turns his head, and while maintaining eye contact with me, bends down and delicately kisses Harry on the cheek. She leaves her red lipstick on him and flashes me a smug smile.

"Hi, baby, so glad we could meet for a coffee," she simpers, plastering a sweet smile on her lips.

Harry goofily grins back at her. "Hi, Liz. Would you like a slice of cake?"

What. The. Fuck.

I blink. I feel blindsided. I've no idea what the hell is happening. What is she doing here?

"Oh, no thank you, I don't eat cake," Liz says with a shudder. *Psycho!* I scream in my head—who doesn't eat cake? "But I would love a triple-shot decaf skinny soya macchiato with sugar-free hazelnut syrup. If they have one," she says again, sweetly fluttering her eyelashes. I have no idea what she ordered, although I am quite sure her pretentious drink isn't on the menu. Harry scrambles away, and I watch him go to the counter. I can hear him mumbling the order back to himself, so he doesn't forget it.

Liz glares at me from across the table. I stare back at her blankly, kind of numbly. She sighs, drops her gaze from mine, and pulls out her phone. She types furiously, ignoring me. Fine by me.

Harry arrives back at the table. I watch dazed as with a flourish he places a regular-looking coffee in front of Liz. He steps back and rubs the back of his head. "It's a normal decaf coffee with…urm, soya milk, they didn't have the other stuff you wanted…" He bounces from foot to foot, anxiously waiting on Liz's approval.

"Oh well," Liz says, again sweetly.

What the fuck is wrong with her? Having her so close and her being nice is starting to freak me out. I know she's not being nice to me, but still, this whole situation is beyond my comprehension. A few short weeks ago, Harry was calling Liz nasty names. She cheated on him! Now he's presenting coffee to her like he has hunted her a prized rabbit. What happened to the whole "I can't be with a cheater"?

"We can go to a better place next time. This place is small, and it smells funny." She sniffs in my direction. Ah there she is...am I weird to feel a little relieved?

"Yeah, next time." Harry beams at Liz and throws himself down into his seat next to her. He sits slumped, with his legs and arms wide. Liz gives me a cocky smile. My bullshit detector sounds—she's up to something. For some reason, her smile makes me want to hop over the table and smash her in the face.

"I am glad you're here, dog..." Liz covers her mouth and giggles over her fake Freudian slip. *Dog.* I briefly close my eyes. It's just a word, and words only hurt you if you let them. I won't give Liz the satisfaction of seeing me react. I sit taller in my chair, fighting my natural hunching reaction, and take a deep calming breath. I cough as I inhale a mouthful of her perfume. God, did she use the whole bottle? "I know that you are *extremely* good friends with my baby and that you want to spend more time with him." She smiles the largest, toothiest, and phoniest smile I have ever seen.

I tip my head to the side. Where is she going with this? Harry is pack.

"What you don't understand is that you can't buy his affection by giving him a shitty house, especially when it was your fault in the first place that he was homeless and classed as a rogue." Liz leans forward across the table and growls. My mouth pops open in shock. *What?* "Admit that you manipulated the whole situation for your own gain and that you staged that phone call." Liz points a red-tipped finger at me, her nails painted to match the tight bandage dress that she's wearing. "Admit it. I am here to tell you that Harry is mine and that you need to leave us alone! You also need to speak to your brother and fix Harry's rogue status. Your lies will come out and you need to fix your wrongs before they do." Liz sits back and raps her coffee cup with her red nails. A smug, satisfied smile flashes across her face.

I blink. What the fuckity fuck fuck? What planet is this girl on? I flick my eyes toward Harry and scrutinise his reaction to her words. I wait for him to tell her to fuck off, but in growing disbelief, I watch as he nods his agreement. He nods his fucking head!

Harry leans forward and with consolation pats my hand, which is gripping the edge of the table. I flinch back and rub away a sharp pain in my chest with my knuckles.

Ouch. I fight to keep my face blank.

"I am sure you're upset. Liz explained everything and what she says makes sense." Harry smiles lovingly at Liz. "You have issues, Forrest." Harry makes a fake sad face and sniffs.

"Her word is no good, baby. Look, she hasn't even bothered to deny our accusations! We have to see this as a righteous intervention. Your pack kept the ungrateful dog safe. What else could you do? She was feral! Why do you think she doesn't talk? She is worried we will catch her out. No one believes her—she's a liar." Liz drops her voice. "None of this would have happened if you would have listened and had her killed when we had the chance." Harry nods his head again, hate shining in his blue eyes.

My heart is eviscerated.

I squeeze my eyes tight. I refuse to cry. I want so much to curl in on myself, but by sheer will, I snap my spine straight.

God, I so wanted to treat Harry with trust and kindness. I wanted to see the best in him. I thought he was my pack, my brother. Yet every time Harry gets the chance, he says something to hurt me, and a piece of me dies. I feel sick, my mouth is dry, and there's a lump in my throat that I can't swallow. The person I thought Harry was, doesn't exist.

I made him up.

The realisation hits me with the force of a double-decker bus—the hole in my chest aches.

I'm an idiot.

"She isn't a pureblood female anyway, right, baby?" Liz strokes Harry's face and sneers in my direction. "She is like part Fae or dwarf or something." She leans into him and whispers, "That's why she is so small and went feral for all those years." Liz runs her fingers through her bobbed hair, and her eyes sparkle with delight as she speaks. "I mean, look at her hair and eyes, what she is wearing—she's a complete freak."

"Part dwarf"—how rude is that. I'm wearing sparkly silver trainers, leggings, and a cute jumper—normal stuff. I force myself not to adjust my grey unicorn jumper. Honestly, what is wrong with this girl? Why does she hate me? The poison dripping out of her mouth is pure fabrication, and Harry is lapping it up. She's crazy, and Harry is nuts to believe anything that comes out of her mouth.

I think I prefer Liz being fake-nice.

The horrible cow can't even address me while insulting me. The least she could do is say this shit while looking me in the eye. I lift my bum off the chair with the sole intention of beating the shit out of her. I might knock both their heads together while I'm at it.

"Sweetcheeks, are you ready to go?" a rumbly voice asks behind me. I sit back down and turn to take in the shifter who has swaggered up to the table, somehow appearing from the toilets behind us. He's dressed impeccably—charcoal custom suit and matching overcoat. I examine Liz, and her face shows zero recognition.

Is he…talking…to me?

I frown. He dips his head, his full attention on me.

Bloody hell—he *is* talking to me.

"Come on, sweetcheeks. I know you wanted to do your normal thing with your *brother*, but we had better get going. We have so much to do today." The strange wolf smiles warmly at me.

I blink at him. Is everyone on drugs, or am I the only person who has not got a clue what the fuck is going on today?

He leans across the table and offers his hand to Harry. "I am Daniel Kerr, it's good to meet you, Harry, finally."

Wow, the strange wolf is good—he gives Liz zero acknowledgement. It's like the mad cow is not even sitting there. I can almost forgive him for calling me "sweetcheeks"— almost. Like bloody hell, that's annoying. Grrr, "sweetcheeks…"

Daniel doesn't even glance at Liz, even when she squeezes her ample breasts together. She's almost propping them up on the table. *Steady, Liz, if you squish those puppies any more, they're gonna pop out.*

"Yeah…" says Harry as he shakes Daniel's hand. Total confusion is written all over his face.

Daniel inspects me with a gentle smile, his blue eyes sparkling. "You are looking beautiful today, little wolf," he whispers as his hand gently cups my face. He runs his thumb across my bottom lip. I am so surprised, I don't react aggressively—I sit and gawk up at him. The gesture is so intimate, I have no clue how to respond.

How many times does an absolute stranger swagger up to you, make out that you are in a fake relationship, and start touching your face? Nothing could prepare me for this shit.

Liz is livid and has gone from smug to downright murderous. She has also gone bright red, the colour closely matching her dress and nails. Her gaze bounces from Daniel to me and back again. Liz again tries to gain Daniel's attention by flapping her hands about, frantically trying to highlight her table-boobs. She's also glaring at Harry—she wants him to do something, but Harry is also clueless about how to react.

I guess this wasn't part of their righteous intervention— fancy that.

"So you're Harry, the rogue? From the dissolved Oakland pack? Thanks for keeping *my* Forrest company, Harry. I know she doesn't talk to you, but she finds you amusing." He slaps Harry on the back, in a supposedly friendly gesture. But his big hand wallops him hard enough to rock Harry's body forward, almost forcing him from his chair. Harry winces. "If you will excuse us. We have a busy day and night ahead. Forrest, come." He takes hold of my arm gently, and I stand. I gratefully allow him to guide me from my chair and between the busy tables. Before I go through the door, I turn and make sure to give the stunned couple a snide little wave goodbye. Fuckers.

"I apologise for interrupting your conversation, but I couldn't listen to that vile girl for one more second," Daniel says when we're safely out on the pavement.

What the fuck just happened? Did this guy randomly rescue me? I look up and up. He's of course, shifter-tall—he must be around six-foot-eight. The top of my head is about level with the middle of his chest. He looks down at me, amusement dancing in his eyes. I give him a suspicious nod of thanks and a little awkward wave, and turn to stomp away.

"She is still watching, Forrest. Come on, I will give you a lift home." I look up into his handsome face. His eyes are blue and his hair is dark. He has that square jaw and heavy brow– look going on that's popular with movie stars.

I strangely allow him to take my arm and lead me towards a posh-looking car at the curb.

CHAPTER SEVENTEEN

Daniel opens the rear passenger door for me, and I slide into the seat. He closes the door and swaggers around to the other side of the car and gets in.

Why I go with him, I have not a clue. If I am honest, I don't want to give Liz the win. She tried to bring me down just now, and without Daniel's timely intervention, I would have entirely and embarrassingly lost my head in there. The only thing I lost today was my rose-coloured glasses in regard to Harry.

I grimace and rub my chest again. I could learn to live with that just fine.

I snap my seat belt into place.

The car sets off and the doors lock, I hope automatically —although the smug, nasty glower the driver gives me from the rear-view mirror suggests otherwise. The driver is male, a shifter with a bald head and a goatee. With a blatant sinking feeling, I realise he is Meathead One, the guy who I knocked out a few weeks ago.

I put my head in my hands and rub my temples. Oh, fucking hell—without being a genius, I now know who Daniel is. I spoke to Daniel once before; he is *Bossman,* the guy who ordered the two meathead wolves to track and take me.

I can't believe I got into his car. I'm a fucking idiot!

I lean my elbow on the door and nudge the electric window button. It quietly moves the window down an inch, which is a good thing. It means I am not trapped. I peek up at Daniel, and he is silently watching me, a satisfied smile on his face.

"Do you know, since our last conversation on the phone, Forrest, I have been more than a little intrigued about you. Your story, your history. In wolf form for so long, trapped. Yet despite the disadvantages, over the last few months, you have thrived. Now that I have met you in person, I am fascinated."

I think Daniel is waiting for me to reply. I don't feel comfortable chatting with a man who has more than likely just abducted me.

One thing I have noticed is, the less you talk, the more others seem prone to do so. They talk and talk. My silence makes them a little uncomfortable, so they fill in my silence with noise. It's such a weird thing that happens—even guys who generally only give one-word answers or have a grunting system open up to me like I am a priest on confessional duty.

"You are so different from other females of our species. Unique. I am almost six hundred years old and even in my long lifetime, I have never had the pleasure of meeting someone like you. It's as if you, little wolf, were created for me." *What?* I gape at Daniel with what I'm sure is a confused and horrified expression. His eyelids droop, he licks his lips. Is he trying to seduce me? *Eww*, I'm not at all impressed. He looks at me as if the sun shines out my bum. Creepy. Apart from our telephone conversation a few weeks ago, I have never spoken to the guy. Yet it's like he's starting on the path of declaring undying love. I wiggle in my seat. The way he's talking...it faintly reminds me of another car-journey conversation with a demon.

"If I hadn't seen the CCTV footage of you taking down two of my best men, I would have never believed it. I am impressed; you are a talented young woman. I'm so glad you made the right decision to leave with me." I have no idea what he wants me to say. Does he want me to give him a gold star?

He inches closer to me, turning his body so he's facing me. He reaches over and tries to paw my face in the same way he did in the café. I growl at him. Instead of taking that as a warning, he leans further into my space with a throaty chuckle. Fear and rage flood my system, and I start to shake. Daniel takes a deep breath in, breathing my scent at the pulse point on my neck. He groans. I growl. Everything inside me screams that I need to get away, that I'm not safe.

This guy is not right in the head.

I move as far away as the seat belt will allow, squishing myself into the corner of the car. I am still growling. His right hand takes hold of my hip, and he slides me back across the leather, closer to him. He puts his hand on my seat belt, tightening it so I can't move, basically trapping me in the seat. With the seat belt across me like this, I won't be able to shift. Well, I can, but I will still be trapped. His hand is blocking the belt-buckle release.

Becoming frantic, I lift both my legs up to try to kick him away from me, but he blocks the movement with his body weight, pinning my legs to the seat. Daniel is almost entirely on top of me. His right hand has managed to grab hold of both of my wrists. I watch him wide-eyed, panting.

I grapple with my rising panic.

What the hell is happening? I try again to escape him, and his grip becomes painfully tight—the lack of room a problem.

"You're not getting away from me again. You. Are. Mine," he snaps. I flinch at the venom in his voice, and he immediately calms. His tone switches to cajoling. "There's no way out of this, Forrest. Hasn't today proven your poor judgment and that you are not safe left to your own devices?

Little wolf, no one will appreciate you as I will. No one will keep you safe as I can." I try to squirm away, unsuccessfully.

I don't know why he's doing this.

The softness now in his eyes is disconcerting. Daniel is the worst kind of villain. He thinks he's doing the right thing. Delusional wanker.

My mouth is too dry to speak, my brain too confused to form words.

Daniel leans forward, and I shudder. He smiles against my cheek and my skin ripples in disgust at his closeness. "Little wolf, I can't wait to be inside you."

Oh my fucking God! I freak the fuck out.

I lose control of myself for a few seconds. The primal fear screaming through my body stops me from thinking clearly. I whine, and I struggle desperately to get away. In those short moments, I forget all of my training. I need to get away!

The meathead driving laughs.

He. Laughs.

I force myself to stop and breathe, to think.

To Daniel, it might look like I have given up or exhausted myself. But I am desperately trying to get hold of my instincts. I am no way used to a grown-ass man talking to me like this. He's got me trapped almost underneath him in a moving vehicle going God only knows where. Does he think it's okay to talk dirty to me in this situation? Maybe some girls would like being trapped helpless with a handsome wolf. But that's another type of story, and this is mine.

I spent years trapped. I dealt with and took so much shit as a wolf. I am not going to deal with this shit as a woman—no fucking way. I have no idea where he's going with this, but I am not a bloody victim, and I am not hanging around.

This is not bloody okay!

My anger triggers another response, and my shifter magic reacts beautifully. My fingers shift into wolf claws for the first time.

Daniel drops my wrists in shock, mumbling the word *magnificent*.

I don't think—I react. Owen's voice screams directions in my head, and I use my claws in one quick move to not only slash the seat belt, setting myself free, but at the same time swiping them viciously across Daniel's neck and chest.

The sudden pain forces him to move away from me— although Daniel, the weirdo, looks back at me with a thrilled appreciation. I take advantage of his distraction, and I smack the window-down button. Before the window has opened fully, and before he decides to try to restrain me further. I shift into my wolf.

I leap through the window, escaping the still-moving vehicle.

I am on the left-hand side of the car, so I don't have to contend with any other vehicles. My shoulder collides with the pavement hard, and I roll with the force of impact.

I shake it off. Apart from my pride, I am unhurt. I run.

Luckily for Daniel, he doesn't follow, as I am so bloody angry I could rip his throat out and chew his nose off with my teeth. I am that cross. I hate feeling frightened. I know it's unrealistic, but I'd stupidly hoped that I would never have to deal with that kind of fear again.

God, am I always destined to be somebody's victim?

The lack of respect he showed me is mind-boggling. I don't know if it's just my opinion, but men shouldn't jump on you like that. Did his mother not teach him not to assault random women, or is it the case that he's so good looking he has never dealt with rejection?

I didn't say *No* or *Get off me you fuck*. So maybe it was my fault—perhaps I should have used my damn voice? Why didn't I use my voice! Harry is right on one thing— I'm bloody weird. I have a voice. I need to use it. What the hell is wrong with me?

Bad things happen if I don't talk.

But Daniel is a shifter, and he must have smelled my fear. He knew I was frightened, yet he continued anyway. He didn't back off, *but he didn't touch me inappropriately either*, a horrid little voice says helpfully in the back of my head.

After I get my bearings, I realise he was taking me out of the city. The car was on the main road leading to the motorway. I was lucky on the timing of my jump, as the speed limit on this road is only thirty.

I know where I am, and I also know Jodie's coven shop isn't too far away. I need to talk to my witch friend. I need a friendly female point of view, so I get my furry ass moving to Jodie's.

As I run, I wonder if it's me and my circumstances that make male wolf-shifters react with zero respect. So far, all that I have been met with is scary misogynist beliefs. They seriously think that they can do what they want to me without consequence.

For fuck's sake, I just jumped out of a moving car to get away from that prick Daniel.

The freaky fuck probably thought it was some kind of foreplay.

I huff. Shit, I was better off sitting in that café taking nasty digs from Liz, and that's saying something…why the hell did I get in that car?

I have spent so much time in my wolf form learning about life from catching the odd TV show through the kitchen window. I have no idea how to behave as an adult shifter. I got lucky just now—the size of him compared to the size of me.

I am not letting myself deeply analyse all the crap that just happened. Being upset, hurt, and frightened isn't going to help. Nor is acting in anger and chewing Daniel's face off, unfortunately.

I have to think of things rationally. If I start thinking like a terrified woman, I'm going to make a mistake and get hurt.

It happened, I am okay, and the best thing I can do is learn from my mistake.

So I shove all this bullshit quite forcibly to the back of my mind. I push it into another mental box, this one labelled *Deal with Later.*

At least today shouldn't get any worse.

CHAPTER EIGHTEEN

It doesn't take me too long to reach Jodie's, as I set an excellent loping pace. I arrive at the shop, and it smells heavily of herbs and magic. I haven't been here before, but Jodie gave me an open invitation to visit. God, I hope Jodie is around and not working at the hospital. I desperately need to see a friendly face.

The magic shop, with a sign written in bold letters above the double frontage, proclaims: 'TINCTURES 'N TONICS' - SPECIALISTS IN PORTABLE POTIONS. The store proudly sits sandwiched between an art gallery on the left and hairdressers on the right. Housed in a modest-sized building rendered in cream with an old bank sign engraved into the stone above the door, it is situated on Birley Street, a pedestrianised street in the middle of the city.

I plop down in front of the closed door. I lift my front paw and give the door a tap-tap, being mindful of my sharp claws and that they don't mark the paint. After a few taps, a young witch in a blue school uniform answers. She swings the door wide in welcome.

"Forrest, how are you doing, come in, come in. Jodie! Jodie! Forrest is here, and she is all wolfy!" The young witch, Heather, squeals her excitement and gives me a huge welcoming smile. I met Heather at the hospital when she helped Jodie bring in a potion order. I find the young witch adorable. "Forrest, can I stroke you? Please, please, please?" Heather wiggles, waving jazz hands at me with a big grin on her face, her short blonde curls bouncing. "You are just so cute."

In response, I nod my head, my tongue flops out, and I give her my best wolfy grin. Heather squeals again in delight. I flop down on the wooden floor, and Heather throws herself to the floor next to me.

Heather gently strokes the fur around my head and ears. She runs her hands along my back. It's sooooo lovely. I've never had my fur stroked before. Thinking about it, I've never known a kind touch in this form. With each stroke of Heather's hands, I find myself relaxing further into the floor.

I glance around the shop with interest. It's brightly lit— natural light filters through the big windows at the front.

Fascinatingly, dozens of magical globes of light float in different corners of the room. As the light in the shop changes throughout the day the floating orbs will move to where they're needed. One has already made its way above Heather and myself. So cool.

I notice that the wooden shelves are filled to the brim with wonders. The tingling hum of energy from the magical artefacts fills the air, and the almost-overwhelming smell of herbs stings my nose.

I close my eyes. Life isn't so bad if you don't focus on the negatives.

"Come on now, leave her alone, you crazy child. She is a woman underneath all that fur." I open one eye, and Jodie is standing in front of a door, for what I presume is the back employee area of the shop. A genuine smile is on her pretty face. "Forrest, so nice to see you, pumpkin. If you change back, I will make you a cuppa." She turns and trots back into the room behind her.

"Aww, I never get to see shifters in animal form. I wanted more time...your fur is so soft." Heather whines her complaint as she scrambles up from the floor and stomps away.

I huff out a wolfy laugh and get up with a stretch. I make my way over to the door, my claws clicking on the floor. I peek in.

The room is large but cosy, decorated in warm tones of green that appeal to me. It has a proper wood-burning stove and a comfy seating area at one end and a beautiful, big, industrial-sized witches' kitchen at the other, with a table that can seat twelve in the middle.

As I enter the room, I allow the shift to take me. The magic transforms my body from wolf to my human form in seconds. It doesn't hurt, and it feels natural. It's not like the human-made racist werewolf films, where the bones break, strange fluid grossness comes out, and the werewolf screams in pain. It's a blink-and-you-miss-it kind of transformation, pure, beautiful magic.

Magic is breathtaking in its complexity. For example, witches handle magic differently from shifters. There are so many branches of magic some witches are potion specialists like Jodie and her coven. Other witches specialise in elemental stuff.

My point is, witches *manipulate* magic. Shifters *are* magic.

One interesting fact I did find out about witches from Jodie is, witches have the opposite issue from the shifters: male witches are extremely rare.

Jodie has her back to me and is making tea. Wow, she is pulling out all the stops. Jodie has arranged delicate teacups, saucers, and a beautiful teapot on a tray. She places on it a little milk jug and a sugar bowl, with actual sugar lumps…so fancy.

I dig out the potion balls from my pockets. I might as well get Jodie to check them, as I am not sure whether the shifting back and forth has ruined them. The shifting magic Jodie gifted me with at the hospital makes my clothing part of the transformation, so I retain my clothing when I change back. It also shifts my weapons—how amazing is that! The only thing it doesn't shift with me is tech, so I am not sure if it will like other magic coming along for the ride. I love not having to strip naked to shift.

"You can put them in the bowl on the side table, I will check them in a bit." I huff. Jodie still has her back to me. *Freaky witch*, I think with amusement. Grinning, I obediently pop them into the bowl.

"Sit down," she says, carrying the tray of tea things to the table. "So tell me, what is wrong? It isn't like you to be carelessly running around in your wolf form."

I sit and chew my lip. I bet half the shit that happened today wouldn't have happened if I'd opened my bloody mouth. I can't let this control me anymore. I place my head in my hands and rub my temples. Where do I start…

"Use your words, Forrest. It's just us here. Please explain to me what has happened." She smiles at me with encouragement. Her brown eyes are warm and reassuring, so I open my mouth, take a big breath in, and tell her.

I explain what happened with Harry, with Daniel. At first, Jodie is livid with Harry and all swoony over Daniel's timely rescue. But the more I elaborate, the angrier Jodie becomes. Jodie is furious on my behalf. I feel so lucky to have such a good friend. I also feel a sense of relief that my friend knows the details about today and agrees with most of my conclusions. Jodie doesn't think I overreacted to either situation. She gives me the impression that I should have acted sooner.

After she calms down on seriously wanting to maim Daniel for the car incident, Jodie finally decides against giving me an exploding dick potion. I think.

"Here, this one is a male impotence potion." Jodie hands me a bright red ball. "It is a witches' version of pepper spray; not only does it make it impossible for a man to get it up for weeks, it also incapacitates even a shifter for about twenty minutes, so you can either escape or as an alternative stab him." She grins.

I stare at the small innocuous ball on my palm and blink up at my friend. I hope she hasn't sneakily given me the scary one. As if Jodie can read my mind, she bursts out laughing. "Your face…" She laughs so hard, tears stream down her face. I watch her with bemusement. When she can speak, Jodie says, "I promise it's not the exploding one, Forrest." Jodie cackles again, slapping her leg, her eyes sparkling. "With this potion, if an afflicted man goes to any witch for help, she will know and will probably extend the life of the impotence potion. So be careful and only use it in a situation like today, as it is a very effective punishment." She rubs the tears from her eyes.

Wow. Note to self: don't piss off a witch.

"Thank you," I say with a cautious smile. The wrath of Jodie is a beautiful thing. I dramatically shudder, and Jodie starts giggling again.

"I wish you had smacked Liz about a bit…" Jodie says wistfully.

Daniel inadvertently stopped me from kicking Liz's ass, which did me a favour, I guess, in the long term. "I just have a new slimy stalker to contend with." That sobers my friend up, and she gives me a sad smile.

"Okay, well, we're going to have to do something about the shifters being able to track you so easily. I do have a few things that will be perfect…give me a second." Jodie claps her hands, jumps up, and starts rooting around in her stock room. After a good fifteen minutes, she producers a gorgeous bracelet. "Now first, this bracelet," Jodie says, putting it on the table in front of me. "If you decide to use it, it's not just pretty; it's also incredibly complex magic. When you wear it, you will be impossible to track."

Use it? I stuff that sucker on my left wrist so fast, Jodie hasn't even finished telling me about it. Jodie gives me a bright smile and shakes her head at me. She pours me another cup of tea and continues. "It is scent-masker magic. It will change your scent entirely and regularly. So even standing directly in front of a shifter, you will smell like a regular mixed human. Oh…" Jodie springs up and returns with an old box, which she places on the table with a thump. "By the time I'm finished with you, these wolf shifters will not know that you're standing directly in front of them. Even your hellhound friend won't recognise you with this next beauty."

"Ooh, is it a glamour?" I ask cautiously. Jodie rolls her eyes and shakes her head.

"No, not a glamour—a lot of strong creatures can see through them. Nope, what you need and what I have here, Forrest, is disguise magic," Jodie whispers conspiratorially. Ooooh.

I leave Jodie's shop hours later, a scrap of paper with a phone number clutched in my hand and my pockets full of shiny fun-filled potion balls. On the good-news front, after checking, Jodie confirmed that my other potion balls had survived my shifts. Which is fantastic news as it tells me that my new magical bracelets will also shift with me without an issue.

On my left wrist, I have my fantastic scent masker, and on my right wrist, I have the disguise bracelet. The disguise magic isn't active all the time, unlike the scent-masker magic. With the disguise bracelet, I have to put my fingers on it and say the word *Betty*—which activates the spell.

It was hilarious, choosing what I wanted to look like. There's nothing like giggling at yourself while looking in the mirror and you have a giant nose and a massive chin. Spending time with Jodie lifted my spirits. I feel lighter.

In the end, because my voice is so deep and husky, we decided on an old-lady disguise, and "Betty" is perfect. I still have my build, height, and hair colour—blue rinse used to be a thing, so why not pink? Popping my hair into a bun, I will be good to go. The less we alter with magic, the less chance of the spell being discovered. Brown eyes, a sharp nose, and lots of wrinkles, happy human wrinkles. Like a lifetime spent laughing and smiling. Shifters don't show our age with lines like humans; our age isn't stamped on our faces and bodies. No, age is measured by the level of power that radiates beyond normal senses. Once a shifter hits their natural maturity, their prime—normally a human-looking thirty to forty years—the body doesn't age. Shifters don't care about age; it's all about power.

With a little bit of artistic dressing up, even if it's just a coat, Granny Betty will be good to go, the perfect disguise.

CHAPTER NINETEEN

When I arrive back at the apartment building, I find out that John has been in contact and wants to speak to me immediately. Apparently, he wants to discuss what happened today with Daniel and the whole kidnapping thing. I've no idea how he found out so quickly.

When John answers my video call, he looks livid. For a second, I'm pleased to see how upset he is on my behalf.

That thought ends up being *hugely* presumptive.

"I had an interesting telephone call with *Councillor* Daniel Kerr." I freeze and my face blanks. Oh bloody hell, stalker Daniel is a council member. Fuck my life. I observe John with growing trepidation.

"You do realise, Forrest, that having a member of the council calling me about my unruly sister is completely unacceptable. What the fuck have you been doing to piss off one of the most important shifters in the country!" John roars.

Shock fills me, and in response, my magic tingles and my fingers partially shift to claws: off-camera, Owen grunts in surprise. I grimace. This conversation isn't supposed to go this way. I bite my lip and twist my hands in my lap. The claws on my left hand inadvertently dig into my thigh, and the scent of my blood permeates the air. Owen promptly takes hold of my hand in silent support, and more than likely to stop me from further shredding my leg.

Unaware, my brother continues to berate me. "The councilman explained what happened today in detail." John rubs the back of his neck and growls, "We decided the whole incident was your fault, clearly due to your lack of life experience. I am so disappointed in you, Forrest—you behaved like a manic child. You obviously misinterpreted the entire interaction with the councilman. Our mother would be ashamed of your erratic behaviour."

My stomach jolts when he mentions my mum. The memory of my mum that day at the warehouse tries to smash into the forefront of my mind. No, that flashback shit is not happening. I grab the memory and stuff it back into its box. No, hell no.

John is wrong; I know in my heart that my mum would understand, unequivocally.

162

"Daniel Kerr was not trying to kidnap you or do anything inappropriate. Bloody hell, you stupid girl, the notion that a council member would try to capture *you* is utterly ridiculous." John shakes his head and curls his lip; his disgust with me is apparent, and it is written on every line of his furious face.

I gather my courage and open my mouth to respond to his unfair accusations. The determination to stick up for myself throbs through my whole body.

"He—"

"No! I'm talking." John cuts me off with a snarl and holds his hand up to silence me further.

My eyes burn as I stare at my brother, silently communicating my hurt.

"Daniel said you assaulted him. Forrest, you assaulted a council member! He could have been seriously hurt. He also mentioned that prior to the assault, he had to intervene in your attack on an innocent female shifter. What the fuck is wrong with you! You need professional help! I convinced the councilman not to take any legal action, and lucky for you he won't be involving the hunters. But we decided between ourselves that you cannot be trusted." Confusion swirls inside of me, and my heart hammers in my ears. It takes everything in my power to sit quietly and not react. Owen squeezes my hand as I struggle to remain outwardly calm. I draw in another shaky, painful breath.

"Daniel was also concerned about how you left his car in such a dangerous fashion. The window, Forrest, really?"

John continues his lecture. "Daniel has offered, at his own expense, his well-trained shifters to take over your bodyguard duty. From now on, when you want to leave the building, they will accompany you. The hellhounds are too busy to deal with you and your shenanigans." John shakes his head in frustration and disappointment.

Daniel has played John well. What a manipulative bastard. I've not got a clue how I'm going to deal with this. Well played, Daniel, well played.

"I did decline the invitation for you to go and live with him." Well, that's real magnanimous of him, refusing my kidnaper full-time access. "I feel as if you've had enough upheaval. But I'm warning you now, Forrest Hesketh, one more mistake and I will wash my hands of you." He meets my gaze, and another growl slips between his teeth. John is terrifying when he loses his temper, and at the moment, he is holding himself together with the thinnest of threads. "You need professional help. Daniel will be arranging that for you. I don't know how you got so fortunate, gaining his favour. Especially after everything you have done." John shakes his head. "The councilman is a better man than myself." John rubs the back of his neck again.

In a quieter voice, he says, "What did I expect from a feral wolf? You behave like an animal, and I will treat you like one. If I could put you on a lead, I would." I suck in a breath. Wow, fucking harsh, a lead? Really, John? Why not get me another electric collar while you are at it? "Now, you've wasted enough of my time. I've got to get back to work. Behave yourself." John ends the call without a goodbye.

I sit in the chair feeling numb. I huff in frustration. Why the hell did I mention that today couldn't get any worse? Bloody Murphy's Law.

Fuck my life.

I close my eyes and repeatedly bang the back of my head on the seat. That whole conversation escalated quickly. Technically I did claw Daniel in self-defence, but what the fuck! He did the assaulting. Now John has invited this powerful and dangerous man further into my life.

If I hadn't spoken to Jodie today, I might have been persuaded that I'd overreacted. The cruel things John said... "One more mistake, and I will wash my hands of you." So easy for him to say, and to believe Daniel's bullshit.

To not ask me for my truth.

I appraise my bleeding leg. The cuts are shallow. I sigh. I have ruined my leggings.

Daniel, the bastard, has manoeuvred us all around like chess pieces and has gotten his own way. A tear rolls down the side of my nose, and I use my shoulder to wipe it away.

I need to hit the gym. I need to beat the crap out of something, and after I am a sweaty mess, I need to spend a few hours meditating. If I don't, I am liable to go hunt Daniel, that fucker, down and show him what assault really looks like. While he's on the floor bleeding, I want to scream and shout at him for frightening me in that car, for turning my brother against me.

No.

I bet he's counting on me reacting like that, without thinking. Going after him with all guns blazing will play right into his hands. Acting like the animal that John claims me to be.

A sob wrenches itself out between my lips. I screw my eyes closed tight.

The best thing I can do is play it smart, keep my head down, and don't react. I am not bloody playing Daniel's sick game.

Daniel needs to think I am scared prey, weak, without friends. To enforce that belief, it might be best if I didn't leave my apartment. With my years stuck in wolf form I have a history of being left in a horrible situation. So this is what he would expect anyway. A predictable pattern of response, to lull him into making a mistake—and given enough rope, he will hang himself.

I think about my brothers and the pieces of my soul that they have destroyed today. I have grown up with neglect and constant pain from my supposed loved ones. Hell—I shake my head—it's easy for me to acclimatise to the callousness of this world, as I expect to be kicked while I'm down. I've dealt with this shit before. Mental and physical abuse—yeah, we're well acquainted.

Life is bloody unfair.

It's how you deal with it that defines you, and I refuse to be a bitter, horrible person who's ruled by my rage.

Why do the men in my life do this? Why are they so fucking cruel?

"That was a bit unfair," Owen says. I open my eyes and blink up at him. I realise we are still holding hands; he has been so quiet, letting me think. Huh, not all the men in my life. I squeeze his hand in a silent thank you. "Will you please tell me what happened?" I let go and poke at my claws. I peek up and give my friend a sad smile, and another blasted tear rolls down my cheek. As I did with Jodie, I start from the beginning.

After I've finished, Owen's angry energy rips around the room. He sucks in a sharp breath, then lets it out in a huff. Eyeing me, he growls.

"John needs to be told—"

"Please, he won't believe me. You heard him. Please, Nanny Hound, you don't have to fight with my brother or Daniel. I...I won't be anyone's burden." The wobble in my voice is pathetic. "It will play right into Daniel's hands. I need to pick my battles and not show my hand." I then go on to explain my thinking and theory.

I meet Owen's gaze; there's fear and anger in his grey eyes. Owen cares about me. I try to convey how grateful I am. My eyes sting and my chest burns. He visibly swallows, scrubs a hand over his face, and manages a surly grunt and a stiff nod.

"Okay." Owen then checks me over; he nods once when he's reassured I'm not an inch away from death. He ruffles my hair like I'm a kid. I then get a whole ten-minute lecture on why getting into a stranger's car is so dangerous. The normality of being told off pulls me away from the teetering edge of hysteria. The warm hug after the stranger-danger talk also helps.

Owen agrees that both the scent masker and disguise magic is a good idea. The less my movements now are tracked, the better.

We both decide that I'm on lockdown and I can't leave my apartment, let alone the building. Not with the new set of shiny henchmen, erm, I mean the *bodyguards* that will be patrolling. Heck, how much are you betting it will be the Meatheads on guard duty? As I am planning sneaky ways to escape, perhaps learning to abseil, Owen tells me about portal doors.

"We have portals? How did I not know that portals were a thing?"

"They are a witch-created gateway system attached to other portals all over the world, using ley line magic," Owen explains. "You have to have permission to go anywhere and know the gateway codes. Otherwise, you're gonna get an unpleasant, possibly even fatal greeting by a ward on the other side." There are local portals all over the city. Owen promises to give me the local codes and the world-gateway portal map later to memorise.

The laziness appeals to me, never mind the stealthiness. The thought of being able to go anywhere in the world instantaneously is mind-boggling. The world is a small place with magic.

Unfortunately, I'm not allowed to play with the newly discovered doorways, because this building doesn't have one.

Owen takes his phone out of his pocket. "I have a lady friend who is a gateway witch." I grin at him. "I can call her—"

"Oh, you have a friend…" I wiggle my eyebrows. Owen is mortified at my teasing. Which encourages me to run my fingers through my hair, flutter my lashes, and pout my lips in a poor impersonation of his hypothetical lady friend. He grimaces in abject horror. I laugh and make grabby hands for his phone. Owen places his big hand on my face and holds the phone out of my reach.

"Stop it. I thought you were having some kind of epileptic fit—don't do that again. Not that kind of friend, Forrest. I can get her to come and install a new gateway in your apartment this evening. The expense will be ridiculous but worth it. Thank God you're rich. I have another witch that owes me a favour, who should be able to come and install a ward after." I bounce on my seat. Whoop! My own portal. "The apartment ward will be extra security; I am thinking to keep this Daniel out of the building will prove impossible. He's a council member with high status. That makes him almost untouchable. It doesn't help that John owns the building and apartments. I could still talk to him…?" I shake my head. "Okay, *we* pick our battles and not show *our* hand." Owen repeats what I said before, meaningfully. "So setting the building ward to blast Daniel or his people, although amusing, would be foolish. So we set a ward to keep them out of your apartment and stop them from getting to you. Meanwhile, you can pretend that you are sitting in your apartment, sulking. It will give us time to find a solution to this mess." Yay. We have a plan. Owen stands and pulls me up from the sofa. "We will use your roof garden for training—using the gym will be out for some time. Starting now, you're on lockdown.

"Right then. Come on, Forrest, get changed. I'm gonna drill you on pressure points, eye-gouging, and your ground game. We also need to make sure those claws don't keep popping out willy-nilly."

CHAPTER TWENTY

When I was leaving Jodie's shop earlier, she stuffed a slip of paper into my hand, insisting that I needed it. On the paper was a phone number for a group that helped creatures in trouble. Jodie swore they were the real deal and that if anyone had any unbiased information on shifter law and how to deal with problems like Daniel, these would be the people to badger. I took the number to be polite. I originally had zero intention of phoning. Jodie must be psychic.

With my stalker slash kidnapper biting at my heels, I have to do something proactive. I have no real allies. Of course, Owen is on my side. But I can't expect him to put his career and his life on the line for me. What kind of person would I be if I did that? The same goes for Jodie. I've made the sad decision to keep away from my witch friend until this thing with Daniel has calmed down. I don't want to get the witches involved. This isn't their fight. Daniel is too dangerous.

I ring the number, but I don't get a response.

A few hours later, after the witches have installed my new ward and portal, I'm making a cup of tea and my phone rings. I glance at the handset curiously. *Who the heck is calling? No one ever calls me.* Staring at the phone like a weirdo won't give me that information, so I think, *Fuck it,* and answer.

"Hello?" I say cautiously.

"Forrest? I'm returning your call…you seem to have a council-member problem? Are you okay?" I pull the phone away and blink at it. *Huh.*

"Everything's a little bit of a mess," I say guardedly. That's a massive understatement.

"Yeah, I get that. Let me introduce myself. My name is Ava, and I'm a security expert. I'm sorry I didn't get back to you sooner. I normally vet my callers before speaking to them, and sometimes that can take a while. In your case, I spent the time productively, gathering available evidence. I am happy to tell you I have footage of today's kidnap attempt."

"You have…footage?" I whisper disbelievingly. "How did you know…what type of footage?" I close my eyes and bite my lip. *Please be ringing to help me. Oh please*, I beg to the universe.

"Yes, of both kidnap attempts. Don't forget, Councilman Kerr has tried this twice now." I can hear the faint tapping of a keyboard down the earpiece. "Camera footage from the lights when you jumped out of the car, footage from the café. Oh, and my pièce de résistance: surprisingly, I also have footage from the car."

"Oh my God." I make a sort of gurgling noise. The sound gets stuck in my throat and turns into a whine. I wobble and almost drop my tea. I manage to slide the cup onto the counter before I sink gracelessly to the floor in the middle of the compact kitchen.

Who is this person? Can I trust her? What does she want in return?

"There, I've sent everything I have to your email address. Now, instead of going to your hellhound brother with this information, I think we should aim a little bit higher, don't you think? If you're up for it and if you can trust me, let's sort out this nightmare once and for all."

"I want to trust you," I whisper. My voice wobbles only a little. "I've had a shitty day. I don't know what to say…Ava, this is too good to be true. But I will trust you. Thank you, thank you."

Ava chuckles, her voice warm. "Jodie will be pleased. It is not going to happen overnight. I will have to arrange a meeting, and in the meantime, Forrest you must keep your head down. I can't protect you until I get this evidence to the right person. That's, unless you want to disappear? I can help with that if you don't want to fight. I think you have an excellent chance to clear your name. But I can help you run instead..?"

"I want to try." I'm so glad she's on my side—I hope. I can't believe that she's got hold of all this information and she knows everything without me telling her. It's awe-inspiring. Maybe Ava is a computer hacker? Is this too good to be true? I have everything crossed and have faith that she will not try to fuck me over. "I will keep my head down and stay here. Ava, thank you. If I can help you in return, you only have to ask."

"It's no bother, Forrest, it is what I do. I will ring you when I know more. Take care." After we've said goodbye, still on the kitchen floor with my whole body shaking, I check my email.

Ava came through.

The camera footage is damning. This is what I needed; I hope it's enough.

I think I've found my rope.

* * *

I am standing outside my portal door. I shift from foot to foot and wriggle as if I have ants in my pants. I am kind of bricking it. I tug my coat into place and with my fingers comb the loose strands of hair back into my bun. I've been procrastinating on using this gateway for weeks. I'm hesitant to leave the safety of my apartment, frightened that either Daniel or John is going to grab me and lock me away. So I've locked myself away in my apartment—how is that for irony?

I'm also nervous I will hit the wrong gateway symbols and end up somewhere I shouldn't. I regret telling Owen I didn't need his help when it was first installed. In reality, I should have done this weeks ago.

I laugh when I remember the gateway witch and her disgust, which was overflowing when I told her I wanted my portal to be inside my walk-in wardrobe—come on, who doesn't want a portal in a wardrobe? Hello Narnia.

She spent hours doing her amazing portal magic to connect my apartment to the ley lines. The witch was seriously not amused when for fun, I asked her if I could send out some of the clothing I didn't like through a random portal, to give someone a present. The *no* was said forcibly, the look of utter incredulity on her face was priceless. The ward witch was much nicer.

I have been spending my time avoiding Daniel's goons, training with Owen, and reading every book that I can get my hands on. Time has disappeared; it has fluttered away while I've been hiding. Now I need to use the portal, and Owen isn't here to help. Owen, along with the other hellhounds, has been sent away—some important council thing that's all hush-hush. I have a terrible feeling Daniel is messing about in the background, but that might be me being paranoid although I doubt it.

The Meatheads and other guards have been outside for the last few weeks, and I have avoided them like the plague. I have been getting my food delivered, but since the hellhounds' departure, my food deliveries have stopped. It's as if I'm in my castle, safely locked in the tower, and Daniel's sieging, trying his best to starve me out. The prick.

Ava got video evidence of the Meatheads accepting and promptly destroying or eating my food. The bastards ate my bloody chocolate cake! My cake! So in cake desperation, I'm going to take the Betty disguise out for a spin. I need to be brave.

I bounce on my toes and examine the gateway with apprehension. I know the codes and where I need to go. I just don't know what the portal looks like on the other side, and it's freaking me out.

I take a deep breath, and with a shaky hand, I start to input the code.

The codes are magic symbols; they look similar to Egyptian hieroglyphics but are closer to cuneiform in structure, a magical language not related to human history—the witches call them "runes." There's a fancy big-ass name for them but don't ask me, I haven't a clue. My magical education ended at age nine.

The first three symbols are like an area code, and the next six are for the portal itself. The one I am inputting *should* take me to a portal door in an alleyway a few streets away from a bakery I want to try. I also need to start talking to strangers more, so I can use this trip as speech and portal practice.

I am stalling. Here goes nothing.

I finish the code, hold my breath, and step through.

That wasn't so bad—I am alive, and huh, it felt like I was plodding through a regular door. So anticlimactic—I expected a little bit of tingling or a flash of light, something. I glance about, pleased to see I am in fact in an alley—hopefully, the one I wanted.

What is a little bit interesting and not expected is the two vampires that are standing in front of the portal door as I step out. I almost career into them. Hopefully, they're using the portal and not guarding it. I shuffle sideways and give a wary nod in greeting.

I don't like vampires.

It's not the undead thing or the blood-drinking thing; it's a shifter thing. My nose is so sensitive, and vampires smell like dead stuff slowly rotting. I think it's the start of decomposition before the human body turns, but it also might be what vampires smell like, as a base scent. Rot. Either way, they always make me feel a little sick. I try not to breathe through my nose or flare my nostrils at them in disgust.

Both vampires look like regular humans. One is fat with a horrendous comb-over, the other is skinny. If I squint they look a bit like Laurel and Hardy—all they need are little bowler hats to complete the look.

"So what is an old human like you doing, using the gateways?" *Huh?* Human? Oh yes, the scent masker and "Betty"...perfect! It works on vampires—that's good to know. Well, if I am going to use today as practice, I might as well use my voice. Hopefully, they're not going to want to try and eat me. Kicking vamp ass because they wanted to use me as a walking blood-bag doesn't scream "incognito."

I clear my throat and say huskily, "I apologise for almost walking into you gentleman. If you will excuse me, I'm on an errand."

They both look me up and down. "Maybe you can be of help, human. We're looking for a female shifter. Pink hair, gold eyes. I don't suppose you know of anyone with that description?"

Oh, crap, the vamps are talking about me. They are looking for me. I give a shake of my head and squint at them with what I hope is a confused and worried expression.

Shit, shit, shit.

"I have never met a female shifter before. Is she a criminal?" I do a little shudder, hoping that will disguise my accelerated heart rate.

"No, but she has an outstanding arrest warrant. She has gained someone's interest. Like I said, pink hair, gold eyes, and she doesn't speak. Here is our card if you see anyone like that. You give us a ring, and we will give you some cash, a grand in cash, for a phone call." I nod my head with fake enthusiasm and take the card.

"How wonderful," I say brightly. "I would love that money so I could visit my sister, how wonderful. I will keep my eyes peeled." I pat my pink bun. "Oh, I have pink hair! I hope no one thinks I'm this shifter." I chortle.

"Do not be concerned, human. No one will mistake the

two of you for each other," Comb-Over Vampire scoffs.

I wish them good luck as I make my way out of the alley. I keep myself calm, hoping the slight rise in my pulse will not give me away. I try to shuffle to make myself appear more human. I probably look like I've shit my pants. I will have to add that to my practice list: my Betty walk. Humans don't prowl.

* * *

Once I am home, I make myself a cup of tea, and I sit in the roof garden eating my chocolate cake.

I thumb through my contact numbers. I first try to call Owen, but his phone is switched off. Before I put the phone down, it rings—Ava.

"Hi, you're home safe? Are you aware of the arrest warrant?" I scamper back into my apartment and throw myself down on the sofa. The ward will stop anyone from eavesdropping.

"Yes. What the hell! I just found out this morning. Two vampires were offering cash for sightings of me. Is it Daniel? What is he doing?"

"Well, yes. I can confirm that Daniel Kerr has instigated the warrant. He's getting impatient; it works in our favour beautifully. Involving the Hunters Guild is priceless." The smile in her voice is apparent. "I will email you a copy of the warrant, now. Fortunately, it's not a substantial amount of money. He will get some sloppy independent players trying to get some easy cash. There are firm stipulations about your health and wellbeing, so he doesn't want to hurt you. I feel the warrant is more for making you desperate and backing you into a corner, covering the bases rather than making a serious attempt at capture. Using the Guild to do his dirty work," she tuts. "This illegal warrant has bumped us up the waiting list considerably. I've managed to get you an appointment with the Guild tomorrow."

Ava gives a satisfied chuckle down the phone. "I couldn't find anything on the Guild's system—there's no official case against you. Daniel has bypassed the rules and issued the warrant without the proper documentation. The document even states that you are to be handed over to him and not to the Hunters Guild for processing. To even have a fugitive handed over to the supposed victim is a big no-no. The whole thing stinks. It is such an abuse of power.

"I'm going to use the vampires that you met today as a distraction for your bodyguards. Keep out of sight in the morning. I will make sure it is safe for you to attend the meeting to get the warrant rescinded. I'll send you a car in the morning." We end the call with a goodbye. It's a significant risk to trust her, but it feels right.

The email from Ava comes through on my phone, and I open the attachment and read. It's the supernatural warrant-for-arrest paperwork. I quickly read through the official document declaring me a fugitive. Huh. In my head, I see myself dashing through tunnels with Tommy Lee Jones running after me. *"I did not kill my wife!" I scream.*

Oh okay, so that was Harrison Ford. But to make the title

of fugitive—even if it's a load of bollocks—makes me feel like a bad girl. I hum a Billie Eilish song, "Bad Guy," as I grab another slice of cake and flick the kettle on.

THE GENERAL

I am going to the Hunters Guild with a demon barrister, yes, a *demon barrister,* whom Ava has arranged to represent me. The demon, whose name is Mr Brown, is accompanying me for questioning in regard to the assault charges against me.

I'm feeling incredibly nervous.

My pink hair is loose, falling to my waist. The hem of the pretty high-necked white dress falls just to my knees. It has lovely ethereal 3D flowers embroidered onto it and a big bow at the back. Underneath I've put on a ruffled underskirt on that makes the skirt puff out. The dress is ridiculous, and because of that, it's bloody perfect. If I'd been tall, the dress would have looked elegant—it's a designer dress, after all.

But on my small frame, it makes me appear more fragile. I seem merely like an innocent, *harmless* young woman. I pair the dress with a soft pale blue cardigan, pale blue tights, and delicate white shoes.

My wrists feel bare without my magic bracelets. Ava had warned me I would be security-scanned for magic, so it's best to leave them behind. I'm good to go.

I mince out the lobby door. The bodyguards left in a big rush about half an hour ago, so the coast is clear. Ava has given me the car details, so I feel confident in leaving the safety of the building and its ward when I see the car waiting.

My knuckles go white on the door handle. I tremble. I close my eyes, steady myself, and open the door. I slip inside and greet Mr Brown—he isn't Daniel, I tell my quaking self—with a nod and a small smile.

The demon isn't what I expect; he's thin, with wispy blond hair and pale, watery blue eyes behind thick-rimmed glasses. He's wearing an ugly brown suit. "Miss Hesketh." He nods back at me and then looks out of the window, not expecting a reply. I sit quietly. I don't put my seatbelt on.

It doesn't take us long to arrive at the Hunters Guild building. The car drops us off at the main glass doors, and we're greeted by a harassed-looking lady who rushes us through a magic and weapon screening. Once we have been security-cleared, she shows us to an elevator, where she flashes a card at the panel instead of pressing any buttons.

We bypass all the marked floors and head to the top of the building. When the elevator doors open, we step out into a very nicely decorated hallway. At the end of the hall is a single door.

That is not ominous at all.

The door doesn't have a name on it. I have no idea who we're meeting. My nerves must show on my face, as Mr Brown looks down at me with a kind, confident expression.

"Now, Miss Hesketh, all you have to do is speak the truth. I will deal with everything else." I nervously nod and twist my fingers together. The lady opens the door and ushers us into the room. She stays in the hallway and closes the door behind us.

The office is massive, and like the hallway, it's decorated beautifully in browns and golds. The very masculine room has wood panelling halfway up the walls. It has a seating area with a bookcase, a leather sofa, and two wingback chairs.

A huge shifter is seated behind a desk that's situated in front of the floor-to-ceiling windows. The shifter stands in greeting as we make our way towards him. I peer up at the massive fucker, and my eyes settle on the bridge of his nose. In a world full of massive shifters, this guy is hands-down the biggest guy I have ever met. He is shockingly so much bigger than any of the hellhounds, in both height and build—although if you looked at him in a photo, you would think he was a normal-sized man as he is so in proportion. Standing in front of him is a whole other experience.

The navy suit he's wearing doesn't have a single wrinkle or mark. It flawlessly fits across his big chest and broad, round shoulders, his taut, tapered waist. Even in his suit, he'd look more at home with a broadsword in his hands. God, his shoulders are so wide! I bet he'd take your head off in one punch. He must be well over seven feet—I estimate around seven-foot-five. I know instinctively he is a dragon shifter.

The dragon's powerful energy makes my skin tingle, and all the hair on my body stands up. I don't know who he is, but I know he must be very important.

I am not too proud to admit he scares the shit out of me.

He sends my instincts into overdrive. I even find myself stepping behind the demon defensively, which is a pointless move as the dragon can still see me. My eyes scan the room, looking for alternative exits.

He is watching me. His face is not showing any emotion, but his nostrils flare, taking in my scent. His face is a work of art—chiselled, angular, with high cheekbones, a strong jawline, and a straight nose. His lips are full, with the bottom one slightly fuller than the top. The dragon's hair is long and silver; even his skin has a slight silver glow. The man is beautiful. I huff. How could he not be beautiful? He is a dragon shifter, rare and legendary, after all.

God, he's a handsome bastard. I let out an almost inaudible sigh.

The dragon's silver eyes flash, and I instinctively freeze.

Predator. I try to act like smart prey. I don't move a muscle. I keep my eyes on him and my peripheral vision on the room as a whole. I can feel my chest tightening, and my breath puffs in and out with my panic.

I am both terrified of him and shockingly turned on at the same time.

There's a knock on the door, I jump and squeak in fright— a fucking squeak! The dragon appraises me even harder.

"Come in," he says in a deep, rumbling voice. The door opens, and a dark-haired male witch enters. Wow, a male witch. The witch appears like he's in his forties; he sneaks around the big desk and stands next to the dragon.

That's it, Forrest, focus on the nice witch and not the scary dragon.

The dragon shifter sits back behind his desk and holds out a hand, indicating the visitor chairs. Mr Brown nods and sits. I stand for a few more seconds, wanting to run like hell out of the room. Prompted by the baffled look Mr Brown shoots me, I rush and take the seat.

I scramble into the chair, the dress bunching awkwardly in my panic. I then have to wiggle around like a little girl, trying to straighten it. What makes the whole thing even more difficult is that the chairs are massively oversized, and my bloody feet are about a foot off the floor. I glance up when I finally manage to get sorted, and all three men are looking at me.

I hope I didn't flash them.

I am so glad I am wearing tights. Bloody dress. The dragon grunts.

I peek up at him. I try to ascertain whether the grunt is a good one or bad one.

"Thank you for agreeing to this meeting, General," Mr Brown says with a nod. "I am Mr Brown, and I am here today to represent Miss Forrest Hesketh in regard to an arrest warrant for assault." The dragon doesn't take his eyes off me. I refuse to move about in my chair. I lift my chin, but I can't help glancing towards the exit with my eyes.

"That is a serious charge, Miss Hesketh," the dragon says in a mesmerising, low voice. I nod, trying not to shiver. The witch hands the dragon a tablet, and he reads through the information. After about ten uncomfortable minutes, he glances up. "Okay, I am going to ask you some questions, and you are going to answer them truthfully, Miss Hesketh. Matthew, the truth crystal, if you please." The witch, Matthew, pulls a clear crystal from his pocket, and he places it carefully on the desk.

"Would you pick that up and hold it in your right hand. Keep your hand on the desk at all times," Matthew says quietly. I nod and take hold of the crystal in my trembling palm.

The dragon waits a few seconds and asks, "Can you give me your full name and age, please." I nod again, and I lick my lips nervously.

Shit, I can do this. *Please, voice, please don't fail me.* I cough to clear my throat.

"Forrest Hesketh, and I am..." I feel ancient. "I am twenty-three." The crystal goes red. Is that bad? It went red! The dragon sighs with disgust, and I glance at Mr Brown in alarm.

"Mr Brown, your client can't even say her name and age without lying! You are wasting my time!"

"General, you have just read Miss Hesketh's file. She has been in her human form for only three months after spending fourteen years as a wolf. I believe her age might be the issue." The room is silent, and everyone is back to staring at me.

"I am sorry, sir," I say, my voice raspy and breathless. I wiggle in the chair. "I don't feel like I am twenty-three. My age is twenty-three. I am twenty-three." The crystal goes red again. I feel like thumping my head on the table. I am trying my best—bloody hell, I'm useless. The dragon is going to eat me!

"Repeat your name!" the dragon barks. I flinch and suck in a ragged breath; my heart is pounding in my ears.

"My name is Forrest Hesketh," I rasp.

"You are here today to deny the charge of assaulting Councilman Kerr?" he asks. I glance over at Mr Brown, and he nods.

"Well, no...urm...I mean, yes, I did," I state quietly. The crystal stays clear. The dragon scowls at me with exasperation.

"Explain!" He barks again, in frustration.

So I tell him.

CHAPTER TWENTY-TWO

When I finish speaking, my throat hurts. I cough—my mouth is so dry. I told the dragon everything, from the beginning. I kept my eyes on his nose, not brave enough to meet his gaze.

The crystal stayed completely clear the whole time I spoke.

Thank. Fuck.

"Show me your human claws. Matthew, will you please get Miss Hesketh a glass of water?" I blink at him in surprise—he wants to see my claws? A shade of impatience crosses his expression. "Miss Hesketh, they are the weapon in question. If you please." Matthew places a glass of water on the table. I mumble a thank you, and I guzzle down almost all of the glass.

Oh my God, the performance pressure, to produce my claws in front of a dragon—a dragon! If I couldn't, would he eat me? My heart pounds anew. I close my eyes, and I centre myself and try my best to ignore my fear. I take a deep breath in and let my shifter magic do its thing on my fingers. I open my eyes to see—to see a blue flame dancing across my fingertips.

Where are my bloody claws! What the fuck is that!

I whine in shock, and without thinking about it, I stuff the offending hand into the water glass.

With my frantic movement, I unbalance, and with no hands free to steady myself, I squeak as I fall onto the floor in a heap. *Oomph.* My dress goes over my head.

I stay where I am, hoping they will forget about me down here. My breathing is panicked, and I am still whining with fear.

What the fuck was that! Fuckity fuck fuck.

There's movement above me and rustling. I peek up at the dragon in shock as he uncovers my face from underneath my dress. I blink. There's a piece of hair that's sticking in my left eye. I blow out a hard puff of air, trying to dislodge it. The dragon squats in front of me; he tilts his head to the side as he studies my hands. I am still clutching the crystal in one hand, and the glass is wedged on the other.

"Have you ever done that before?" I shake my head no. "I need the words, Forrest," he says quietly in his smooth chocolate voice. He brushes the annoying strand of hair away. I gulp and stare at his hands. Big hands, the biggest I'd ever seen. He's proportional, so it shouldn't surprise me. He is so close; the dragon towers over me.

"No, never, I was trying to show you my claws." The crystal stays clear.

"What were you thinking at the time?" he asks me intently. His voice is deeper, softer too. He is almost hard to hear. I lean forward, and for the first time, we make eye contact. Wow, his eyes are such a beautiful silver. He smells fucking incredible, the smoky musk of burnt wood. I hum.

"I was frightened that I wouldn't be able to show you my claws and that you would... eat me." The dragon huffs out a laugh, stands, and helps me back to my feet.

"Let us try that again, shall we, Miss Hesketh." He shakes his head at my still-full hands and picks me up and puts me back on the seat, arranging my dress perfectly around me without effort. I stare at him in shock. He pulls the glass from my hand with a wet plop and puts it back on the table.

"Okay, claws please, Miss Hesketh," he says as he prowls back around the desk and sits.

"What if I—?" I wiggle my wet fingers and make a weird flamey sound at the back of my throat.

The dragon smirks at me. "You will not."

Okay then, okey-dokey—let's do this. Instead of closing my eyes this time, I focus on my practice time with Owen.

I think of the slice of chocolate cake I am going to have this afternoon.

My magic tingles and my claws come out. I smile brightly in triumph.

The dragon's eyes drop to my lips, and his eyes dilate. A rumble vibrates in his chest, almost like a purr. "Very good," he praises in a deeper and slightly gruff tone. The dragon tilts his head to the side and again breathes in my scent. I don't know if he's aware that he isn't so sneaky about smelling me. He holds out his hand across the table, palm up. My mouth pops open, and I blink at him in confusion. "Your hand please, Miss Hesketh."

Oh. I put my wet hand in his, and he frowns. "Sorry," I mumble.

Then he inspects my claws. "Matthew, please update the file to say Miss Hesketh's claws are approximately three inches in length." He taps the end of my index finger. "They are not weapon class," he says dismissively.

It's my turn to frown at him.

What is wrong with my claws? They're awesome! Not a weapon? I huff. "Daniel thought that they were," I mumble under my breath.

"Okay, if you will excuse me, stay where you are, Miss Hesketh." The dragon gets up and walks away from us. "Matthew, test Miss Hesketh for all magic, including residual. I want a full report." He disappears behind a hidden door near the seating area. Huh, It's a portal.

The room is suddenly colder without him in it. His smoky musk of burnt-wood dragon scent lingers.

The scary dragon smells so good.

I glance at Mr Brown, who nods at me. I bounce in my seat a little, relieved that my part in this debacle is almost over.

I take the opportunity to tidy up my hair, which is still all over the place from my fall. Matthew disappears into the hallway and returns with a magic scanner.

"Please put your claws away and place your palm on the scanner." I do as he asks. I have been using my claws to run through my hair like a comb. Unfortunately, my lap is now full of little pieces of hair. Note to self: sharp claws are not suitable for hair-brushing. Thank God my hair is thick—otherwise I'd be bald.

I place my hand on the scanner and watch in fascination as the scanner lights up. I saw one before at the hospital, and I know from my reading that hunters carry a basic version. This one isn't a basic one, and even Mr Brown is watching on with interest. It also pricks my finger and takes a sample of my blood.

We wait for the dragon to return; he has been gone for what feels like forever. Well, okay, a tad over two hours. But I have a date with a chocolate cake. Waiting for him is nerve-racking. It would be just my luck that the handsome bastard hands me over to Daniel.

Matthew orders tea and coffee for us while we wait. I stuff two shortbread biscuits into my mouth quickly before anyone else grabs them. I love shortbread, and this is the good stuff from Scotland. My mouth is full, and I probably look like a hamster.

That's when the dragon decides to walk back into the room.

He appraises me with a frown, taking in the scattered pieces of hair. The dragon raises an eyebrow at Matthew. "Miss Hesketh brushed her hair with her claws," Matthew explains.

The dragon rubs his hand across his temple and sighs. "Nutty," he says with a shake of his head. He sits back behind his desk and takes the tablet back from Matthew, I presume to read the magic scan report.

"So the anti–body-hair potion and the shifter–clothing-retention potion are active in her system? Traces of a scent masker and basic disguise magic also." I chew the shortbread that's still stuffed in my mouth, trying not to choke. Bloody Jodie and that hair potion! I can't believe the dragon knows about that. I told him about the scent masker and my disguise, although I didn't go into detail—Betty is a disguise, after all. I can't say to a dragon that I am planning to dress like an old human lady and sneak about.

"Who is your potion supplier?" I have almost finished eating my shortbread, but I puff my cheeks out a little to make out that my mouth is still full. I hold up a finger and point to my cheeks. I am attempting to give myself more time to think. The dragon frowns, not buying my move.

What do I say? Will I get Jodie in trouble? I scrutinise Mr Brown, and he does his typical nod. My eyes fly to Matthew, but he isn't even looking in my direction. I have finished chewing. I shake my head no. "You're not telling who supplies your potions?" The dragon asks incredulously. I shake my head again.

"Miss Hesketh, they will not get into trouble—you have not used anything illegal. You can answer the question," Mr Brown says, trying to encourage me. I still shake my head. Jodie is my friend, and I will not send a dragon to her door. Even if he employs a male witch. No way. Nope. The dragon will have to eat me. I cross my arms across my chest but uncross them quickly, as the move reminds me of something Liz would do. Matthew has lifted his head and is now looking at me with interest and a small smile.

The dragon puffs out a breath of frustration. "Lucky for you, I haven't got time to torture you for information," he says drolly; he rubs his temple again. "I have cancelled the arrest warrant with immediate effect. The evidence Mr Brown provided before our meeting corroborated your story. I have informed Daniel Kerr that I have placed you officially under my protection. I can't believe the hellhounds were not more of a deterrent." He regards me. Sternly he says, "You are a trouble-maker, Miss Hesketh, and you need better guidance. I have spoken in person to your brother. I showed him the video evidence of Daniel Kerr's attempted sexual assault." My eyes widen. *Shit.* Incredible shit—John knows the truth. He can't argue with evidence and a scary-as-hell dragon. *Boom.* I love this guy. I wiggle in my chair, almost doing a happy dance.

"After today, with you producing fire magic, he agrees that you will be better off in my care, for the short term."

So it *was* fire magic! Of course it was—I am such a divvy. I can't believe fire magic scared me so much. "Does that make me a hellhound?" I ask eagerly.

"No, Miss Hesketh. Hellhounds are warriors. It makes *you* a liability."

CHAPTER TWENTY-THREE

That's how I found myself moving into the lair of a dragon. I wasn't listening to him properly at the end of the meeting, and all I heard was *cancelled warrant, protection blah blah blah,* and then my brain got stuck on the fire-magic thing. I may have mentally nodded off at the end.

Anyway, before I knew it, Mr Brown was standing up, and we were being shown back to the elevator.

Owen met us by the car. Which was a surprise—Owen told me the General had cancelled the mission and ordered him to accompany me home.

What I didn't realise at that moment was, I was only going to the apartment to pack my shit.

I thanked Mr Brown and asked him to send me a bill for his fee; he informed me that my guardian had paid the bill. When I had looked at him blankly, he told me the General had paid. *Huh.*

So here we stand on top of an actual cliff, the dragon's portal gateway at our backs. I stare at the view—my mouth is almost catching flies, it is hanging open that wide. Wow. Perched on the rocky cliff, hovering over the untamed beauty of the wild Atlantic, is the dragon's Irish lair—a square building that's made entirely out of glass.

It's a breathtaking ultra-modern James Bond villain house.

Shit, I hope that's not a sign of things to come.

The sound and smell of the sea fill my senses, the taste of saltwater heavy on my tongue—the waves of the Atlantic crash into the rocks below. I never thought a house could be so impressively beautiful. It must be at least two hundred and fifty feet above the sea. The sheer scale and dramatic impact of the cliff and house are awe-inspiring. It makes me feel small and humble.

The surrounding countryside is lush and green. The springy coastal grass at my feet is dotted with yellow, purple, and pink wildflowers. In the distance are mountains and trees. For some strange reason, for a split second I miss my trees around Temple House. But I dismiss the thought; I don't want to see them again. So missing them is pointless.

This is the first time I've left England, and I'm in Ireland. The land of the Fae. Typically shifters are not permitted on

Ireland's shores. But the dragon, because he is a dragon, is the exception to this rule. Now so am I! How exciting.

The dragon opens his door when Owen knocks, and we enter a bright white hallway. I hide behind Owen's bulk and greedily take in the house, forcing myself not to gawk up at the dragon. I end up watching him out the corner of my eye anyway. His very presence is impossible to ignore.

Oak-and-glass stairs—the perfect blend of old-fashioned and modern—lead upstairs, and another set of stairs goes down, to what I presume is a lower-ground floor. Halfway down the hall, there's an oak door to the right and another on the left, with another double-glass doorway further ahead, perhaps leading to the living room. The smoky scent of the house is a delight to my senses. I weirdly feel like I'm home.

Owen places my two small bags on the polished concrete floor, shakes the dragon's offered hand, and then turns to me with a small smile. I look worriedly into his warm grey eyes.

"You be good. Don't be getting into too much trouble," Owen says gruffly. "You have my number if you need me. I don't want to hear from someone else that you beat up some troll or Fae creature, you understand me?" I grin. Owen folds me into his arms and gives me a gentle hug. "You're safe here, I promise," he whispers. I nod.

"I will miss you, Nanny Hound," I say, my voice rough. I wish he could stay.

"Okay, that's enough—you will see plenty of the nutty hellraiser. You can go now, hellhound Owen. Thank you for dropping her off." The dragon glares at Owen, who nudges me gently away, and with a smile at me and a respectful nod at the dragon, he leaves.

I forlornly watch Owen go.

I peek up at the dragon. Shit, I have no idea what to call him. I can't keep calling him "the dragon," even if it's in my head. Everyone has been calling him the General, but that isn't his name, surely it's his job title? Mr Brown said he's my guardian. It's all so confusing; I must try listening better and ask more questions.

I am also frustrated that my bloody brother keeps on passing me off to others without asking me first. What is wrong with him? I don't understand why John can't find the time to talk to me and ask me what I want and where I want to live. I have money and I am supposed to be an adult. I feel like I'm in a game of Pass-the-Parcel and the music has stopped for another layer of me to be removed. If this keeps happening, nothing is going to be left. Now I am staying with a scary dragon! This is happening so fast it makes my head spin.

"Come along, Miss Hesketh, let me show you to your room." The dragon has been quietly observing me. He picks up my bags, and I follow meekly behind him. "I thought you would be comfortable on this floor. My bedroom is upstairs if you ever need me." I nod politely.

The gorgeous bedroom smells of fresh paint and is at the front of the house. I am relieved that at least in this room I won't be asleep dangling over the cliff. The external walls are glass, and the internal walls, ceiling, and woodwork are painted a magnificent dark navy. The floor is oak in a herringbone parquet. The navy should make the room feel small and dark, but it does the opposite, and the two glass walls bring the outside inside, highlighting the spectacular view of the mountains. The navy blue reminds me of the first time I saw the night sky after years of seeing nothing but bars. It's the colour when the sky is clear, the short time before the stars come out and it hasn't quite gotten fully dark. The smell of paint hints that the dragon had the room painted for me.

The bed is king-sized, and I run my hand across the mustard-yellow bedding with delicate blue flowers. There's a round mustard-yellow rug on the floor. I step further into the room and notice the floorplan narrows towards a door to the left, which I presume is a bathroom. It has open-style oak wardrobes on either side of the doorway. I glance behind the wardrobe, which is not flush to the wall, and see the reason for the narrowing. Next to the floor-to-ceiling wall of windows is a little hidden nook, also painted in the navy. I gasp as I take in the empty shelves begging for books and the substantial squishy-looking navy bean bag on the floor. It's the perfect reading nook. I want to squeal. I hold in the noise by the skin of my teeth and instead grin like a loon.

My eyes catch a familiar photo frame alone on a shelf, and for a second, I can't breathe. My knees go weak. I trace the glass with my finger, and my mum and sister smile back at me.

My eyes fill with tears.

"I hope you find the room agreeable." I spin and see that the dragon is still watching me from the door. I react without thinking. I rush towards him, throw my arms around his waist, and give him an impromptu hug.

"Thank you," I whisper into his abs. I might as well be hugging a tree for all the reaction I get from him, and wow his muscles have muscles. The dragon is solid. But I don't care at this moment; the dragon deserves a hug. I bury my face in his shirt and breathe him in. After twenty or so seconds, I pull back and glance up. "Thank you...the photo..." I say, trying to hold in a sob; I swallow it down, and my eyes shine up at him. "The room is perfect. It is so very thoughtful of you to have it painted." The dragon is standing awkwardly with his arms out at his sides, holding a bag in each hand. I step away and give him a watery, bright smile.

I don't know when I stopped being terrified of the dragon.

"You're more than welcome," the dragon says roughly; he coughs to clear his throat. "I will put your things here for you to deal with. Feel free to explore the house." He places my bags on the floor next to the wardrobes. He then turns, quickly leaving the room. As he is closing the door, he says, "Dinner in an hour." The door clicks shut.

I kick off my silver-sequined trainers, scrub my face, and wait for a few more heartbeats. I open the door, peek out of my bedroom. I don't see any sign of the dragon. I hold my breath and intently listen. I think I can hear him upstairs. The excited anticipation of looking around the dragon's lair wells inside of me, and I quietly pad into the hallway.

I poke my head into the room opposite mine and find an empty spare bedroom. Huh. It's nowhere near as lovely as mine. I can't go up, but I can go down. I ignore the room at the end of the hallway, and instead, I scamper down the stairs. A slight hint of chlorine and more of the dragon's smoky, musky scent fills the air. At the bottom of the stairs, the room opens up, and an impressive state-of-the-art gym greets me. I guess this is the reason why the dragon is so massive.

I open doors and cupboards and squeal when I find a cinema room through a door to my right.

Past all the gym equipment ahead of me, outside behind a wall of glass, I can see a pool. I slide open the glass door and step out; I find the dragon has a fancy jacuzzi, a sauna, and a steam room. The heated pool is what holds my fascination. It's incredible and made entirely of glass. I wobble and feel slightly dizzy as I stare down—I can see the sea through the glass bottom. It gives the impression that the water is flowing over the cliff edge, into the crashing sea below. Swimming in that pool will be an adventure. Eeek, this house is phenomenal.

An hour later, I leave my room and this time head towards the smell of food. I amble into an open-plan room that has a kitchen, a dining table, and comfortable-looking leather sofas. Everything is modern and elegant—it's lovely. Like in my bedroom, the external walls are made of glass, but as the room is so big, the glass walls are on three sides.

My feet follow my eyes in an almost-trance; all I can focus on is the view. The sun is slowly sinking into the horizon. The bright colours bounce off the glass and make rainbows on the walls. It's incredible. The whole room is a backdrop of fading sunlight, sea, and sky. I can almost imagine I am flying or on the deck of a ship out at sea. The thought of being here watching a storm roll in, the sea wild and the wind gusting, thunder and lightning lighting up the sky, like the best natural show imaginable...how incredible would that be to see? I don't think anyone could get bored with this magnificent view.

"Miss Hesketh, please take a seat at the table." I turn and blink. Wow, I am rude. The dragon has put our plates on the table without my noticing. He is standing in front of a chair, waiting to sit down.

"Oh, I am sorry, the view took me by surprise. Your home is exquisite, and that view is epic." I want to ask if there's anything he needs, but that would be weird as it's his home. I clamp my mouth closed and I hurry to sit down. I aim for the chair opposite, but the dragon shakes his head. He indicates the chair he's standing in front of. Oh, he is holding the chair for me to sit, wow. No one has ever done that before. I sit with a mumbled, "Thank you."

I watch as he prowls around the table. He looks very nice. He has changed out of his suit and is wearing light blue jeans and a tight white long-sleeved top. The top is *crazy*; it hugs every muscle on his torso, so much so I could count them.

It's that tight, he might as well not have it on. It reveals the most muscled body I've ever seen. It's hard not to drool. I peruse my food quickly to hide my ogling, and I don't look back up until he has safely sat down.

"What do I call you?" I blurt out.

He observes me. His head tilts to the side with his consideration. "Do you not know who I am?" He doesn't say it arrogantly; he says it as if he is genuinely perplexed that I don't know. I smile apologetically and shake my head no. I have not got a scooby who he is. "Oh…Miss Hesketh, please tell me, what do you know?" I feel my face go pink and have the urge to wring my hands with embarrassment.

"I know that you are important…urm, I can see that you're a dragon." I wave my hand about to encompass him. "Everyone calls you, urm, 'General'…I have no idea what you are a general of, but I presume it's something to do with the Hunters Guild? Mr Brown said you are now my guardian? After he told me you paid his bill. Thank you for that. I can pay you back." I glance down at my food; he has made steak. Steak, mashed potatoes, and broccoli, with a peppercorn sauce. Yum.

"Eat your dinner," he says gruffly. He doesn't have to tell me twice; I dive in.

I try my best to use my knife and fork correctly. I am getting better.

The dragon makes an odd noise. I peek up at him; he has his fork raised to his mouth and such a sad expression on his face. I glance back down at my food and continue eating. I hope he is okay. I don't like the idea that he's sad. It has been a while since I've eaten red meat, so I let my inner carnivore take over.

It's difficult to eat like a lady when you have the urge to stuff your face into your food and eat as quickly as you can before someone takes the plate away. I don't know if I will ever not have that worry, that inbuilt fear at the back of my mind. Being starved for such a long time...when I eat, I find it impossible to eat slowly. I unconsciously hug the plate towards myself, my arms circling it protectively. Huh, at least I didn't growl.

"You were starved." Momentarily I come out of my frenzy, and I peek up again to see him watching me with an indescribable look of compassion in his silver eyes. I drop my eyes and shrug. I guess that explains the sad look from before. It isn't something I want to talk about.

Now that I've had a few bites—well, okay half the plate—I can try to control myself and slow down a little. I listen intently as the dragon starts to talk. His voice rumbles around the room, much like the ocean below us.

"Yes, I am a dragon shifter. My title is General. I have a long and boring history of being a warrior and commander. I currently oversee the Hunters Guild, and the hellhounds are also under my jurisdiction." His big but elegant fingers tap the table. "Mr Brown is correct—as you are under my protection, I am classified as your guardian. You may call me Aragon."

CHAPTER TWENTY-FOUR

After dinner, I'm horrified to find out he doesn't have any dessert, *nothing*. Who doesn't have dessert! At the abject horror on my face, the dragon, urm, Aragon, roots around in the freezer and finds a sad-looking tub of vanilla ice cream. It's an icy lump frozen solid to the bottom of the container. But I sit happily stabbing at it with a spoon while sitting cross-legged on Aragon's leather sofa.

Aragon talks about his rules expectations, and we got to the real reason why I'm here.

It isn't all about keeping me safe from Daniel.

"When you first went to the hospital, there were several issues raised," Aragon says. "The front part of your brain is called 'the prefrontal cortex,' and it hasn't developed properly. It is the area responsible for planning, prioritising, and controlling impulses."

So basically Aragon has medical data to suggest my brain is stuck in teenage mode. Huh.

I want to moan that I have no issues with my impulse control—the number of times I have chosen not to do something reckless is mounting up to impressive levels. I am an absolute fucking guru of control. But I don't say a word. I am smart enough not to argue with a dragon and his medical data.

Ha, perfect control.

I smell bullshit, though—there's nothing wrong with my brain.

As well as my teenage brain...cue eyeroll. "You are stronger than an average shifter," Aragon continues in his mesmerising, low voice. "Even with your small stature, you are at a level of hellhound strength." Smugly I bounce on the sofa. I am a super-shifter! "Nutty..." The dragon mumbles as he rubs the bridge of his nose in frustration. I stop bouncing. "The onset of your fire magic has raised serious concerns. Miss Hesketh, shifters should not develop that type of magic until they're at least six hundred years old, if at all, as it is such a rare gift. To have the ability to partial-shift at twenty-three is also unfounded. I believe your brother was over a century. Combined with your shifting at a young age, you are a complete anomaly. A magical and medical conundrum." *Way to go, Mum, and your lotto DNA.*

Aragon assures me that there's a slight possibility my brain could develop adequately over time. But I'm not that worried, or that bothered. There's nothing bloody wrong with my mind.

Of course, I think I am a little crazy, but come on—who wouldn't be, with my history? I've been through Hell and come out smoking. What all this testing comes down to is an excuse to control me. They can't let me go wandering about and not have control of me. I narrow my eyes at him. Being a young female shifter with fire magic, I understand now why I've been parcelled off to Aragon.

"Who better to keep an eye on me and keep control of me than you?" I say, raising my eyebrow.

"I assure you, Miss Hesketh, that I will do whatever it takes to protect you. I want nothing more than to keep you safe. The council isn't aware of your fire magic. I'd like to keep it that way. I'm officially your guardian. It is a task I have not entered into unadvisedly or lightly." The immense burden contained in Aragon's gaze just then is disturbing. It freaks me out. He clearly believes what he's saying. Has appointing himself my guardian put him at risk? Am I that much of a danger? Aragon's expression is heart-wrenching, and something inside me rips wide open. I hate this. I drop my chin to my chest and scrutinise my hands, unable to meet his intense gaze.

"Okay, well, thank you," I mumble around a lump in my throat.

No matter what the dragon believes or what I want to think, I have to get it into my head that I am on my own. I am a survivor, not a victim, and I'm not just going to accept my circumstances. I can't. Eventually, I'm going to find a way to gain control of my life.

It's not going to happen overnight, and I can't allow myself to mope like I have been doing for the past few weeks. At the moment I have a bloody scary, powerful dragon claiming that he wants to protect me. Daniel can go swivel, and John can also fuck off.

I have loyalty to Owen and Jodie. Ava has also earned my respect and trust. But the only person whom I can rely on is myself.

* * *

I am back in my room, getting ready for bed. I have showered and changed into my PJ's, which are workout shorts and a t-shirt. Since I got control of my shifting at the hospital, I have been sleeping in my wolf form. I can't sleep in my human guise as I feel vulnerable. I am used to sleeping as a wolf. Also, beds are too soft, my skin is too cold, and even trying to sleep on the floor in my human form doesn't help.

Ultimately what makes me choose to sleep furry are the nightmares that plague me. Strangely, they don't find me when I am a wolf.

I pad towards my hidden nook and place the photo frame on a lower shelf. I allow the magic to transform me. Aragon wants us to run at five a.m. I am sure he thinks I'd object, but I enjoy training, and the early time doesn't matter to me. It isn't like I have to drag myself out of bed.

I curl up in a wolfy doughnut, my nose on top of my fluffy tail. I face the silver frame; *I love you both so much*, I say to my long-dead pack. Each blink gets a little longer as I try to keep my eyes on their happy faces until I fall asleep.

* * *

I run behind Aragon as we follow a thin strip of a track, worn away naturally bare from previous footsteps. The morning is dry and fresh. The path takes us through a wood, heathland, and peat bogs that surround the base of a mountain. The landscape is breathtaking.

As the miles disappear under my feet, it becomes apparent just how remote Aragon's home in this part of Ireland is. Interestingly, I discover there isn't even a road leading to the house—Aragon must only use the portal or fly, I guess. I feel as if we could be the last people on Earth. Even with my excellent hearing, all I can hear apart from animals and the crashing ocean is the crunching of our feet.

Oh, and the freaky buzzing of Aragon's ward.

I didn't notice the ward yesterday when I arrived, as it's miles from the house. I am astonished to see it this morning. Instead of covering only the house, it circles out and covers miles and miles. It isn't the gold colour that I'm used to seeing either, like the ward at the apartment. No, it's multicoloured and glows and crackles in the dark. You can feel it buzzing through you, deep into your bones. No one could say that they missed seeing this ward if they stumbled up to it. It's the magic equivalent of a laser field. I'd hate to see what it would do to anyone unwelcome.

The sky lightens as we dash across the wind-whipped cliff, the waves rolling endlessly below us. Aragon points out that the coastline has tiny coves and natural swimming spots protected from the full force of the Atlantic by a reef. He explains the different flora, the delicate sea champion, cat's ear, and sea pink.

We continue for a good hour at a fast pace. I've never run with anyone before as a human or as a wolf, and it's terrific. If I had been my wolf, I would have had my tongue hanging out and a silly wolfy grin on my face. As it is, I don't think I stop smiling the whole time. My cheeks hurt. It's epic.

When we return to the house, the sky is just lighting up further with the dawn. Aragon tells me to be ready to leave by eight a.m. and to help myself to breakfast.

I fret over what to wear, and in the end, I wear black leggings and a cute green jumper. Aragon informed me last night that I couldn't wear my magic bracelets—that I am under his protection blah blah blah and he needed to be able to track me. So I wrap the scent masker bracelet in toilet paper and put it into the handy pocket of my leggings, and the Betty disguise bracelet, I put around my ankle so it's nicely hidden. Time for breakfast.

The bloody dragon's kitchen is made for a giant. I huff, prop my hands on my hips, and glare.

All the countertops are higher than standard; luckily, he has almost everything in the lower cabinets. But the strawberry jam is in a big larder cupboard, and it's on the top shelf about a hundred foot in the air. I tip my head back and glare at it. I am sure it's okay if you are a humongous dragon that can also fly, but for me being five-foot-two, it's like mission impossible.

I hum the "Mission Impossible" theme tune as I scale the counter in my socks. I balance on my tiptoes and lean across the gap. My fingertips can just brush the jar, but I can't get hold of it. I growl at the jar in frustration as I plan my first free-the-jam attempt.

I am going to jump and grab it.

Just as I am getting ready to make my first jump, Aragon appears by my side, scaring the ever-loving shit out of me. I let out a shriek at his sudden appearance, and my sock-encased foot slips.

Oomph. I find myself in Aragon's arms as he catches me.

"I was drawn by the incessant humming. You should have called me to get that for you," he says gruffly.

"Oh, urm…nice catch, sorry about that, you, urm… scared the shit out of me," I squeak out. I gawk up and meet his beautiful silver eyes—he doesn't seem angry—his eyes are dancing with mirth.

His forearms hold my weight with ease.

My proximity to Aragon confuses the hell out of me. But it doesn't frighten me the way it would have with just about any other person. Instead, I brace my hands on his chest and lean forward. All the way forward and brush my nose against his neck.

I inhale.

His smoky, musky scent fills my nose. I shiver, and my stomach flips.

I hum.

Shit, it feels good in his arms. Why does it feel so good? I know he's dangerous, and it isn't hard to assume that he's one of the most powerful shifters on the planet. When did I stop being frightened of this huge man?

I groan deep in my throat.

Since I first laid eyes on him at his office, it's like every dormant hormone in my body has awakened at once—all clamouring for my guardian's attention.

Aragon turns his head, and I feel his breath on my lips. I open and taste his exhalation.

Goosebumps break out on my skin. I am being inappropriate. What the hell is wrong with me? I straighten up, my face burning.

"Urm…sorry. Sorry! I've never done that before. You…urm…caught me at a bad time. I'm in a hunger mood. I'm urm…hangry…" Gibberish. I'm flustered, I've no idea what I'm saying. I cringe and try to keep my eyes from looking crazed. Why did I sniff him!

"You are absolutely nutty. What will I do with you?" Aragon sighs as he gently lowers me to my feet. My body brushes against his on the way down. A shiver wracks me; it leaves me strangely breathless—warmth pools deep in my tummy.

Wow, oh…urm. My heart feels like it is beating out of my chest, and my stomach flips again. I like being close to him. Aragon smells so good.

Aragon disappointingly moves away. I sigh in frustration. He keeps his hand on the back of my neck as he easily reaches for the jam. He places it on to the counter next to the toaster.

"Nutty, please don't climb on the furniture. Hurry, you have five minutes." I grin at the nickname: *Nutty*. He squeezes my neck gently, and then he prowls out of the kitchen.

I watch him leave. He is wearing a dark grey suit today, and it looks good against his silver hair and skin. I let out a breath, and my hands tremble as I finish making my toast.

God, that was hot.

CHAPTER TWENTY-FIVE

Aragon takes me to work with him, how weird is that? We arrive in his office through the portal. "Okay, Miss Hesketh, it looks like you will have to entertain yourself. Please let Matthew know if you need anything."

"Is there anything I can do to help?" I ask, excitement budding inside of me. I bounce on my toes a little and my eyes flick around his office. "Any work that you need doing? I am sure I can help out with the Hunters or even help with paperwork? I can answer the phone?" I smile and nod encouragingly.

My thoughts drift away slightly as I imagine myself saving the world, and I have an urge to practice my shocked look for when the Hunters Guild honours me with a medal for my bravery. I hum.

Aragon tilts his head to the side with a frown. "Miss Hesketh, do you even know how to read? Your records do not give any indication of your literacy skills." My mouth drops open, and it's my turn to blink at him. How rude—of course I bloody know how to read! I was nine when I was trapped in my wolf form, not three. It's not like I forgot the alphabet. I growl at him.

Then I reconsider. Of course my education wasn't a priority for the council—who cares if a walking womb can read or write? Lucky thing I was home-schooled. Aragon doesn't know the details of my mum's schooling agenda, though.

"Please don't be offended; it is an honest and genuine question." I screw my face up and give him a sharp nod that he must take as confirmation. "Well, I have a bookshelf full of fascinating reference books." He waves his hand towards the seating area and the full shelves. "Why don't you start there?" He smiles encouragingly and leaves.

Bloody handsome nobhead!

I don't want to read boring shitty books. I love books, but not those type of books. I want to do something fun! I huff, closing my eyes and tapping my foot. I need to suck it up. I do need to learn more about shifters. I don't know anything about my race apart from the basics I learnt as a kid. Nothing useful.

Ideally, I should at least learn the laws, not only to keep myself out of trouble but so I don't have others taking advantage of my ignorance. If I know the code-of-conduct rules inside-out, I'll know when I can kick someone's ass and when I can't.

I seriously need to find a solution to what is turning out to be a massive clusterfuck: my life.

I know that I cannot trust the council or the dragon, even if I have a strange new sniffing fetish. It's only a matter of time till I fuck up and Aragon gets rid of me. Hell, if my own brother—I close my eyes. *Don't think about it.* I worry the end of my hair. At least I had the foresight to bring the bracelets with me, because I have a feeling that given the opportunity, Aragon would make them disappear. If I know anything, I know that.

I glance at Aragon's bookshelves.

I meander over, dragging my feet with a total lack of enthusiasm, and start to read the titles. Bloody hell, I need a help book to navigate this shit. Do they have a handbook—*Shifters for Dummies,* or something similar? I have to learn as much as I can about *everything* as quickly as I can. I wonder if he has a book on fire magic. I hum. If I can learn to control my fire magic, it would be difficult for some bad guy to kidnap me.

Especially while on fire and screaming. I grin, imagining lighting Daniel's pants on fire. I rub my hands together and do a mental *mwahaha.*

A few books catch my eye, and they're surprisingly perfect. Nothing on fire magic but the books do have the information I am looking for. I grab six of the most essential and settle down on a chair to read. I am back to humming "Mission Impossible."

The vast law book has blacked-out text that draws my attention. My dry eyes widen in horror as I make sense of the passage I'm reading. I nibble on my bottom lip and do a full-body shiver.

The place where the shifter bites is blacked out, but from what I can gather, there's a way for one shifter to control another. It freaks me out. Mind control! I cover my mouth. It's banned mate-slave magic.

Oh, that's bad.

Oh my, it's not banned because it's sick as fuck and highly immoral—no, it's forbidden because if a male shifter does the biting and he dies, the female he has bitten will follow him into death. I shiver again, and the hair at the back of my neck stands on end.

That's it. I think whoever wrote this book, the council who made our laws, are missing a huge point. It's fucking slavery! Evil. What the hell is wrong with shifters? I huff out a shaky breath and slam the book closed, disheartened. Female shifters are screwed—no wonder we're so rare. You can't fix stupid.

Shifter society is rotten.

"Miss Hesketh, I am free for the rest of the day— nothing pressing needs my attention. We shall be going out for something to eat. If you are agreeable?" I glance up, and Aragon has returned with Matthew at his heels.

"Yes, sure," I say, my voice glum. I spring up and put the books that I have finished back on the shelves. The law book, I poke with my finger and give a snarl. That thing needs burning.

Aragon nods at Matthew, and as we head for the portal, I give the witch a friendly wave. I follow quietly behind Aragon. I try not to skip in excitement. He is taking me out for food. My first date!

We make our way to a small restaurant in the city. It looks like a nice place; they specialise in gourmet burgers. Aragon opens the glass door for me and follows me inside. His big hand curls gently around my neck as he guides me to a table. My heart skips a beat. I enjoy the heavy hand on my neck, a bit too much.

We sit opposite each other at a two-seater table, made smaller by Aragon's bulk. He has no choice but to stretch his long legs underneath my chair. I can't help but enjoy the feeling of our legs touching. As it's early for the dinner crowd, the restaurant isn't busy, and most of the tables are empty.

My whole focus is entirely on Aragon. Who has removed his suit jacket and is now in the process of deviously rolling up his sleeves. With each turn of the fabric, he slowly uncovers more of his muscled forearms. How can one innocuous body part be so attractive? I have no shame in watching his yummy forearm striptease.

Our human waitress is equally fascinated with my dragon's forearms. She doesn't acknowledge my presence as she runs her hand through her hair and along her collarbone, fluttering her lashes at him as if she's attempting to get those fuckers to fly off. I frown at her. Aragon is his usual polite self, and his gaze doesn't linger.

The handsome bastard needs a bag over his head.

I don't read the menu when I order; I just pick a random burger. I cough and glare at her to get her moving.

"So how was your day?" Aragon asks me in his low, rumbly voice.

"Good. You haven't got a lot of picture books," I say petulantly. Aragon rubs the bridge of his nose and sighs.

"I am sorry, Miss Hesketh, I spoke out of turn. Please forgive me." A line appears between his brows and his beautiful eyes become distressed. I keep my sad-face for a few seconds longer. But I can't stop the cheeky grin from slowly spreading across my face. I wave away his apology.

"It is fine; I'm only messing with you...your books are...urm, scary. The shifter laws in regard to women are shit." I wiggle in my chair and debate with myself about whether I should say anything.

Aragon tilts his head and raises an eyebrow. I wave my hands about and word-vomit my anger. "My purpose in life is not to be a bloody pup-maker. I'm more than my womb! The world I have experienced so far? It isn't a world that I want to bring my children into. If my DNA is so unique and I do beat the odds and have little girls, do I want them to be born into a world where their whole existence is about what is between their legs? To be fought over like little pieces of meat and sold like property?

"I'm an orphan; my father died before I was born, trying to protect my mum and three sisters. Only my mum survived. Not even ten years after that tragedy, I had to watch while my mum killed herself and my two-year-old little sister, Grace..." I lower my chin to my chest with sorrow. "She would be sixteen now. Aragon, that's just *my* pack. Five females that died for nothing—nothing! This shit needs to stop. The laws protecting us are non-existent. You are strong, can't you do something?"

Aragon gives me a pained look. I drop my eyes and take that as a no. Why did I even bring it up? I lift my head and my bottom lip trembles. I sigh and square my shoulders. Fuck it, I will do it myself. It isn't in my nature to ignore injustice and go down without a fight, even when things seem insurmountable. "So, urm, when do you want to teach me about—" I lower my voice to a whisper—"my fire magic? The sooner we get started with training, the better." So I can start helping others.

Aragon shakes his head, and before he can answer, our food arrives. The waitress literally throws my plate down in front of me. She must think I'm human, or she's crazy.

I wrinkle my nose in disgust and scrutinise my burger with growing horror. I let out a pained whimper. I have somehow ordered a veggie burger. I am so disappointed. I cut it into quarters and poke at it. I have eaten excellent vegetarian stuff, but this burger isn't a good one. It's falling apart, looks dry, and it's a strange colour. I give it a surreptitious sniff; *eww,* it doesn't even smell like food.

Not long ago, I was eating dog food. So I should count my blessings that it's warm and just eat the thing. I lift my top lip and snarl at it.

Aragon watches me with fascination, his eyes sparkling. *Yeah, yeah, dragon boy, laugh it up.* His double burger with bacon oozes cheese—it looks so good. Aragon methodically cuts his burger into quarters. Without saying a word, he takes my plate and exchanges it for his. I glance down at his plate, my new plate and the yummy burger.

My heart swells, and I am now feeling just as gooey as the cheese.

"Thank you," I say while trying and failing to get a whole quarter into my mouth. Aragon just gives me a nod and a warm smile. He eats my veggie burger without saying a word of complaint, but I catch the odd wince.

I focus on the seriousness of eating. Once I have practically inhaled my burger, I try to bring the conversation back to before. "So, the fire training?" I ask Aragon again.

He sighs, throwing the veggie burger back onto his plate and wiping his hands with a napkin. "There is no rush, Miss Hesketh. Hellhound Owen has agreed to continue your self-defence training. Once you are up to a good standard, we can address the subject of your magic again." I huff out a frustrated breath. "It takes a lot of mental control. You have dealt with a lot of challenges over a short amount of time." He meaningfully raises his eyebrow. "There is plenty of time to master your magic." Aragon gives me a gentle smile; his eyes are open and honest.

"Your brother has been trying to get hold of you," he says, changing the subject. I flare my nostrils at him and stuff an onion ring into my mouth. Aragon patiently waits, his head tilted to the side, watching me.

Oh, bloody hell. I wiggle in my chair in discomfort. "I know it is childish. But I don't want to speak to John." I examine my plate and choose another onion ring. "The whole Daniel thing? He said some horrible things…" I close my eyes. "I just need some time." Aragon puts his big hand on mine and squeezes it.

"I will explain. You don't need to speak to him until you're ready. If it is any consolation, he is aware that he has made a serious error in judgement." I shrug. John keeps believing the monsters over me. One time is forgivable, but he keeps on doing it. I will never trust him. I will try to forgive him for my mum's sake. But it's hard—to be honest, I'm not the forgiving type.

When the waitress returns to our table and we both order dessert, another button on her top has become undone!

I think I am going to scream. I know we're not on a real date, but she doesn't know that. *Oi, you, blondie,* I have the urge to say, *why don't you take a seat if you are that interested in him? Pull up a pew and grab yourself a bite of rancid veggie burger. While you are sitting down, would you like my lemonade? Why don't I work your tables while you tell the dragon what your star sign is.*

I growl until she scurries away.

I'm growling as if Aragon is food and I'm starving. What the hell… am I…am I jealous? I turn the idea around in my head. Huh. I have never felt jealousy before. I have no reason to feel like this; Aragon isn't mine. I scratch the back of my head. Even surrounded by attractive hellhounds and shifters, I have never liked anyone before. It's disconcerting.

I huff. I can't understand how he has not picked up on how inappropriate she's being. Maybe he likes her? *Shit.* I clack my teeth. I don't like that thought.

I get down to the serious business of cake-eating, so I don't notice while eating my hot chocolate fudge cake with cream that Aragon hasn't started his. Okay, I lie. Of course I bloody noticed. It's chocolate!

Again he makes the plate exchange, my empty plate for his full one. He gets a beaming smile, and I happily hum as I eat my second dessert.

Aragon has set the date bar high. I don't even feel the need to guard my plate. *Not when you're guarding Aragon,* my snide, not-so-helpful internal voice pipes up.

I finish, and I swear I have a little food baby going on. What a relief that I'm wearing leggings and I don't have to undo a button.

The blonde waitress is back to clear the table and to ask if Aragon wants a coffee, and she unbelievably just gives him her number. It's like I am not even sitting here! Who does that!

"I swear, Miss Hesketh, if you growl at our waitress one more time, I will put you over my knee, in front of all these people, and spank you, and we will see just how well you do with being a brat." I blink up at him in shock. I cut off my growl.

When the wannabe Aragon-stealing waitress sashays past our table again, I let out a growl so loud that it frightens her and she drops the plate she's carrying. I bounce happily on my seat and watch the mayhem I've caused. I have zero regrets. I peer up at Aragon from underneath my lashes and grin cheekily at him. He rubs his forehead and shakes his head. I'm sure the forehead rub was a tactic to cover his smile.

CHAPTER TWENTY-SIX

Aragon stalks outside, muscles rippling along his bare torso. His black swim shorts sit low on his hips. *Oh, my bloody God*. I grip the edge of the pool.

"You don't mind if I join you?" he asks in his low rumbly voice that's currently made of liquid chocolate.

No, I am not dreaming. When we got back from lunch, I decided to hit the pool. It seems like Aragon had the same idea.

I shake my head vigorously, almost smacking it on the glass side. I bite my lip—fucking hell. Aragon is lean rather than bulky, but there's so much of him—I didn't know a body could have that many abdominal ridges. I fight to keep my gaze on his face, not his beautiful body.

He looks chiselled from stone. Bow-chicka-wow-wow.

My mind wanders, in a rude direction…my imagination skids to a halt as some figmental voluptuous female dragon shifter tries to drown me for looking at Aragon in *that* way.

Without thinking, I blurt out, "Will your girl not get mad that I'm living here?" Shit, shut up, oh hell. I drop my eyes and rub the edge of the floor tile with my finger. I can feel my cheeks going red.

"No," Aragon says softly.

No, she won't mind? Or no, you haven't got a girl? My brain prompts my mouth. I so want to ask, but I swallow the question.

Aragon steps down into the pool. The steam off the warm water wraps lovingly around his body.

"So, are you single?" Fuck it. I come out with the words. They almost speak themselves. *Shit, don't look at him.* I can't look. I shouldn't look. I do.

He has moved to the opposite end of the pool. He surveys the view. His face in profile is a marvel. So perfect. A stunning symmetry. The dragon is so beautiful—defined jaw, pronounced cheekbones—all that incredible silver skin. What the hell is wrong with me?

"I currently do not have a female. Do you have a male?" I drop my head and grin, I giggle, I meet his serious eyes. Oh, he isn't joking. Isn't that in my file? I make a gesture of weighing tough options with my hand. Aragon scrutinises me and his eyes narrow. I giggle again, and I shake my head no.

I let myself float on the water, looking at the sky above. I wonder if this pool can be used in winter. The whole pool area must be freezing that time of year, but as I'm floating, I can see the shimmer of magic, I guess to keep the entire area temperature-controlled. Magic is amazing.

I get bored, so I hum the music from *Jaws* as I do handstands and rolly-polys, entertaining myself. I also attack Aragon's toes. After a while he leaves me to it.

As I'm bellowing "Part of your World" from *The Little Mermaid*, Aragon returns with a towel. His eyes sparkle, and his lips twitch.

"Come on, Nutty, it has been hours." I grin at him and scramble out of the pool, and he envelops me in the towel.

* * *

The rest of the week goes the same way; we run together in the mornings, and then we go into his office. Mostly we stay until lunch, and then Aragon will work from home—although a few times we have spent the whole day at the Guild. Owen comes every other day for my combat training.

I am disappointed that I have not been able to do anything at the office but read. I spend my days pretending to be engrossed in the stuffy books, making mental notes as I can't be arsed to jot anything down.

When we get home, I pop the current text onto the shelf in my reading nook. I need to go for a run in my wolf form and afterwards I need to do some training. Owen has set me a new kick combo, and I will have to spend hours working on it to get it perfect.

Aragon's fancy, well-equipped home gym has everything I need. The heavy bags are hung a little high, but they're actually at a perfect height for me to practice my overhead kicks.

I haven't asked if the dragon will spar with me. Could you imagine? God, I wouldn't want to take a hit from him. But I would love to work on my ground game. I don't hold out much hope. Pervy girl. My hormones are raging out of control when it comes to Aragon.

I shift and go for my run.

The dragon is quietly waiting for me when I return. "No fur in the house, Forrest," he says sternly. Oh, I am "Forrest" now? Huh. He has called me "Miss Hesketh" all week. I let my magic turn me back into my human form, I start towards the gym, and his voice stops me.

"Forrest," he says, "I would like to talk to you about something I am concerned about. Please go into the living room." I nod. I don't like the expression on his face; it's a look that makes me revert to being bratty. This is usually about the time when I get in trouble. I want nothing more than to either salute him or maybe stick both middle fingers up at him and shout *fuck you*.

I sigh...and they say I have poor impulse control. I manage to dawdle into the living room quietly and sit. Aragon must know about the bracelets. I find myself wanting to fidget as he prowls into the room. I watch him out of the corner of my eye; I am unwilling to look at him directly. I pick at a loose thread on my leggings.

"Forrest, when we're at work, I have some Fae come into the house to clean—they are brownies." Okay, where is he going with this? I had wondered who did all the cleaning. Is this when he shows his hand and maybe admits that the brownies went through my stuff? Looking for my magic? "I have been informed that your bed remains unslept-in. So my question is, where do you sleep?"

What? I stare at him. I didn't expect him to go with that. What on earth am I going to say? Will he use it against me? Probably. I keep my mouth shut and shrug.

"I know you don't leave the house at night."

I study my hands. The best thing that I can do is not answer him. I can feel him looking at me. I bet his face wears a fake mask of concern. What does he care where I sleep?

"Forrest, why are you sleeping on the floor in wolf form?" I peek up at him at that. "The brownies found your fur on the floor," he explains as I nibble my lip. "You will answer me."

No, I bloody will not.

"I had a whole chocolate cake ordered for you...It would be a shame for the order to be cancelled."

What! Nooooooo! No, he can't do that, it's so mean. I glare at him.

"Chocolate cake is for good girls who answer questions." He raises his eyebrows. Is Aragon going to hold a chocolate cake over me as a hostage? Damn it. I haven't had a bit of chocolate all week! I have to give him something.

I wrinkle my nose. "I get cold. I find beds strange," I tell him honestly.

"I can understand you find sleeping in a bed strange, but it has been over three months since you shifted back—you need to adapt. No fur in the house from now on, Forrest." I glare at him, but I shrug and think it's okay because I will sleep outside.

"Also, no sleeping outside. You will sleep in your bed." He leaves the room.

A single tear falls down the side of my nose, and I quickly wipe it away. This is shit. Why does it matter to him that I sleep in my wolf form? Controlling bastard.

I go into the gym, and I work out like a crazy person. When he calls me for dinner a few hours later, there's a bag on the table. I look at it without interest. It isn't cake-shaped.

"I bought you something that will hopefully make you feel less cold," Aragon says from the kitchen. I peek into the bag and see something fluffy. I pull out what turns out to be fluffy pyjamas and some equally fluffy bed socks. I stare at the thoughtful gift in shock.

"Thank you," I say, my hand stroking them; they're so soft. The long-sleeved top and bottoms are covered in little pink unicorns, and with the socks, they should cover me completely. It was a good idea; it was also very kind. I give Aragon a small smile.

CHAPTER TWENTY-SEVEN

I haven't slept for three nights; I have started stumbling and knocking into stuff. Running this morning, I opted to run as a wolf as my poor coordination couldn't handle two legs.

I am so fucking grumpy. I want to bite the dragon on his bubble-bottom for making me do this. Food has started to turn my stomach, and I've almost stopped eating. The only thing I can force down is the traitorous chocolate cake.

Aragon hasn't said anything to me, but I can see his frustration building. I am sure the dragon thinks I am stupid, stubborn. I haven't told him how sleeping as a human makes me feel, and I haven't explained about the nightmares. Perhaps if I did, he would let me be?

It's too late now to even try and explain; in my experience, he probably wouldn't believe me anyway. John certainly wouldn't.

I am sitting at the table, pushing my food around the plate. My head occasionally dips down towards the table, nodding, as I force myself to stay awake. Aragon snaps and his big hand thumps down on the table; the plates jump with the impact.

"Forrest, this is getting ridiculous. You have lost weight, and you look ill. You are leaving me no other choice but to get you a sleeping potion!"

"What?" I look up at him, suddenly wide awake. Oh my God, I can't think of anything worse—the thought of being magically put to sleep in my human form, lying in bed vulnerable.

It absolutely freaks me out.

Would the potion trap me into my nightmares? So I wouldn't be able to wake up? I can feel the utter panic take hold of my body, and I desperately shake my head no. My eyes plead with him as I hunch in my chair, enveloped in the scent of my fear.

"What will you have me do! You will sleep tonight, Forrest. As a human in your bed, or tomorrow, I will get the potion and use it without your permission."

I spring up from the table, my chair screeching across the floor. I narrow my eyes at him; I am shaking in fear and anger. The only good thing is that the high level of adrenaline in my body is making me feel almost normal.

"You are a monster!" I shout at him. I turn and run to my room; I dramatically throw myself onto the navy bean bag in my book nook. I wrap my arms around myself and curl into a ball and silently cry, my head almost on my knees.

I don't want to go to sleep in this body! I don't! But I am so tired, and I can't risk him forcing a sleep potion on me.

Most of the time, when I'm awake, I can convince myself, force myself, to believe those bad things didn't happen.

Except in my dreams.

In my dreams, the boxes in my mind that are stuffed full of bad memories rattle, and the lids loosen. The memories creep out across my mind and plague me.

At the hospital, when I first started getting the nightmares, Owen would hear me screaming and gently shake me awake. He would then sit up and talk to me until I felt safe. It was Owen who suggested and encouraged me to try sleeping in my wolf form, and it worked. I never had a nightmare again. But now…I should have told Aragon the truth. I stare at the photo of my mum and Grace.

I'm a silly coward. The bad dreams can't kill me.

I shower and then put the stupid fluffy cute unicorn pyjamas on with the socks. I eye the bed with disgust. Pulling the duvet, I get in. The bed is so soft it's like sleeping on a cloud. I hate it. I pull the cover up to my chin, close my eyes, and try to quieten my mind. I huff, chuck one of the pillows onto the floor, and thump the remaining one to flatten it. I start a simple meditation exercise, and before I have finished, I fall asleep.

* * *

I am in my silver cage in the garage. I am naked, and my skin is cold.

My mum is with me. I can't quite believe she is here with me and that I am not alone. It has been such a long time since I have seen her beautiful face. God, I have missed her. She sits upright, leaning against the silver bars, and I can smell her skin burning.

"Mum," I whisper urgently, "your skin is burning. Please, you need to move away from the bars." I take her wrist and try to pull her away, but she won't move. Mum has a doll in her arms. The toy has blonde hair, and it looks familiar. She starts giggling strangely, hugging the doll to her chest.

"You have to be quiet, Mum; please stop laughing. If Vincent hears yo—"

"If Vincent hears what?" A voice comes from the darkness, I start to shake in fear, my teeth chattering I cover myself the best I can with my arms.

Why am I naked?

Vincent steps forward, the yellow hose in his hand. Cold water suddenly blasts into the cage. "You are such a dirty and disgusting thing, look at the mess you have made!" he roars.

My mum continues to giggle, and I watch in growing horror as her throat slowly starts to open up, and her blood pours from the wound down her chest. The blood is bright red in the darkness. The cold water from the hose hits her, the water and blood mix, splashing red against my face. I put my hands up to her throat to try and stem the bleeding. But this causes the wound to open further, and her head rolls from side to side, her neck unable to support its weight.

The doll falls into my lap as my mum takes hold of my wrists and squeezes them. "You are…" over the pounding of the water, I can't hear what she is saying, so I lean closer. "You are such a disappointment. Why didn't you die like you were told? You are cursed." My mum pushes me violently away from her.

Her throat is gaping, and she makes a horrible gurgling sound. She is no longer bleeding. Her chest stops moving, as she slumps to the side. I know she is dead. Heartbreaking sorrow grips me, and I sob. I feel like my heart is being slowly ripped out.

"Mum, Mummy," I whimper.

The doll in my lap suddenly starts to scream, making me flinch. I realise my mistake—that it isn't a doll, it is my baby sister, Grace. I look down at her, and with trembling fingers, I move her hair from her face. I meet her wide glassy dead eyes. Grace is dead, but she still screams...

"Forrest, Forrest, wake up. Wake up!" My eyes fly open, and I am sobbing, my throat is hurting, I've been screaming. My wrists are held in Aragon's grip. I don't understand why he is holding me so tightly until I notice the flames.

My arms are shockingly on fire. I am on fire!

The flames light up the room in hazy blue. The smell of smoke fills my nose. My once-fluffy unicorn pyjamas are burned black, and my bedcovers are smouldering. I sob harder. What have I done? I have ruined everything. Aragon waves a hand, and the small flames around us die. He scoops me up into his arms and takes me out of the room. He rushes me through the house, and we go up a flight of stairs.

"I am sorry, I am so sorry, I didn't mean to, I didn't mean to ruin the lovely things you bought for me. Nev—" I sob, "—never happened before. Just the dreams, never the flames. I am sorry…" I mumble over and over through my sobs. The shock of everything makes me cry harder, even more than remembering the horror of the nightmare.

"I need to get these off; then you can shift to heal." Aragon carefully starts to strip me out of my damaged pyjamas. The top has melted, and pieces of the fabric are embedded in the skin of my arms. Aragon painfully picks out the material, which makes my arms bleed.

"This is the reason I was concerned about the witch magic; messing with something you don't fully understand is dangerous. Without the potion in your system, you could have shifted. I have no idea if it will stay in your skin if you shift now." He finishes quickly, "Shift, Forrest."

I transform into my wolf, and I don't want to turn back. Aragon holds my furry head in his large hands, with a firm voice and pleading silver eyes—almost with his will alone, he forces me back to human.

I return to human naked and shaking, but thanks to Aragon, I am completely healed. Aragon grabs a long-sleeved t-shirt from his bed and tugs it over my head. He folds me back into his arms. I am no longer crying, but with his stillness, I can feel how much I am shaking.

He gets into bed and pulls me with him so that I lie on top of him. I struggle. What happens if I burn up again? I'm going to end up hurting him. Aragon ignores me and firmly holds me to his chest. I belatedly realise that his torso is bare.

"I am a dragon, and I am fireproof. Be still." I am too exhausted to fight him, and he feels warm, he smells good. I rest my cheek on his chest and close my eyes. I breathe in his smoky, musky scent. I listen to his heartbeat, and it calms me further. He cups the back of my neck in his massive palm, holding me to him. His other hand runs up and down my spine gently. My heart starts to slow, the rhythm no longer pounding in my ears. My body slowly stops shaking. I've never been held before, and I soak up his affection. "Have you had bad dreams before?" Aragon asks quietly. I nod. "Is that the real reason you didn't want to sleep in this form?" I nod again. "Do you want to tell me about your dream?" I shake my head; I really really don't want to think about it. "Sleep, Forrest. I will watch over you." He pulls the covers around us; I don't think I will ever sleep again.

But in his arms I feel warm and safe. Lying on top of his hard-muscled form is the most comfortable I have ever been. My body fits on top of his like a perfect puzzle piece.

* * *

I awake more comfortable than I've ever been in my life. Warmth surrounds me. My face is pressed to warm skin. Aragon. I open my eyes. My eyelashes brush gently fluttering butterfly-kisses across his skin.

I've moved in my sleep, and I am straddling a warm naked silver torso. My legs are on either side of him; he is so broad they don't touch the bed. One of my hands is resting on his chest, the other has gone rogue and is wrapped around his long silver hair. The hair is so soft; it's like silk.

I reluctantly let go of his hair. I raise myself slightly on my hands, using his chest for balance. I peek up into his face. It is then that I realise his warm skin is *everywhere*. My eyes widen in shock—I haven't got underwear on! I am straddling him. My breasts that were happily pressed to his chest a second ago gently scrape across him as I move and my nipples go hard. The intimacy steals my breath, and I let out a little gasp as his energy tingles along my skin.

Aragon meets my gaze. His eyes are heavy-lidded and his pupils are dilated. I panic and try to scramble off him. But his hand gently grips the back of my neck; his other hand wraps around my thigh underneath the T-shirt so close to the curve of my bare bottom, and he presses me back down onto him, keeping me in place. He slowly sits up, and leaning forward, he brushes his nose against my ear. His warm breath tickles the back of my neck, making me shiver.

I let out a little moan. He breathes in my scent and lets out an appreciative growl.

The hand gripping my neck has now moved slightly and is cupping the back of my head. He tips my head back, his eyes on my lips. His thumb gently rubs my cheekbone. My tummy flips as he moves closer, his lips almost touching mine, and he pauses. My lips part, and we breathe in each other's breath.

His eyes close, Aragon groans deep in the back of his throat, chest rumbling under my fingertips.

He sighs sadly.

"How do you feel?" Aragon rests his big palm against my forehead, his fingers smoothing back strands of my hair, thumb caressing my skin.

"I'm okay…"

Aragon pulls me back into his chest, my head tucked underneath his chin, and he holds me close like he never wants to let me go.

CHAPTER TWENTY-EIGHT

We are outside, and I nervously bounce on my toes. My dragon is going to teach me how to use my fire magic. After last night—I'm shitting myself. My hands are twisting around my grey unicorn jumper, and I'm gnawing on my lip.

"Nutty, what are you afraid of? Your magic won't harm you. The fire magic is a part of you, just like your wolf magic." Aragon is trying hard to waylay my fear. I don't know who he is kidding. I blink up at him in wide-eyed disbelief. So he tries a different tactic. "Without proper control, you could hurt others, and we can't have what happened last night happen again. I couldn't bear it. So I'm going to teach you how to control your fire magic. I should have done this weeks ago. Now, as a precaution..." Aragon pulls a beautiful silver necklace from his pocket. "It's platinum." With two fingers hooked underneath the delicate chain, Aragon dangles the necklace for my perusal. It spins and sparkles, the light reflecting from the teardrop diamond's many facets.

"It is beautiful," I husk out.

"It's Fae magic, and it will help you gain control."

"What...How? Will it stop me from hurting people? Will it stop me from burning down your beautiful home? I'm so sorry about—"

"Forrest, I'm the one that's at fault. I let you down. I should have respected your decisions." Aragon pulls my hair away and places the necklace over my head. The chain is long, and the diamond settles warmly between my breasts. "I let you down. I should have realised that there was more to this sleep issue." He kisses the top of my head. "Now close your eyes and let's begin." I close my eyes; I can still feel the slight imprint of his kiss. Aragon moves behind me. In his deep, low voice he says, "Relax your mind, feel your magic. The fire magic will be hotter than your wolf. The magic will feel different, pulsing. Bring it forward gently in your mind." I feel for my magic.

The almost playful tug of my wolf magic makes me smile. Behind my wolf magic is a flame. Hot. Angry. Scary. My whole body starts to shake.

My fear makes my wolf magic rush forward, and I shift.

I huff my disappointment. Aragon smiles down at me. "Shift back and try again. I promise you can do this. Please don't be frightened." Disappointed, I turn back to human. "Now, close your eyes…"

* * *

I am at the Guild office, and because of my constant begging over the last few weeks, I have been allowed to help Matthew. It's my first job! In the first few weeks, I found coming to the Hunters Guild so dull. But now that I am allowed to do something productive, the time here goes much quicker.

If given a choice, I'd be on the street kicking ass as a hunter—chasing down warrants and catching bad guys. I find the work that the hunters do for the Guild fascinating. My imagination goes a little nuts with the excitement of it—*Hunter Hesketh*— oh my God, how good does that sound? I repeat it back to myself a few times, nodding. I will have to think of an appropriate theme tune.

Between phone calls and running around, I practice my fire magic. After weeks of solid training, I can handle my magic without much thought. I practise so much that I can make a small flame dance in my hand and make it skip from one hand to the other. I privately think that with my skills, I put John to shame. I can shape a flame in the air, and today I am working on a butterfly; it's going to be epic.

Aragon is encouraged by how quickly I've picked everything up. In a few decades, he says, I should be able to use my fire while in wolf form and light myself up like a proper hellhound!

Flaming fur! Oh my God, how cool is that!

Aragon is the real reason I have picked everything up quickly; he is an impressive teacher. It helps that he has total control of the element. Aragon can not only control his fire magic but that of others as well, and ordinary fire.

I munch on a giant chocolate chip cookie that has appeared on my desk as if by magic. Matthew must have left it for me—he is so thoughtful. It tingles strangely on my tongue. I spin my office chair and roll it across the room to answer the ringing phone. Why walk when you can roll..."Good afternoon, the Hunters Guild, how may I help you?" It's Friday afternoon and I haven't seen Aragon for hours. He has been busy with meetings all day.

"Ms Hesketh? I'm so glad I caught you. I have a buyer for the house who wants to discuss the opportunity to purchase more land than the listed ten acres," the lady on the phone says, taking my grunt of surprise as confirmation that she has gotten the right person. Huh, a call from the estate agent who is selling Temple House. I have no idea how they got this number. I drum my fingers on my desk. I had earmarked the five hundred acres to keep, but do I need all that land?

"I could probably sell a bit more land." It would be good to get Aragon's advice. Maybe John should have input too? Although I still haven't talked to my brother, since the

Daniel incident. I know it's petty of me; I should do the right thing and give him a call. I guess I need to gather up my nerve to return his calls. "I need to think. Can I call you back on Monday?"

A wave of dizziness hits me, and with the heel of my hand, I rub the aching spot between my eyes.

"Ms Hesketh, the reason for my call is that the buyer is unfortunately looking at other properties and will only be available tomorrow for a viewing. She's adamant that she will only discuss the purchase in person, with yourself. She's a cash buyer, and if she loves Temple House as much as I think she will, the sale could be finalised within the month." The fee for the agent was astronomical, so you would think they could deal with this without having to involve me in the viewings. I groan and huff down the phone. I open my mouth with the intention of putting the agent off, but I find myself agreeing instead.

"I guess I can meet her at the house at…urm, midday?" I shrug to myself. It will be fine. Realistically, I want to see the back of that house as quickly as possible. Left up to me, I would have burned the place to the ground. But Temple House is my mum's legacy, so I should at least take the time to sell it to a proper custodian. Besides, my head is spinning and I don't want to negotiate—I just want to get off the phone.

Once she gets my agreement, the estate agent quickly finishes up the call. God, I hate that house. I am not looking forward to tomorrow.

I push off from the desk, roll into a clear space, and spin again. Instead of a butterfly, this time I'm going to aim for a little dragon.

Thinking about dragons, disappointingly I have yet to see Aragon's dragon. Aragon is incredibly private; I don't think anybody has seen his dragon form in centuries. I yearn to see his shifted form. I am not brave enough to demand to see the other part of him. I wonder how huge he is and if like his human colouring, he is silver.

The flaming blob looks nothing like a dragon; I scowl at it.

I can't wait to go home; today has been boring. *Only 'cause you want to go back for cake and then bedtime*, says that helpful snide internal voice. I huff and go red at my inner monologue. God, I'm such a weirdo.

Yeah, so at night Aragon insists I join him and sleep human in his arms, so he can keep me safe. I spend my nights curled on top of him, wrapped safely in his muscly arms. Unfortunately, Aragon is a total gentleman, and he makes sure to cover me from head to toe in fluffy pyjamas so the incident that shall not be named doesn't happen again. Urm, you know, the whole naked-parts-of-me-on-naked-parts-of-him incident. Oh my.

Thinking about it, I have yet to have my first kiss. Nonetheless, I've moved to the unplanned impressive level where my bare vulva sat on a dragon shifter's eight-pack. Since the incident, I can't help thinking more naughty thoughts. I regret not pressing my lips to his.

But my experience in everything is so lacking; I have zero chance of making the moves on anyone, least of all a legendary dragon shifter. Could you imagine? What if he said no? Of course he'd say no! Then I'd die of embarrassment.

As if thinking about him has conjured him up, Aragon prowls through the portal. His jacket buttons are undone and his hair is dishevelled, as though he has repeatedly been running his fingers through it. Aragon's brief smile and tight eyes relay a lousy day, and in his wake, angry energy smashes around him like a livid wave. If I didn't know him as well as I do, I'd be hiding underneath the desk.

"Are you okay?" I spring up and rush to him. I reach out and rest my hand on his forearm. The wariness within him sets me on edge.

"Yes, I'm fine thank you, Forrest." Aragon washes his hand across his face and closes his eyes, and when he opens them, his crashing angry energy has dissipated. He holds up his arm, and I nestle underneath. "I apologise. A meeting didn't go my way. I will not bore you with unnecessary details." Aragon hugs me to his side and kisses the top of my head. "My schedule has become inundated, and I have to work later than planned. Would you like me to arrange for Owen to escort you home?"

"No, that's okay, I can go by myself." Aragon runs his thumb across my cheekbone, a soft expression in his eyes. I beam him my best smile. "Oh, the estate agent called about my mum's house. I have a viewing—" The office door slams open, and Matthew hurries in, his hands full of paperwork and a harassed, crazy look in his eyes. "I can see you're busy—it can wait. I'll see you at home." I stand on my tiptoes and kiss his cheek, then wiggle out from under his arm. I almost sprint to the portal. No way I'm helping Matthew with all that shit. "See you Monday, Matthew," I yell.

CHAPTER TWENTY-NINE

The taxi drops me off outside the main gates.

It's so strange being back here; memories whisper through the trees as I meander down the driveway. My boots crunch on the leaves that have fallen unchecked, and more red, orange, and yellow leaves swirl around me. The light breeze also tugs at my hair and teases strands from the fancy side plait.

Initially, I hadn't known what to wear; it's the middle of November, and although it isn't too cold, I still get cold. I was going to put on jeans but then thought better of it. I appear young, and the buyer might be difficult if I don't at least look like I own a big-ass manor house. So I chose a warm black jumper dress, thick black tights, and boots, and I topped off the outfit with an expensive long red wool coat.

I tug my coat closer around me and bury my cold hands in my pockets as I amble towards the house. Something inside me doesn't want me to go near the place. Maybe I should have cancelled the viewing…no, it wouldn't have been fair to the lady wishing to view the house.

I can see that the buyer is already here; their empty car is parked by the front entrance. I presume they're looking at the grounds.

I wish Aragon or Owen were here. I made the mistake of leaving everything to the last minute, and my head has been kind of fuzzy. I rub the aching spot between my eyes.

I guess I've not worked on the whole time-management thing; today, lazily, I was relying on my missing dragon to do all the planning work for me.

I didn't leave home till eleven, and it takes a good thirty minutes to get to this house from my old apartment portal. I had hoped to spot a friendly face at the apartments, to beg one of the hellhounds to drive me and play bodyguard. When I didn't find a handy hellhound and Owen didn't answer my call, I got a taxi and fired off a text to Owen to explain. I still haven't told Aragon I have a viewing today— he's inundated with work, and he left for the Guild early.

I didn't sneak out intentionally, and I scribbled a note. I bet I will be back home before Aragon anyway.

I unlock the main door and leave the door open behind

me as I traipse into the house. I glance around with a shiver; it feels like a lifetime since I have stepped foot here. All the pack photos and portraits have been removed and safely stored. The walls have a fresh coat of paint, the floors have been freshly waxed. I appointed a cleaning company to make sure the house remained pristine.

It isn't as scary as I remember, but the past still echoes in its walls. I know on some level it wasn't the fault of the house—what happened to me had been the result of the actions of two men. But it still makes me a bit sick, and I feel uncomfortable being here. My instincts scream at me to leave, to run.

My phone rings and I fish it out of my coat pocket—Owen is returning my call. "Hello, Nanny Hound," I say brightly.

"Forrest, where are you?" Owen demands, his voice urgent. I hate it when he uses that tone; it means I'm in trouble.

"I am at my mum's house, meeting a buyer. Is every—"

"Forrest, get out of that house now! I am on my way; you need to leave now! I will meet you up the road from the house. Head towards the village." He disconnects the call without saying goodbye.

Oh, crap. Owen is pissed, and Aragon is going to be pissed. I don't know what I'm going to tell the buyer.

I turn and rush back down the hall towards the entrance, my keys in my hand, ready to lock the door. I grind to a halt.

Liz Bloody Richardson is standing at the door with a sick-looking smile on her face. *What the fuck is Liz doing here?* In greeting, she gives me a strange little finger wave. I shake my head at her and scrunch my nose in disgust—God, she's a loon.

"I can see the persuasive magic worked. Did you enjoy the cookie?"

What? Oh no! Before I can tell her to fuck off I am grabbed from behind; my head hits a hard chest, and my arms are pinned to my sides.

I react without thinking. I drop and shift my weight to the side, which handily opens up my line of attack onto the idiot's groin. I slap my hand with the keys back hard, nailing him; it makes him flinch with pain and gives me room and a few seconds to twist out of his grip.

I should now run like hell, but I am pissed. He tries to grab me again, and I drop the keys to the floor and throat-punch him. I then do a little skip and use my elbow to strike his temple. As he goes down, I recognise him. It's Meathead Two, the one with the brown hair. Oh, bloody hell. I knee him in the face for good measure. He flops to the floor, out cold.

I turn to leave, and Liz is standing right in front of me. I don't see the knife in her hand until she stabs me with it.

"Why?" I gasp.

"You killed my lover Paul with your stupid dinner stunt. My brother found him and killed him. Now, dog, any time I get even a sniff of your happiness, a hint that things are going well for you, I will be there to fuck it up. Harry says hello…" She jams the blade deeper into my side to make her point. She grins. "I hope that hurts."

The wound burns, which indicates that the knife must be silver—the crazy cow. I keep my face blank, not giving her any opportunity to revel in my pain. The silver will slow me down and stop me from shifting. But I lived in a silver cage for ten years, so while I'm not immune, I have built up a tolerance to its effects.

I punch her in the chest, and she's knocked away from me. With a sucking sensation, the knife pulls free. Liz still has the bloody blade in her grip, and she waves it at me, a snarl on her lips. I narrow my eyes and follow her. I dart to the side, cup my palm, and slap her hard across the face. I kick the knife, knocking it from her hand, and with satisfaction, I hear her wrist crunch. Liz drops to her knees, holding her broken wrist to her chest; she starts wailing. I scoop up the blade.

I stumble past her and out of the house, clutching my side.

"What the fuck, Liz, you were supposed to be a decoy, not fucking stab her with silver. That's my mate you have just marked up," a voice chastises. I glance up, and Daniel Kerr is there, looking like a textbook villain in a custom black suit. He swaggers towards me.

I slide the blade into my coat pocket, and I don't react when Daniel grabs hold of my arm. There's no fighting my way out of this. He has a group of twenty shifters at his back, and I am bleeding all over the fucking steps.

I'm starting to feel the effects of the silver, and it isn't pleasant. Everything around me echoes and reverberates like I'm underwater. I shake my head to try and clear it. I almost fall to one knee, but Daniel's grip on my arm stops my descent. The pain in my side shoots to the tips of my fingers. Slowly my skin grows numb and cold, marking the paralysis of the whole left-hand side of my body. Fuck, that can't be good...well, at least it doesn't hurt anymore.

"Forrest." Daniel pulls my head back by my hair. If he didn't have a grip on me, I would have fallen. "I have missed you, little wolf. Look at you, all elegantly dressed up." He is such a dickhead. Wordless snarls erupt from my mouth, which he ignores. "Let's go into our house and get things sorted. Try not to get blood on my suit." He chuckles and pulls me back around. Daniel half-drags, half-carries me back into the house. We pass Liz, who is still crying on the floor. "You lot, wait outside! I don't need an audience for this. Marcus, Ron, come. I want you to watch the office door."

Daniel drags me into the small downstairs office; he must have been inside the house before. I am struggling to stand, but at least the bleeding is starting to slow. According to my research on silver poisoning, it should be out of my system within the next ten minutes or so if I am lucky. I can then shift and chew his nose off.

Daniel smiles at me in triumph; he lets go of my arm and leans towards me. I take a small, unsteady shuffling step back. My bum meets the wall, and I use it to prop myself up.

"It has taken me months to get you away from that fucking dragon. Yesterday the council permitted me to pursue my claim. I told them that you were my mate. He let the vote pass."

He what? I don't believe him. Why would Aragon do that? I brace my knees and lift my chin. The back of my head smacks against the wall. Daniel is still a delusional wanker.

"I know that fucking dragon isn't going to let me near you—he will burn every favour he has to keep you away from me. So I thought I'd up the timeline. I don't need his permission; I have the council's." Daniel snarls, "I know he's been fucking you for months." He yanks me away from the wall and into his arms and spins me so that he is standing behind me. "I forgive you for that, Forrest." I attempt to turn my head to keep my eyes on him, but my vision is swimming with black dots. I feel like I have taken several punches to the head. It takes everything I have to keep on my feet.

Daniel pulls me to his chest and takes hold of my right wrist, pulling it away from my wound, where I had been applying pressure. He pulls my arm across my body. The silver is making me slow, and I don't react as he does the same to my other arm. He holds both my wrists firmly. Daniel kicks out the office chair, sits, and hauls me onto his lap. His breath is on my neck.

I hear him open his mouth, the slight click of the jaw, but nothing prepares me for him biting me.

BROGAN THOMAS

He must have shifted his teeth. He bites the back of my neck, his upper and lower canines on either side of my spine. I let out a pained whine.

It hurts. It hurts. It hurts.

The sheer pain cuts through the effects of the silver. I manage to struggle for a few moments, but it's useless. He continues to bite me, and everything falls away. It is as if I am trapped inside myself, unable to move at all. Dark and twisting, I feel his rancid mate magic ooze through my blood, into my head.

He finally lets go of my neck; I come back slightly to myself, my breathing shallow. My heart is beating too slowly.

My neck feels wet and what I presume is blood from the bite trickles down my back. *Daniel has bitten me...*the words bounce about my head as I try to remember the significance.

Daniel stands, and he shoves my shocked, useless body across the desk. Putting his hand underneath my coat and dress, he starts lifting everything. "I have to make this quick as we have to go. I won't leave here without finishing our mating—I have waited too long." He painfully rips my tights and knickers down; I still can't move. "Look at that fucking ass—fuck me, you are fucking perfect. I am a lucky bastard." He slaps my bottom, and he laughs. My heart has sped up and feels like it is now beating out of my chest.

In my head, I am screaming.

His fingers brush between my legs, and I suddenly wake the fuck up. I find my voice. "No." It comes out as a whisper;

I say it louder. "No! Get off me, this is rape," I croak out.

"Oh, sweetcheeks, you silly girl. You can't rape your mate. I know you are not going to enjoy this, but I will." The scraping descent of his zipper brings tears to my eyes.

No God, no, I won't survive this.

I flinch, and the knife wound pounds rhythmically, waves of agony in tune with my frantic heartbeat. Energy suddenly slams into me from out of nowhere. It fills me, and I know the silver is finally out of my system. I want to sob in relief.

Whatever the bite has done to me, will not stop me.

I fling my head back, catching him in a head butt. Daniel is knocked away from me. I roll off the other side of the desk.

The idiot laughs. "I love it when you fight."

"Then you're going to love this," I rasp out, "but not as much as I will." Daniel won't be laughing soon.

I slip the silver knife from my coat pocket into my hand. I then let my returned fire magic heat my palm. I send the flame up the blade and push the heat level to violet, my hottest level. The silver knife quickly starts to melt.

Daniel pulls me towards him, and he smiles in sick excitement.

I bring the knife up, and I press the melting silver blade to his face.

Daniel screams. I smile.

I don't have time to do anything further or see the damage I have done. I adjust my underwear and tights, shift into my wolf, pounce on the desk, and hit the window of the office.

The window shatters. I run. I run so fast.

I hear shouting behind me. Daniel has stopped screaming. What is it about that asshole that has me jumping out of windows to get away from him?

A vindictive, cruel part of me knows there will be no healing the damage to his face. Silver scars; it scars horribly. I can imagine that Daniel's face now matches who he is inside. He isn't so pretty anymore. The thought makes me smile and gives me some measure of peace.

CHAPTER THIRTY

I have to wait for only a few minutes and a car arrives. There's an electronic whirring as the boot opens. I exhale out of my nose, and my body sags in relief as I smell Owen's scent on the air. I creep out from underneath the thick hedging where I've been hiding and spring into the back of the car. The boot closes electronically behind me with a click, and the car sets off.

I shift back to human and climb into the front passenger seat. As I move, I shed little bits of crusted blood and glittering specs of silver that were clinging to my coat and dress. Owen grips my hand and squeezes it in relief. That relief turns to concern when he catches the scent of blood.

"What the fuck happened? I got your text message at the same time as a phone call from a contact. He said that Daniel was on the move with a load of heavies and it had something to do with you...?"

We head back towards the city. I settle into the seat. "It was a trap, an ambush. Liz Richardson stabbed me—silver knife to the side. I will be fine." My voice sounds cold and robotic to my own ears. I warily watch Owen's reactions as I curl sideways and lean my weight back against the door. My right cheek presses into the leather and I huddle into myself.

Owen's nostrils flare. "What the hell was that nasty cow doing there? The wound will scar. Are you feeling okay?" Owen flicks his eyes from the road and glances at me with concern. I smile sadly; he has entered nanny mode. "You shifted, so it must have cleared your system. Are you feeling dizzy or sick? Is your breathing okay?" I nod as he continues to give me a visual once-over. I ignore his worried questions; they aren't important at the moment.

"What happens when a male shifter bites a female's neck," I ask dully.

Owen slams on the brakes. I brace a hand on the dash as the tyres squeal on the tarmac. The car skids to a stop. Owen turns in his seat and grips my chin gently in a shaking hand. "Let me see." I peer up at him with dead eyes, unwilling to dip my head for him so he can inspect the back of my neck. Owen starts to growl.

"Who? Did Daniel do that? Did he bite you? Mate you?"

Owen growls out the words. My eyes fill with tears that I refuse to shed. If I start, I'm never going to stop. "It forces a mate-slave bond, makes the female more willing. Easier to control. Real archaic and illegal. Did…did Daniel bite you?" His grey eyes beg me to say no. I wish I could. I force a stiff nod. Owen roars and slams both hands on the steering wheel. His left fist smashes into the dash, and the plastic crumples.

For a few minutes, there's silence.

In a quiet, horrified tone, he says, "Daniel will be able to track you. Is the bond entirely in place?" I look at him blankly. "Forrest, did Daniel….did Daniel rape you?"

What Daniel did was rape—the bite, his touch—but I know that isn't what Owen means.

"No," I whisper. Owen's whole body sags. "And he won't be able to track me for a while." Owen's eyes are glowing red; his hellhound magic is raging inside him. I reach across the console and place a trembling hand on his arm. "I stopped him, burned a silver knife into his face. He should be down for a while." I say this matter-of-factly, not elaborating that I used Daniel's face for anger-management therapy. But Owen gets what I'm saying, and he stops growling. He takes hold of my frozen hand.

"The bond will be only partly formed, then. If the bond is consummated, you will be stuck with him. Till death do us part, in the most literal sense. Fucking hell, Forrest, we can't let him near you. I don't recommend we kill him either; I have no idea what it would do to you. It could kill you too."

"Can the bond be removed?"

Owen turns away from me and stares out of the window. The worry and anger are evident on his face. I don't think he can bear to look at me.

"No…yes, theoretically. It is attached to your wolf; if you're willing to give up your wolf, I know of a curse. The curse will cut you from your wolf. In Daniel's mind, it will be as if you have died." Owen lets go of my hand and grips the steering wheel. "It will make you human. Cut off suddenly like that from your magic, it's not healthy…it's risky. Without shifting, you will age. *If* you live that long. It's a curse for a reason…" Owen restarts the stalled car, and the vehicle moves off.

I contemplate his words. The bite mark feels sore and heavy on my neck. I curl my lip with disgust as I skim the back of my neck with trembling fingers. I trace the ragged scar with my fingertips; it seems as if slave-bites, like silver wounds, don't heal from shifting. I huff out a breath; I am glad I messed that fucker up.

I glance at my hands, and in a split second, I decide it's what I am going to do.

I want out. I want the curse.

To choose this, after the trauma I have just experienced, is crazy. I must be insane. But when is the right time to make this choice? I want out.

I'm ruined. I let out a self-deprecating laugh; I'm half-bonded to a fucking psychopath. He won't stop till he has full control of my body and mind. Daniel will never stop coming for me, and if not him, there will be other Daniels.

I realise that my mum is no longer the winning *DNA EuroMillions ticket*. No, that's me.

In my nightmares, my mum told me again and again that I was cursed. All this time, have I been prognosticating?

My heart has just one instruction left— run.

I let out a strangled laugh. What the fuck had I been thinking! Floating around in my happy bubble. My childish, pathetic antics, the embarrassing shit attempt at being a sweet, happy, lovable person. That stupid childish kitchen-climbing, chair-spinning idiot died in that office when Daniel bit her. I scrunch my nose, and my lips turn up in self-disgust.

I let out and nurtured every spec of childish hope that I had hidden away from the rotten parts inside me. I believed my own lies. My innocent, sweet mask got so wedged onto my face, I forgot for a while that it was just a guise. I forgot I'm rage, hate, and ruin.

Sometimes the people you love aren't safe for you, and sometimes it's you who are the toxic one. I am not safe. I'm cursed. Will it take one curse to end another?

I should never have been let out of that cage.

I forgot for a while that I was never meant to be safe in this world. The illusion of safety, of freedom, of contentment, of fucking love. It is all a cosmic joke, and I'm the biggest joke of all, with my stupid childish dreams. I thought I could make a difference. I naively thought I could alter perceptions.

Help others. I can't even help myself.

I run unsteady hands over my face. I feel utterly overwhelmed and exhausted.

My fingers creep to the chain miraculously still around my neck, to the diamond Aragon gave me. Aragon...I think about him, and my heart flips. Devastation slams into me and my eyes fill with tears.

How is all this happening?

Aragon and the meeting yesterday. The council meeting. The reality of what Aragon has done makes me sick to my stomach. It was a meeting about me; it was about my life. He didn't even bother to tell me, to warn me about Daniel.

My head drops back on the window behind me, and the cold glass touches the bite mark on the back of my neck.

I love him—stupid naïve lost wolf—I have fallen so hard for my beautiful dragon. A life with him, to even contemplate it? To dream it? Loving Aragon, and him loving me back? The idea is preposterous. Impossible.

God, it is a selfish muscle—the heart.

I rub my face again, refusing to cry. Aragon will forget me. I have previously been forgettable. For fourteen years, I was forgotten. Now I will be again, perhaps remembered as collateral damage from the council's scheming.

I am so tired of being used and so overwhelmed with trying to work out different people's motivations.

I close my eyes. *Be brave.*

I am a cool calm void.

The strange calm that I feel spreading through my mind feels less like acceptance and more like the calm before a storm, made up of pure, unadulterated hysteria. I let out another strangled laugh.

Fuck, I will do this. My fear will not stop me. Without my wolf, it might be a slow death sentence, but I will be free. Freedom is the only thing that matters now.

"I want the curse," I say quietly. More strongly I say, "I have a plan. I need to speak to my friend Ava. Can you help me?" Ava once offered me a chance to run. I'm going to take her up on that. I open my eyes and give Owen a pleading look. "Will you help me?" Owen shakes his head and runs his hand through his hair in frustration. "Do you trust me, Nanny Hound?" I meet his conflicted gaze; I swallow down my sadness and my shame as I look at Owen, I beseech him with my eyes.

He growls at me— a real snarl— then scrubs a hand over his face, muttering unintelligible things to himself. His hand drops and some of the fury dims.

"Yes, I trust you." My heart hurts; Owen has faith in me. That's when I start crying. Big body-wracking sobs leave my lips, and Owen folds me into his arms. So much for being brave. "I don't want to," he says quietly into my hair, "but I'll help."

NORTH-WEST NEWS

Police are appealing for information to identify a woman who was witnessed falling into the sea this evening at around nine o'clock. Police were called after witnesses reported seeing a girl jump from the sea wall in a presumed suicide. The coastguard will take up the search for the missing young woman in the morning, as sea conditions have made it impossible to search for her this evening.

The police have asked the Hunters Guild for assistance, and foul play has not been ruled out. A police spokesman said, "We will know more about the circumstances when the woman's body is recovered, but a curse or mental influence has not been ruled out at this time. Please call 111 with any information. We would like to identify this young lady and inform her family. Thank you for your help."

The police, with the help of a local technical expert, have released the following CCTV footage to piece together the woman's last movements.

Some viewers may find this disturbing, and viewer discretion is advised.

The footage shows a broken-looking girl in a red coat at a bus stop in Singleton village. She's captured on the bus's CCTV and on the local fire station's camera that's located near the bus stop. She gets on the number 75 bus and pays her fare.

She gets off the bus forty minutes later in the town of Cleveleys, and the cameras track her movement through the town via the police CCTV system and also through a few local shop cameras. She looks like she's sleepwalking. The girl isn't moving as if she's injured, but there's a dark patch and a hole in her bright red coat.

She doesn't interact with anyone, nor does she react to anyone around her. She just traipses towards the seafront and the promenade.

We see her clearly on several CCTV cameras walking across the road, across the tram tracks, and towards the sea wall. The waves pound the sea defences, and when the sea spray hits her, she doesn't react.

Her long distinctive pink hair catches the street lights as it's whipped around by the wind. She removes her red coat and drops it to the floor at her feet. She then climbs up onto the sea wall.

The camera pans to the savage bite mark on the back of her neck.

She takes one look behind, a glance, so her face is caught one last time on film. Then she turns, and with one step, she falls, disappearing into the sea.

A clear photo of the woman flashes up on the screen, asking the public again for their help.

* * *

Morning News: Police have identified the woman who was witnessed falling into the sea yesterday evening at around nine o'clock. Police were called after witnesses reported seeing a young girl jump from the sea wall.

In a presumed suicide, the woman has been identified as Forrest Hesketh, a wolf shifter. The woman's pack has been informed.

The shifter community has responded with shock, disbelief and sorrow, the loss of such a rare female a blow.

The police have thanked the public for their assistance and request any further enquiries to be directed to the Hunters Guild.

The police are also warning that the promenade has been closed to vehicle and pedestrian access. For the time being, all humans should avoid the area.

Reports of a silver dragon aiding in the search have also been confirmed.

CHAPTER THIRTY-TWO

Sunshine warms my face. It glows orange behind my closed lids. I blink my eyes open. I move, and the white duvet cover underneath me stirs the dust motes into the air. I watch them dance and twirl through a beam of sunlight.

I blink. I gasp as the general awareness of yesterday immediately bludgeons me. It hits me so hard I want to curl into a ball and wail.

Don't look back...be brave.

I don't allow any of the terrible details into the forefront of my mind. I stuff everything again into another fucking box.

Soon there will be nothing left but boxes rattling around in my head.

A tear runs down the side of my nose, and I angrily swipe it away.

I instead focus on the moment. On the here and now.

I sit up and knock a thick envelope that has been left next to me onto the floor. I scoop it up and tear it open. Contained inside are my new identification documents.

I sit on the side of the bed, my body slumped. Physically I feel okay, tired and slightly sluggish, but not as horrendous as I'd expected. I am disappointed that I can no longer feel my fire magic. It looks like the curse took both wolf and fire.

I huff and shrug. I lived my whole life without access to magic, so to be trapped in my human body is less challenging than being stuck as a wolf. I guess it's a different side of the same coin. I had access to magic for only six months, not a long time in the scheme of things.

I thumb through the documents. According to my new identification, I'm eighty-three–year-old Betty Green. I huff out a breath, and a morose smile pulls at my lips. I prod at the disguise bracelet on my ankle and notice that my scent masker is back on my wrist.

I'm in Ireland.

I grip my thighs tightly and hunch over in an attempt to stop the pain from crushing my chest. I'm in Ireland. I haven't a clue how Ava managed it. It's risky; shifters aren't welcome here. I will have to be extra careful, although with the curse, I am as close to human as I possibly can get. Being so close to my dragon, yet so far away, is going to be a challenge. I swallow down the rising bile. I'm dead to him, and I know he isn't my dragon anymore. It's something I will have to get over.

Don't look back...

I'm now living in County Sligo. I stand and lug myself away from the bright bedroom. If I don't leave this room, I will pull the covers up over my head, as if they can protect me from the world and I'll never leave. I unenthusiastically explore. The traditional Irish cottage is lovely; it's modern and set over one floor. Ava must have spent a lot of money on making this cottage perfect. The bungalow style consists of one large bedroom with an ensuite bathroom and open-plan living room, with a beautiful farmhouse-style modern kitchen. There's a hallway linking both the front and the back doors with a small utility room and another bathroom. The cottage is also in the middle of nowhere; my nearest neighbour is about six kilometres away.

The tiny little blue car in the driveway is a shock. I have an Irish driving licence, yet I have not got a clue how to drive. The cottage came with a kitchen full of supplies, so I am not going to be hungry anytime soon. But being so remote, I decide that my priority must be learning how to drive, with hitting YouTube as my first port-of-call.

If I had any light in me, it would be exciting. But I feel dead inside.

CHAPTER THIRTY-THREE

It's a cold April morning, and I decide I want to go to my favourite café on the seafront at Strandhill. I love the place. They serve the best ice cream in the country, but I want to grab a hot chocolate and a slice of chocolate cake. I haven't left the house in weeks, so I do my best to make an effort. The stray dog I found in December isn't for moving; he hates leaving the house. He takes it upon himself to be my perimeter guard and gets miffed if I make him leave the garden. He's a character.

I spotted the big beige dog, alone with his head in some bushes, sniffing about quite happily. I whistled to get his attention, and he turned to me and growled. I growled back.

The dog blinked as if trying to work out who the heck I was—his expression hilarious. He's big, a giant breed, well over 100kg, and after a few internet searches, I found that he's a Caucasian shepherd.

I love his company, and he's delighted with his new living arrangements, especially as I will not under any circumstances feed him standard dog food, for obvious reasons. The bloody dog, whom I name Lucifer, eats better than I do. He's an exceptional guard dog, and we get on tremendously, especially when the opinionated monster realises that I'm in charge and he can't get his way.

I set off in my little blue car.

When I arrive, the parking spaces are almost empty. I imagine that when summer finally comes, it will be difficult to park. There's already a steady stream of surfers, braving the Atlantic all year round, so I can only imagine how busy it will get in summer.

I order my drink and cake at the counter and find a table. The traditional ice cream parlour has a warm beachy theme. The walls are a mix of blue and grey, with a black and white checkerboard floor; there's even an old wooded surfboard attached to the wall. I find a seat with my back against the wall. As I sit, I slide the block of wood with my order number onto the distressed-wood table. I can see little grains of sugar that have fallen through the cracks. I stroke my hand across the wood and feel some of the grains; they're rough underneath my fingertips.

I'm sitting next to a big picture window with a view of the sea. I watch the waves rhythmically crash into the sea wall, and my mind wanders to a different location. I'm glad it's the same ocean—I miss Aragon's glass house terribly.

I keep myself busy, but even with Lucifer's help, I still feel alone. Should I care that the solitude that broke me as a wolf now brings me solace as I'm stuck as a human? Without using my rage, which is the only emotion left inside me, I'm nothing but a numb shell.

My body and senses have turned human-slow; I don't need to try to walk like a human anymore. I lost that shifter prowl. I also find that I sleep more. Mercifully I don't have many nightmares, but I wake in the middle of the night or early morning with the feeling of Aragon's arms around me. In that time between sleep and wakefulness, I let myself for a few heartbeats imagine I'm in his arms. I live for the imaginary moments. When I awake fully, I feel like my heart is being ripped out of my chest. I think missing him is the worst part of my new life. I wonder if he misses me, but I know that is wishful thinking.

A chair scrapes against the floor, and I glance up to find two strange men sitting down. One of them sits on the chair next to me, blocking my exit, and the other sits opposite me.

Their whole attitude screams aggression, and they aren't human. Even though I no longer have my wolf senses, I can tell the guy opposite me is an influential, powerful, older Fae. With shock and fearful trepidation, I realise that the guy sitting next to me is a wolf shifter. That alone scares the crap out of me; his nostrils flare as he picks up the fear in my scent.

I take a deep breath in and close my eyes. Why is my life so fucking shit?

I can't get away from them—even in Ireland, the shifters manage to find me. Without my fire magic and the strength of my wolf, I'm in real trouble. I open my eyes turn my body so I can keep both of them in sight, and I wait. I wait for them to make the first move.

The waitress comes up to the table with a smile and drops off my order. I smile at her with thanks. I'm too frightened to say the words, and there's no reason to put her in any danger by attempting to run.

The Fae opposite me is elegant and deadly. Enormous pale blue eyes and pointed ears betray him as a full-blooded Aes Sídh, a warrior elf. His black hair is long as is their custom, styled into intricate plaits. I know enough to recognise his warrior markings—they look like human tattoos, and they start at his right hand and go all the way to his neck. He is dressed in all black, combats.

I'm so fucked.

The wolf isn't as big as the hellhounds back home, not that I have seen him standing, but sitting, he still towers over me. The expression in his eyes is hard, and he screams "old shifter." He looks as if he has been to Hell and back. His light hair is shorn to his scalp, and his eyes are brown.

Both men are looking at me like I have stolen the last slice of cake. Maybe I have?

"You're not human—I can see the witch magic all over you, covering your identity. You shouldn't be using appearance-altering magic in my territory," the elf points out acerbically. He narrows his eyes at me, but all he gets back is a blank stare. I shrug. What does he want me to do? Remove it?

"I demand you remove the magic."

Okay, then. I glance about to try to work out how to get away, but my options are limited. I've stupidly cornered myself.

"You are not going anywhere. Whatever you are, you are dangerous, especially if you have had to alter your appearance."

"This one is unusual or stupid, as it is more frightened of me than you. How strange. It reeks of fear," the wolf says in a growling voice. He lifts his top lip and shows me his teeth–*my, what big teeth you have.* It hasn't been that long since I was last called *it*. Instead of it making me want to rage, my stomach flips and the sadness gets me for a few heartbeats. I shake it off.

Not having much of a choice, I reach for my ankle. The elf pulls an iron blade on me and points it in my face. The wolf growls. I glare at the pair of them—they either want me to remove my disguise, or they don't. Can they make up their fucking minds? I hold up my hands to show I haven't got any weapons, and I roll my eyes when they both look pointedly at my ankle.

The elf puts his big-ass knife on the table with a *thunk* and pulls my foot towards him, almost pulling me from my chair. I let out a squeak of protest, and the fucker pulls my leg harder. I want to scream at him, *my bloody legs aren't that long, you prick!* In the end, he seems to come to the same conclusion, and he ducks underneath the table.

He pulls my leggings up and my boot off. He finds both my disguise- and scent-masker bracelets, and I feel the magic disappear. The wolf's eyes widen as he takes in my young face and gold eyes. He makes a slightly shocked sound, which causes the elf to spring up from underneath the table, his iron blade back in his hand and pointing at me.

He too stares at me with absolute shock on his face.

"What the fuck? I wasn't expecting that," says the wolf.

I sip my drink as they continue to study me. I am not wasting it—it's hot chocolate, plus it gives me something to do with my shaking hands. The wolf leans towards me, sniffing. I glare at him. Fucking rude.

"She still smells wrong, of magic," the wolf grumbles. "I can't believe she's a wolf shifter. How old are you, kid? You look about...twenty? Where the fuck have you come from!"

"She has a curse on her," says the elf. Just like the wolf, he's looking at me with fascination.

"What type of curse? Why are you alone, kid? What the hell are you doing in Ireland?"

I ignore his questions and continue to drink. I also stare longingly at my slice of cake, which is on the edge of the table. The wolf grunts and slides the plate closer to me. I nod my thanks to him. I have no idea why—sometimes I can be too polite, but my mum drilled manners into me, and it's an excellent habit.

"A curse to stop her shifting. It has blocked her shifter magic completely. It's killing her," the elf says matter-of-factly, tipping his head to the side as if he's studying a strange bug. "Why would someone curse you?" I pick up the cake, ignoring the fork, and stuff half of it into my mouth.

The wolf lets out a really angry growl that makes me, embarrassingly, squeak. I spray little bits of cake onto the table. I glare at him. What a dramatic reaction to a few unanswered questions! I'm trying not to cough; my eyes water a little. I feel like I have inhaled some crumbs—what a bloody waste of cake.

He ignores me, his focus behind me. He grabs the back of my chair, dragging it around till he can get a good look at the back of my neck. I wonder for a split second what he's looking at, what is so—the ragged bite mark. My stupid mate-mark. I want to slap my forehead; I can't believe I forgot about it. I hunch my shoulders and quickly move my chair away from the nosy wolf.

I am not going back.

I hunch further into myself. I worry my chapped lips with my teeth, and the taste of blood fills my mouth. I need to get back to the cottage for my dog. Fuck. I won't look at either of them. I try my best to stem my rising panic. I don't want to have to fight them. I know there's no way I can win. I remember a quote: "Appear weak when you are strong, and strong when you are weak." By Sun Tzu, *The Art of War*.

I sit up straighter and wolf the fuck up. I will do whatever is necessary, even fight them if I have to. My dog needs me.

I peek at my cup, contemplating what would happen if I threw my cup of hot chocolate in the elf's face. He might spring to his feet; then I could grab his big-ass iron knife off the table and shove it up his left nostril.

"Well, we now know why she is wearing a disguise and why she is hiding out in Ireland," the elf says matter-of-factly. "Runaway mate? You shifters can be barbaric."

The wolf growls, "Says a member of the Aes Sídhe. She is still innocent, and I can't smell a full bond on her. The evil bastard bit her—that shit isn't right. I'd like to use my teeth on his throat, to rip it out. Female shifters are rare and should be protected, not fucking mauled." I glance down at the table and notice his hands are balled into tight fists. "What about the curse?"

"It's a bloody awful crude thing, presumably to stop him from tracking her?"

"Yeah, I guess? You said it's hurting her?" The wolf shifts in his chair.

"*Killing* her."

"What the fuck, kid. The wolf that almost chewed the back of your neck out, he that bad you'd rather die?" I finally look up at the wolf. I let the sadness show in my eyes; I don't hide it from him. I nod. "Fucking hell. Madán, we can't leave her like that. Must be something in your fancy magic box of tricks." The elf, Madán, shakes his head.

"It is none of my business, none of yours. We came to check out a threat. She has been warned not to use witch magic." He narrows his eyes at me. "Do not use disguise-magic, wolf." I nod. He pockets my bracelets and gets up. That's it? God, I hope so. Madán strides away, and just as I am about to sigh in relief, he looks back at me. "No shifters in Ireland. Even ones that can't shift. Out of courtesy, I will give you a few weeks to leave. If I see you after that, it won't be a curse that kills you." I nod.

Maybe if I get online shopping and never leave the house, I will be fine. I stuff the last bit of cake into my mouth. I've had worse odds; I am not leaving. I have nowhere to go.

"I will talk to him," the wolf says gruffly; I don't respond. "My name's Mac." I blink up at him, nod, and give him a small smile. "In case you need anything." Mac flicks a business card onto the table and follows Madán out the door.

"Goodbye, Betty," I whisper.

I glance at the card; it has his name, number, and the bold claim of *Warrior*. I pop it into my pocket. I have no intention of calling him.

I grumble as I hunt for my discarded boot underneath the table.

CHAPTER THIRTY-FOUR

I find it impossible with my new shitty driving skills to tell if anyone is following me. So instead of trying to drive while keeping an eye in the rear-view mirror, I just drive around for a bit. I also fill up with petrol.

I get back, and Lucifer is barking at me like a nutter. I know I am not wearing my Betty disguise, but he's used to me without it. He spends ages sniffing around my car, barking at it. My only thought is that some other dog has peed on the tyre.

I'm feeling so down I don't bother eating—I just feed Lucifer and go to bed early.

The morning comes, and I ugg like a zombie to the toilet with my eyes still closed, not wanting to wake up from my dragon dream. I know I'm a bloody idiot, but my sleeping brain will not behave.

Lucifer is going nuts at the back door, barking as if he's ready to kill something. It's still dark out, so I flick on the outside lights. Hopefully, the light will scare away whatever creature is upsetting him, before I let him out. We have a young fox that likes to come to wander about and pee in Lucifer's territory. I quite like him for his boldness but not for his driving Lucifer crazy, as some nights I can be fast asleep and then the damn dog is going mad with his barking. There was also a badger that Lucifer fought with—the badger won. He kicked Lucifer's ass. I had to take Lucifer to the vet in the town to get a couple of shots and his leg stitched up. Lucifer has his own massive first-aid kit now...well, we both do, as I can't shift to heal.

I open the door and he runs out like the house is on fire, continuing to bark, so I slip on my wellies and pop outside to make sure he's okay. He's using his big angry warning bark.

I stand in my driveway looking at the two men I met yesterday—they're outside my gate. Really? Couldn't they have waited till it got light?

Well, I am doomed now that they know where I live. I can wave goodbye to the home-delivery idea. I grab the keys for the gate and let them in; I might as well get this over with. It's not like I can hide under the bed.

As I pass the car, I remember Lucifer's behaviour towards it yesterday, and I want to smack my forehead for being so stupid. They must have put a tracking spell on it—something that six months ago I would have been able to pick out with my own nose. I also wouldn't have been taken by surprise this morning. Being human is shit.

Madán is looking me up and down—of course he is, I am in fluffy pyjamas. I just got up and wasn't expecting an ambush.

"Cute PJs," Mac remarks. I growl at him.

Lucifer continues to bark at them from behind the safety of a tree. His beige fur and black muzzle don't camouflage well. Even in these circumstances, he makes me smile. He's supposed to be a scary guard dog, but he's way too smart to come close and take on these two. It makes me oddly proud of him; he's a good dog.

We go into the house, and I excuse myself by indicating that I need to get dressed. I get changed and return to both men looking around my home.

"Your place is nice," Mac says gruffly when I catch him looking through my kitchen cupboards. I point to the kettle, and he nods. I politely make us all tea, with Mac happily telling me how they take it. We all sit in the living room; this is so weird.

Lucifer has gotten braver and is barking at them through the window. I keep my mouth shut and wait for them to tell me what they want. According to Madán's get-out-of-Ireland-and-I-won't-kill-you speech, I still have thirteen days left.

Madán starts the conversation. "Do you know what I am used to? Begging. You tell a grown man that you are going to hunt him down and kill him, and they either run, or they beg. The amount of begging..." he sighs. "Even the most insane beg, trying to appeal to my sensibilities. You get the idea." He takes a sip of tea. "Then there is you, a pink-haired girl on her own in a hostile country, with your sad, angry eyes. Unbelievably just giving me a shrug and a nod. You at least could have cried." He shakes his head. I narrow my eyes at him. Is he disappointed that I didn't cry? What. A. Wanker.

"It got me thinking, Forrest..." My stomach drops when Madán uses my real name. They know who I am, which is just great. "You look good for a dead girl...although it won't be long until you die for real with that curse. Is that what you want?" He widens his eyes at me, mockingly. "How long are you sleeping at the moment, around twelve hours?" It's more like sixteen, but why does he care?

"I have an old friend who turned England inside-out in your name, Forrest. Do you know what has been happening while you've been dead?" Madán has my full attention. Shit. I feel sick. "The council has been decimated. England almost had a shifter civil war. Replacing the council, a new assembly has been founded, with members voted into power. Their first official act was to introduce an emergency law to protect all female shifters—'Forrest's Law.'" Madán raises his eyebrows. I carefully keep my face blank. "Forrest's Law"? Oh my bloody God, I wonder if they will amend the name once they find out I am still alive and kicking? "The shifters' old laws are in the process of being updated or changed.

Modernised. It has had a positive knock-on effect on shifters all around the world. The other races are looking on with interest." Madán drops the information bomb on me as if he is talking about the weather. He sips from his cup, his eyes never leaving mine.

I wiggle in my seat. I feel a tad uncomfortable and a bit like a fraud. It was never my intention to be a martyr. I selfishly ran.

Will this new assembly fix the rot in shifter society? I'm unsure, but anything positive is a step in the right direction. I think about Madán's words: *the council has been decimated.*

"The Hunters Guild, Aragon? The General, is he okay?" I husk out. My heart beats faster. Worry hits me full-force in the chest. I haven't got the energy to care about myself, but what about Aragon? My dragon.

"Shit, you *do* talk," Mac says happily, smiling at me. "Yeah, the dragon is fine. He kicked everything off, knocked heads together, set up the whole assembly, and then disappeared." I puff out a relieved breath to hear that my dragon is safe. The world is a better place with him in it. Thank God.

I make a mental note to check on Owen, and indirectly, my brother John.

"Killed over half the council, is more like it," Mac says with a laugh.

"You might be interested to know that your mate is still alive," Madán says. I wrinkle my nose and narrow my eyes. Does he mean Daniel? He's no mate of mine.

"Fuck me, kid, you did a number on that fuck-pig—you burned half his face off. He looks like Harvey Two-Face from *Batman*." He shakes his head, chuckling, "You have some impressive skills, or you did…." Mac says, looking me up and down. He frowns at me. Yeah, I look like shit. I admit it, the curse is eating me alive.

I shrug, unconcerned.

Madán continues, "Yes, well, Aragon left him alive after spending a few hours questioning him. I think the dragon was happy to leave him with his life as a warning to others. Especially after the punishment you gave him. Though Aragon cut his right hand off and pulled out all his teeth…I'm sure they returned with his shift, but it must have been an unpleasant few hours." Madán looks at me, a curious expression on his face. "I didn't understand why he had left him alive, until now. I don't believe Aragon would have risked killing him if there was any chance that you could be alive. He didn't find your body…well, for obvious reasons."

"It is safe for you to go back now, kid," the wolf shifter says. "The new laws will protect you."

I am so glad, so proud that Aragon made changes to help others and the whole of shifter society. The council had ruled for too long; the laws had been for a different time. I feel overwhelmed, knowing what has happened—gratified that I made the right decision in leaving. Aragon did all that because I wasn't there to be a toxic distraction. I am still better off dead. "I can't," I say huskily, looking at my hands.

"I don't want to," I say quietly. I peek up and meet Madán's eyes. "I can beg." I will go on my knees if I have to. His eyes widen, and mine plead. *Please don't send me back; please don't. I want to die free.*

A muscle ticks in Madán's jaw as he continues to stare at me. "Aragon misses you." I shake my head in denial. Madán sighs. "He is going to murder me…Okay, Forrest. I can see you are not for changing your mind. I will help you. Foremost, we have to remove that bloody curse…" When I shake my head in panic, he holds his hand up to stop me. "And the half mate-bond. I will link you to my court as a warrior, like Mac." He tilts his head towards the wolf shifter. "The magic is omnipotent; it will clean up all that fragmented magic." He scrunches his nose and waves his hand around, indicating me. "It also means that you will be able to stay in Ireland without any repercussions. As a warrior of the court, you will be asked to help out on low-level missions, similar to being a hunter in the Hunters Guild. I will not ask for any more than you are willing to give. I offer protection, and you commit to a minimum of twenty hours a week. I will contract you for three years, to which you must commit. It isn't a permanent position—after three years you may leave. I must be getting soft in my old age," Madán says, tucking his hair behind a pointed ear. I sit in shock; the Aes Sídhe can't lie.

Mac gives me a big smile. "What do you say, kid—no dying, no psycho-mate bond, and you can have your wolf back, and a job where you can help people. You do any more hours than twenty, and you'll even get paid." Mac winks. I nod in agreement.

"Thank you," I whisper.

Madán's offer is more than I could ever dream of. I glance down at the cup in my hand. It's more than I deserve. "If you're willing to help me, it would be an honour to serve the court and help others." I lift my eyes and meet Madán's pale blue gaze. "I will not hurt the innocent, but if you point me at the bad guys, I will be good to go—I have a lot of repressed anger."

"I'm able to ascertain why he is fond of you," Madán says gruffly.

"When do I start work?" I ask. A small, repressed voice at the back of my head whispers that I will need a theme tune.

"You need to recover from the curse; we can do the warrior link now. I am worried that if we wait any longer, we might be too late." I nod. Wow, I guess I am so not dying today, and I get my magic back!

"I will need to put my hands on your neck. Is that going to be a problem?"

"No, that's fine."

Madán moves closer and puts both of his elegant hands on my neck. They easily wrap around; he holds me gently. His eyes close, and he starts to chant in a language that I don't understand. His hands heat up, and even my human nose can smell the scent of grass and flowers. A light breeze from the magic ruffles my hair. My vision goes slightly cloudy, and my right arm tingles.

Once Madán releases me, I pull up my sleeve, and we all look at the silver markings on my arm. I blink up at Madán. The surprise on his face is a tad concerning.

"Warrior markings," he says quietly, with awe.

"Is that normal?" I ask, poking at them.

"No," he replies, knocking my prodding finger away with a frown. He pulls my sleeve up further. Of course, my strange magic has to act up and give me proper Fae-warrior markings when it shouldn't. The markings are silver and not black, so they're different. I wonder if they do anything. Another Forrest record-breaking feat, which is freaking Madán out. I hope he doesn't put the curse back on. "Would you please remove your jumper." I nod and wiggle out of it.

My warrior markings are on my right arm; they start at my fingers and go up to my shoulder. At first, I presume that they're a random pattern, but after staring at them from various angles, Madán deems that the markings depict the tree of life.

Instead of worrying about them, I will embrace my inner freak—as long as Madán and the other Fae don't get angry and try to kill me, which could still be a possibility. My eyes start to close of their own volition. The magic has drained me.

"All right, Forrest, you are going to need a few hours of sleep to recover. We shall see ourselves out. Mac will be in touch to let you know when your training starts. Do not mess with the markings," Madán says firmly. I nod in sleepy confirmation, and he leaves the room. Mac takes hold of my arm and guides me into my bedroom and to my bed.

"Sleep, kid. When you wake up, you're going to feel so much better. You will be running as your wolf this afternoon."

I mumble a thank you, my eyes already closing. I sleep.

CHAPTER THIRTY-FIVE

It has been over three-and-a-half years since Madán removed my curse and that godawful mate bond. I have my freedom, and I'm healthy.

I'm also haunted by the nagging voice in the back of my head—the voice that gets louder late at night, whispering Aragon's name. Half the time, I convince myself that Aragon wasn't that special and that eventually he let me down, or at least he failed to give me enough information to protect myself. I try to convince myself that I am still not grieving the loss of him.

The warrior training was brutal. My first week, the guys on my course (all no shorter than six-foot) made jokes about me being the token shifter mascot—the pet freak. I am sure that in their eyes the five-foot-two pink-haired shifter was a joke. They thought they had every reason to mock me. I didn't rise to the bullying—I mean, come on, I have handled so much worse.

At first, hidden deep inside I was devastated. Who doesn't want to be liked? I found their gibes and nasty comments hurtful. Mac was furious, but I made him promise that he wouldn't interfere. I kept my chin high acclimatised and got over it.

I proved my point and got payback a week later when we started physical training.

One class, my favourite, was fight-training. In one afternoon, I kicked the absolute fuck out of every guy in my class. I was so aggressive that by the end of the day, the training staff decided to pull me from sparring, for my classmates' safety. Funnily, no one talked about my mascot status again. Mac spent the whole afternoon clapping and laughing.

The Fae I worked with became warier of me. I guess I should have stuck with being the joke mascot instead of the psycho shifter with the creepy dead eyes, fire magic, and stolen warrior markings.

I wore another mask and learned it was better to be feared than liked.

I couldn't kid myself that I would fit in, and part of me didn't care.

Fuck them. I'm dead inside.

My soul is lost in buried memories.

The best parts of me remain with a dragon. I'm just the remaining shell.

I made sure to keep my chin held high and to walk with extra swagger. My new warrior theme tune: "Broken People" from the film Bright, playing in my head.

Years later—after they realised that I wasn't going anywhere, I think—I slowly earned their respect.

Always the hard way.

Being a warrior is a tad anticlimactic. It isn't how I thought it would be. Sometimes you want something so badly you get caught up; you lose yourself in the dream. You find out that what you wanted isn't what you initially thought it would be.

It's December, and ugg, today I am training an idiot. I huff out a frustrated breath, yawn, and scratch the back of my head. I'm glad I opted to have the magical cameras, as no one would believe this shit. I've set them to track my movements. It's like your own film crew following you around. The magic cameras film everything that's happening, circling above and below, getting the best angles. It helps with information-gathering and prosecution. Some warriors choose not to have them. But it's something I don't mind. At first, they were something that Madán had insisted on. But over the past few years, I've come to be so glad he did, as they have helped to exonerate me from many claims of excessive violence. No guy likes the idea of a tiny female warrior taking him into custody, so they claim loads of fake shit. The cameras are so small; it's almost impossible to see them, even with my eyesight.

"What is that!" The new warrior-in-training shrieks in a total panic. He's freaking the fuck out, and it's amusing. The Slime Monster he is screeching at is an amorphous, shapeless, gooey creature that's leaving bits of itself on the pavement outside my favourite ice cream place—the same place where years ago, I first met Madán and Mac.

The newbie warrior pokes his iron blade at the blob-monster, and the knife just disappears. Huh? I have no idea where it goes, but there's a kind of sucking sound as it vanishes.

"I wouldn't get too close to him, Noel," I say helpfully, licking my ice cream—what? It honestly would be rude not to grab one while I was here. A yummy waffle cone, even if it's freezing today—I have a scoop of Belgian chocolate and a scoop of cherry. Yum, the best ice cream in Ireland. Noel screams and dives away from a tentacle of goo; I roll my eyes.

He then produces a flame. He has a fire gift, which is why I have had him dumped on me. "Noel, don't use a flame on him, fire doesn't work." Noel has just fallen on his bottom as he has tripped over a bollard that he didn't notice behind him, as he's so panicked. He flails on the floor. I frown as Noel screeches in a pitch higher than I could ever hope of achieving. My ear that's closest to him rings painfully. I frown and rub it on my shoulder. As he cries, Noel throws his flame at the Slime Monster.

I wince and rub my forehead. With a *whoosh*, the whole monster is now alight and is dripping not just goo, but flame-y goo all over the pavement.

Noel screams again, the sound grating. I finish my ice cream and decide to rescue the situation. I circle the monster and make my way to Noel, who is still on the floor wailing. I smack the back of his head. He finally shuts the fuck up and turns to me, his eyes wide in panic.

"Get up, you idiot. Noel, you need to listen better. You haven't even noticed that the creature is not trying to hurt you; he is just standing there!" I huff out a frustrated breath and point at the flaming goo monster. "You have set him on fire for no reason at all, apart from your total lack of control and your fear." I march up to the scary-looking Slime Monster, wave my hand, and call the fire that surrounds him into my control.

I have learned a lot over the years, and the fire listens to me as if it's my own. I wave my hand again, and the fire dies completely.

"Hi, Bert, thanks again so much for helping with training. I appreciate your time. Sorry about the fire…" Bert, the Slime Monster, nods his head, burps, and the missing iron knife tumbles to the pavement. "Tell your family hi from me." Bert gives me what I interpret to be a slimy wave and goes off to his car.

Bert and his family are so helpful. They help a lot in training newbies to react to a situation and not to what a creature looks like. It's usually a good lesson—unfortunately, it's one at which Noel has failed miserably.

I scowl at Noel, who is still on the floor. His mouth is opening and closing. He's doing a good impression of a goldfish as he watches Bert leave.

"You let him go? He is getting away!" I roll my eyes; this idiot needs a miracle to pass his training. Thank God I got this on film. I chuckle evilly.

CHAPTER THIRTY-SIX

I am playing bait this evening, as we're hunting some big bad. The evil bastard has been killing young girls; we presume it's a male solo predator. He has moved across the country, killing as he goes. He has murdered fifteen young girls, and three girls are still unaccounted for. He started in Dublin, and it didn't take the local police—the Garda Síochána, more commonly referred to as the Gardaí or "the Guards"—and the Fae warriors long to connect the dots. The public is pissed. The human papers are blaming the Fae, and the Fae are biting back, with everyone pointing an accusing finger at everyone else. It's turning into a total clusterfuck, a nightmare of epic proportions.

All I am focused on is the big bad, and I let the higher-ups deal with the shit that's going down. The state of urgency demanded from everyone is nothing compared to the pressure that, as warriors, we put upon ourselves. We need to find this guy, and quickly.

For some reason, he doesn't mind who he picks—human or Fae, it doesn't seem to matter much. He does have a type, though: he likes the girls young and delicate-looking. So it stands to reason that I'd volunteer to be the bait to try and catch him. We know he's heading to the Sligo area, but we don't know when, so this week my evenings have been filled with me sashaying around Sligo town centre in a pretty dress looking irresistible. We have yet to get him, and I've become disheartened. On a plus note, we have already arrested three idiots who thought it was a good idea to try and take advantage of me.

The self-control I have mastered in the past few years is impressive; I don't have the worst record for beating the crap out of the bad guys. I want nothing more sometimes then to punch a few predator dickheads in the face. Women should feel safe to go anywhere after dark, without risk. I hate that in our modern multi-creature world, that isn't the case.

Tonight is Saturday night, and I'm wearing a lovely gold dress. It has long sleeves and a high neck. It's mega short, and I have to keep reminding myself not to tug at the hem. I am bloody freezing, as I am not wearing a jacket. Apparently, young humans like to freeze when they go for a night out. I am twenty-seven and find it ridiculous. A coat would be nice. I hate the cold.

"Peter, ya burger, did ya want cheese?" Arrah, I bloody hate having these idiots in my head. Bloody mind links...luckily, it's a spell used only on these kinds of assignments. But the guys on duty with me tonight, all they have done is eat.

"Yeah, and bacon." I huff out a cloud of hot breath. I am cold, and now I am fucking hungry.

I wander to the next pub and grab a drink and a snack from the bar. I find a great place to sit, in the corner, where I can watch everyone and get myself warm.

I am also isolating myself, screaming: *Hey predators, look at me, the easy prey, oooh all on her own, looking lost.*

Two members of my team keep up the chatter about food. Mac tells them to shut the fuck up, but not until after he orders his meal. Such a bunch of twats. My tummy rumbles in agreement.

I like this pub. It's situated next to the River Garavogue in Sligo town. It's the right mix of traditional Irish and modern. I love that it's still privately owned, with its character intact, and not owned by a pub chain. There's a long bar running down the left-hand side of the room. Small wooden tables are scattered around, with half a dozen booths along the right-hand wall. Chart music is playing at the moment; the live music has finished for the evening. The majority of the customers are braving the cold weather in the beer garden, which is the smoking area outside.

I sip my half-pint of Guinness and blackcurrant. I also nibble on a bag of salt and vinegar Tayto crisps. Obstinately I allow my crisp-crunching to echo in my thoughts. *Crunch. Crunch.* Mac groans—he hates food noises. That will teach them to have burgers without me.

"Hi, you on your own?" A guy takes the seat across from me, without asking—creepy fucker. I have to remind myself that I am playing bait. I peek up at him from underneath my lashes and smile in what I hope is a timid way. I always wonder if they will notice my dead eyes and realise I'm not what I pretend to be. But I have this down to a fine art, and they see what they expect.

"No." I shake my head, and then I shrug my shoulders and let out a little sad-sounding laugh. I lean forward and glance around as if I don't want anyone else to hear me. "Sort of, I guess. My sister has my phone and my purse. I went to the toilet, and she held them for me, and she wasn't around when I got back. I searched for her; I couldn't find her, so I thought I would come to this pub to see if I can find her here instead." I shrug again, tucking my hair behind my ear. "She always comes to this one. I don't think her friends like me too much." I widen my eyes in fake horror, then glance about again, searching for my non-existent sister.

The creepy guy nods. "I can help you find her if you like. A beautiful girl like you shouldn't be on her own." I nod and give him a smile, dropping my eyes coltishly back to the table and my drink.

"Thank you," I say, and he smiles at me, showing a little too many teeth.

He is a troll, although he's attractive in a greasy-hair, slicked-back, 80's-troll kind of way. Trolls usually are quite easy to like. They're big and dumb, and they work a lot in security. But this guy, even if he isn't our killer...he's bad news. My creepy-bad-guy warning alert is pinging like crazy. You know that feeling? The female lizard brain that warns you, someone or something is dangerous and to run? I think mine is a bit defective, as it always encourages me to run *at* them and punch them in the face. This creep makes my hand itch with the overwhelming need to slam the heel of my palm into his nose.

"Please, could I borrow your phone? I might ring my dad and ask him to come and get me," I say shyly.

"Sure, beautiful." The creepy guy pulls out his phone. He looks at the screen with a mock-sad face, waves it at me, then taps the phone on the side of his head. "No signal. We will have to step outside." I give him a sweet, timid smile, gulp down my Guinness, and get up. I let myself wobble a little as I stand.

"Oh, room spin," I say with a hiccupping giggle. Creepy takes hold of my arm and instead of leading me to the front of the bar, he puts a hand around my waist and muscles me towards the emergency exit at the rear.

"It's a go, leaving out of the back exit. Please be ready for my signal," I say, pushing my thoughts into my team's heads.

They confirm.

"Thank you so much for helping me. My name is Mellisa, by the way," I say as we stride out into a back alley. I stumble a little; then I turn towards him with a small smile on my face. I hold my hand out for his phone. "So if I could just use your phone?"

He leans towards me and puts an arm above my head, resting it on the wall at my back. He looks down at me and flashes his teeth in a sinister smile. "Sure, beautiful. Gosh, you are a tiny little thing...so perfect." He hands the phone over to me, and I take it. I try to keep my attention on him instead of the phone, but as soon as my hand grazes the handset, I lose focus.

"What the hell..." A spell comes over me, and I realise my touch on the handset activated it. It takes only a few seconds for my magic to burn through it. If I were human, as I'm pretending to be, I'd be in serious trouble.

But a few seconds is all the creep needs. He grabs me and *steps* us to somewhere else.

Oh shit.

CHAPTER THIRTY-SEVEN

Adrenalin rushes through my system, and my heart picks up its rhythm. Well fuck, that is interesting—a troll shouldn't be able to *step*.

Stepping is like the gateways but without a portal. Powerful Fae can step; they usually have to be as old as shit. It's like how you would imagine teleporting to be. We had been unaware of how he moved his victims—at least now we know. Creepy must be our guy.

I let Creepy think the spell is working. I slump against him, which is totally gross, but when you are playing the part of prey, you have to go with it. I am not surprised when we end up stepping into a basement.

Not knowing where I am is disconcerting. I hope I'm still in Ireland.

I keep my eyes down, feigning disorientation, and use my other senses. I can smell blood, vomit, and some seriously scary scents that I won't put a name to, for my own sanity. I can hear crying and four other heartbeats. My tummy dips as I feel a monumental sense of relief that Creepy has bought me straight to the missing girls. Thank God.

Surreptitiously I roll my head back and to the side, throwing in a moan for good measure. My eyes dart about the room. Creepy has everything set up, a serial killer's paradise: chains on the walls in various metals and half a dozen iron cages, the whole shebang. I hope this fucker doesn't attempt to put me in a cage.

I will lose my shit if he does.

You know you're messed up in the head when you feel relief when the serial killer you're hunting only handcuffs you to a wall. Attached to the wall, I sag in my chains, the substantial steel chains heavy and biting on my wrists. He leaves me, murmuring that he will play with me later when I wake up as I'll be no fun if I don't scream. Fucker. The door slams behind him.

I am so glad that playing human is working out for me this evening.

I stand straight and roll my shoulders to loosen my stiff muscles. I twist around in my chains as I take in the basement. One door in and out.

"Jenny, Sarah, Mary?" I say in a calm, gentle tone. The girl who's crying stops. "I am sorry, I don't know who the fourth girl is. My name is Forrest, and I'm a warrior with the Fae Court. I'm going to do everything in my power to get you all home. Can you tell me if that creepy bastard is working alone? Have you seen anyone else?"

The sobbing girl answers, surprising the hell out of me. Brave girl. "My name's Sally. He took me this evening. I haven't seen anyone else."

"Okay, thank you, Sally."

"He is working alone," a quiet voice says; she's in the cage in the corner. "I have been here for a while. It feels like forever. He rapes and k— he kills. I think he eats; I think he has been eating us. I am Mary..." She makes a heaving noise. When she gathers herself, she crawls to the front of her cage, a bitter smile on her cracked lips. "What are you going to do? Chained to the fecking wall! Who is going to rescue you? We needed a proper warrior, not some girl." Mary bangs on her cage and whimpers as the iron burns her hand. "This is a bag of shite...ya rippin' the piss," Mary mumbles as she turns away, nursing her hand. The other two girls don't respond.

I know from the files that he has had Mary who is Fae for around three weeks. I won't take her words personally. Mary won't be the last person to underestimate me, and she's a scared kid. I'm kind of proud of her angry words— it gives me hope that she will have enough piss and vinegar to get through this experience.

I listen for any movement outside the room. Sweat drips down my back and makes the gold dress stick to me like a second skin. I cautiously send my flame into the handcuffs, delicately destroying the locking mechanism. I am convinced that all the girls are victims, and I feel the time is right to get this shit sorted. I desperately need to check on the two unresponsive girls. The cuffs rattle as they fall from my wrists and hit the wall.

"Mac, have you got a track on me?" I direct my thoughts, with no answer.

Well, shit.

I rub my wrists. Now comes the difficult decision on whether to unlock the girls who are awake, or leave them. If I undo them and they panic, it might be an issue, but if I leave them and I get taken out…fuck that. They need every opportunity to try and rescue themselves.

I undo Sally's chains, whispering to her to keep still and silent until I tell everyone to move. I kneel in front of Mary's cage door. The concrete digs into my knees and shins. My flame makes short work of the lock and the cage swings open.

I channel Owen, and some of the first words he said to me pop out of my mouth. "Mary, I can see that you are frightened and that you have been through Hell. I can also see the fire inside you. Keep using that fire—your anger. Don't let it go inwards. What has happened to you is not your fault. The blame rests on him, not on you. Do not let him win and don't let him take any more from you. Sometimes it's better to bury the memories until you are strong enough to deal. It's going to be hard, but you need to keep moving forward one step at a time. Do you understand?" Her eyes meet mine, and we take stock of each other. She nods. "I need you to trust me. Stay in this shitty cage for a while longer, just until I kick the sicko's ass. If anything happens to me, I'm trusting you to grab Sally and run like hell. Got it?" I hold out my fist to the girl, who is still huddling at the back of the cage. I wait. Slowly she lifts her arm and bumps her fist to mine.

I miss my friend Owen; he's always in my thoughts, like an emotional ghost. I regularly ask myself the question, *"What would Owen do?"*

I close the door and move on to the first unconscious girl. She's naked, badly hurt, and is bleeding profusely. I stroke her dirty blonde hair away from her face. Her breathing is shallow and her heartbeat is weak. I remember her name from the files—it's Jenny—and my heart aches for her. I slip my hand underneath my dress and dig about in my bra for the little tubes that hold condensed Fae tracking-magic and a sleeping draught. I need these girls to stay asleep; I can't afford to add any more variables to this shit-show. I tip the plastic vials and let the magic seep into her chest; I then place my fingertips on her collarbone. My warrior mark starts to glow; the silver light bleeds through the fabric of my dress. Pulled directly from the Fae Court, the healing magic rushes into Jenny. I wait and listen. It isn't long until I can hear that her breathing has become better and that her heartbeat has returned to a normal rhythm. The bleeding stops, and the wounds that I can see heal. I bow my head in relief.

We were all a little surprised when my warrior mark turned out to be defensive magic. The marks channel innate magic—healing, shields, wards, and a whole host of cool defensive stuff.

The last naked, unconscious girl is Sarah. The dark-haired girl has a nastily broken arm. I use the sleeping draught first, I pour the vial and wait for a few seconds, and then get myself into position. I brace myself. I cringe as I grip her wrist and shoulder. My warrior mark lights up again as I sharply pull the broken limb. It crunches, snapping back into place as it heals. I blow out a shaky breath—I will never get used to resetting bones. I'm glad she was asleep for that unpleasant job. Sarah's face relaxes from a pained grimace into a peaceful expression.

I heal Sally and Mary; I also put a tracking potion on all of the girls, so if the worst happens and I can't rescue them, a member of my team will still be able to track them—or at the very least, locate their bodies. I shudder and swallow the bile that's doing its best to crawl up my throat. I close my eyes for a second. I take a breath. Rage, panic and determination fill my lungs in place of air. I need to save these girls. I can't fail.

I hustle back to the wall and get back into position, looping the broken handcuffs back around my wrists. As I wait, I analyse what has happened to these girls, and I can't help thinking about my situation, my past. I have been running forever. I huff out a sigh and grind the back of my head into the wall. I'm happy to fight for others, but I have never once fought for myself. Never. I always run. I still love Aragon. My self-inflicted broken heart has never healed. I've just learned to live with the cracks.

The job I do is dangerous, and perhaps I need to meet my internal demons head-on once and for all. I can't have my trauma define me; maybe it's time to open and deal with my boxes? Deal with Daniel and tell Aragon how I feel.

CHAPTER THIRTY-EIGHT

It isn't long until Creepy arrives back. The basement stairs creek ominously with the troll's footsteps the evil bastard slams the door open. It hits the wall and bounces closed. Sally and Mary both shudder. I stand against the wall and glare at him. I can't have Creepy paying attention to the other girls; I need him to focus on me. I'm hoping my defiance will do the trick. Creepy smiles.

Showtime.

He flashes his pointed teeth. I tip my head to the side, wondering if I can knock a few of them out. He swaggers towards me, and I let him get close enough that I smell his rancid breath.

I keep my face carefully blank and my big gold eyes wide.

"Ahh, you're awake—that's good. I can't wait to show you my—" Fuck this. I am not waiting for his villain speech or for the creepy fuck to grope me. I already think this whole assignment will give me nightmares without having to listen to him. I kick my leg out and aim for his knee. I put all my strength into the kick, and I hear and feel the knee crunch. His body goes one way, the leg the other; the shock on his face makes me smile.

I grab hold of the back of his head and smash his face into the basement wall. Once: "It's not so lovely…" twice: "when your prey fights back…" three times: "creepy bastard." I let go of his head. Wrinkle my nose and wipe my hand on my dress as he slumps to the floor.

Huh, that felt a bit anticlimactic.

I was expecting a bit more of a fight. Creepy is out for the count. I give him a kick in the ribs for good measure, urm, just to make sure he isn't playing games. I'm slightly disappointed when he doesn't make a sound. I grab some iron chains from the wall and cuff his hands behind his back. I grab some more and cuff his feet together. I hum as I loop the chains and attach both sets so that his hands are linked to his feet—he is like a Fae pretzel.

Dragging his body by his feet, I pull him towards a conveniently open iron cage. With a bit of huffing and kicking him, I manage to squish him into it. I lock and then chain the door. To make sure he can't go anywhere, I place a ward on the cage with another handy bra-vial. Hopefully that will stop him from stepping himself anywhere. For my final touch, I send my flame out to surround the cage. The fire hits six feet in height, and I coax it into a dome. Overkill? Too damn right it is. This fucker isn't going to be hurting any more girls, not on my watch. If it were up to me, I would have killed him. But I have to stick to the law; I can't go around killing people, even if I want to. Looking at the frightened girls here, the smell of what he has done to them in my nose, I want to. God, how I want him to suffer.

I wipe my hands again on my dress; I don't want any part of him on my skin.

"Okay, ladies, let's get out of here. I need your help in carrying Jenny and Sarah. If I carry one, will you be able to carry the other girl between you?" Mary bravely crawls out of her cage, and she raises her eyebrow at the flaming cage. I shrug and make a "meh" face.

Sally needs a little coaxing. I get them to hold the previously bleeding girl, who I think is Jenny, between them, while I pick up Sarah. I dig my shoulder into her stomach and lift her over my shoulder. Luckily Sarah is only a little taller than me, which makes it easier than, say, hefting a guy.

I open the basement door quietly. Creepy was so confident, he hadn't even bothered to lock it behind him. I dance my magic onto my right palm, letting it grow more and more until I form a sword out of the flames. Holding onto Sarah's thighs with my left hand, I make my way up the stairs, leading with my sword. I am not leaving these girls in that basement for one more second with their kidnapper. They follow me, doing an excellent job of keeping close and quiet.

As soon as we clear the basement staircase and enter the ground floor, something in my head pops. I can hear my team again, and more importantly, speak to them. *"I have our big bad contained. I also have Mary, Jenny, Sarah, and Sally with me. I need clothing, healing, and urgent assistance."*

Everyone talks at once, making me wince. Madán gains control, and with a few gruff words, he has the rest of my team silenced. I grit my teeth, and my lips straighten into a firm line. Shit. It is always an issue when your big boss gets involved. The guys must have been shitting themselves when that nobhead creepy fucker stepped away with me.

As Madán talks, I quickly clear the ground floor of the house. As I am on my own and my priority is the girls in my care, I don't bother checking the rest of the house. I won't leave them, and I can't smell or hear anyone else in the vicinity. I use another vial and set up a ward in the hallway by the front door. It's a small area, with peeling flower wallpaper, and it should be easier to defend, much safer, than taking the girls outside.

I am still in Ireland, which is good to know—the cavalry is on its way. Madán steps through before the portal is in place, bringing Mac and a healer with him. He lets me know, using the mind link, so I can open the door to the house and allow them through the ward. I inform Mac that I haven't checked the rest of the house, so he disappears to do a sweep, iron sword in hand.

I leave the healer to check on the girls. Madán gives me an assessing look, nods, and then pulls out his phone. He holds up his finger at me to let me know he will be only a minute. I can hear his side of the conversation, but he has a spell on his phone that stops creatures from listening to the caller, so I have no idea who he's talking too. I presume that he might be speaking directly to one of the girls' parents, or it could be about me.

"I have eyes on her now; she is okay. Looks to be completely unharmed. Yes, not a hair out of place. I will debrief you when I know more. Yes, well, it was something we couldn't have anticipated. I do my best; you know I make every effort t— Yes, well, I will let you know more when I have the information. I care about her too. I will speak to you soon." Madán ends the call and marches back to me.

The other warriors have arrived. "Forrest, will you take me to the creature you have apprehended, please?" I nod and take a final glance at the girls to double-check that they are okay. Healers now surround them.

I show Madán and my team to the basement, warning them that any mind links that they have will be blocked as we move down the stairs.

We go down.

Peter whistles at the room, which is now our grim crime scene...well, it will be once we have removed the creepy bad guy. Then the whole place will be magically processed.

They all stare at my fire dome. I shrug. I ask my flame to come back to me, and it quickly obeys, shrinking back until it's a small flame. It dances across the room and comes to my outstretched palm happily. I close my fist around it, and it dissipates.

They all look from the pretzel troll in the cage to me. I shrug again.

"How the fuck did you fit him in that cage?" Peter asks. I don't even bother answering, With fucking difficulty. The creepy guy is awake, and he moans. I open the iron cage at Mac's timely arrival, and he helps me to drag out the creepy pretzel. My fellow warriors are all Fae and avoid the iron cage like the plague.

Creepy moans again, so I kick him in the head. Mac lets out a chuckle, Madán tuts at me.

"What? We don't want him stepping anywhere, and he looked like he was about to," I say calmly, without any inflexion. We uncuff him and replace the cuffs with our own, and Mac slaps a plastic magic-voiding wristband on him. As soon as it snaps and wraps around his wrist, the magic activates.

We all watch as Creepy's shape changes. Instead of a troll lying on the floor, he's now a goblin. Huh, interesting. No wonder the takedown was so easy. I glance at Madán with eyebrows raised as if to say, are we done? He nods.

"Do you need any medical assistance, Forrest?" I shake my head no. "Let's get you off home then—you have done enough for this evening." Madán holds out his hand, indicating for me to go first back up the stairs. I wave a one-finger goodbye at the guys.

"Am I in trouble?" I say when we get outside. I breathe in the cold winter air, clearing my nose of the horrors of the basement. I start to shiver.

"No. Please debrief me. I am aware that everything that happened tonight was recorded. If you could tell me in your own words what happened, I will add your statement to the report." Madán takes off his jacket and holds it out to me. With a smile and a thank you, I slip it on. It's still warm from his body heat. I am relieved to hear that the magic cameras have been filming the whole evening and that they kept up with me, even when I'd been stepped away.

I yawn, rub my hand across my face, and explain what happened in detail.

When I finish, Madán nods.

"Thank you; I will take you home myself. I shall get one of the warriors to drop your car off in the morning." He waves his hand above my head, and my team-link chatter disappears. I sigh in relief, massaging my temple—that will stop me from getting a massive headache. I also know with that wave that the cameras stopped filming.

Madán takes hold of my arm, and we step back to my home. Lucifer goes nuts—I can hear him barking in the house. I have been working for only about six hours, but it has felt like forever. It has been a long-ass week, trying to catch that evil bastard. I can't believe we did it.

"Take the rest of the week off, Forrest, you deserve it. I am so glad that you are okay and unharmed. You did me proud today—well done." I turn and impulsively hug Madán. Inside it makes me laugh, as my affection always makes him uncomfortable. Surprising the hell out of me, he hugs me back. "Go sort that monster dog of yours out—he sounds like he is trying to eat through the door. Mac will be in touch for when your next shift is." I nod, and he disappears before I can say anything else. I still have his jacket on.

I have to jump over my gate as my stuff is back at headquarters, with my car. I unlock my door with my spare key and Lucifer goes nuts, sniffing and squeaking in excitement to see me. "Hey, squeaky boy, you missed me?" Obviously not so much as Lucifer pushes past me, almost knocking me off my feet, crazy dog. He dashes outside, his fixated priority a perimeter sweep of the garden. I leave him to it. I am that hungry, I could eat a scabby rat.

Luckily for me, I have a whole chocolate cake with my name on it calling for me. I skip and bounce towards my kitchen.

Come to me, yummy chocolaty goodness; you want in my belly.

CHAPTER THIRTY-NINE

I hate time off from work. It has only been a day, and I'm already bored. If I didn't have Lucifer, I'd be working every hour, in a sad attempt to keep busy. But I have to be home for my dog, even if he isn't arsed in spending time with me. Lucifer is content to sit on guard, watching the road and chasing birds that dare to land in his garden.

We have a red weather warning in place for storms and heavy snow. The weather is horrendous, and the public has been warned to stay off the roads and stay at home. My Irish colleagues would say it's a day for looking out, not looking in.

Being cold isn't my thing, and I think my moaning about the cold weather in the past has been slowly driving my colleagues nuts. Mac told me, when he dropped my car off, not to come back into work until the temperature rises.

I didn't know how to take that, but I handled it with my usual maturity by waving goodbye and running back into my house, giggling with glee. I hate not being at work, but I hate the cold weather more. Even though I have fancy solar-powered heating, nothing says homely to me like a fire in the log-burning stove, so I'm staying inside and having the fire on.

While I'm getting ready for bed, the snow is coming down heavily, and lightning dances across the night sky. Freaky thundersnow—I had no idea that it could do that. The power goes out. I peer out of the window and shiver; I am not even attempting to sort out the electric in that. it can wait 'til morning.

Unexpectedly I hear a tremendous bang outside and the whole cottage trembles, and what sounds like a glass in the kitchen falls to the floor, smashing. Cue Lucifer going nuts. I rush to the back door and let him out before he does damage to the door. Lucifer tears off around the back of the house, barking.

I should probably go outside and check it out. I quickly grab my big coat, and I hop on one foot while stuffing my other foot into my wellie. Once both feet are clad in my bright orange Hunters, I make my way to Lucifer, and what I see has me jumping the fence and running across the field like a madwoman.

A bloody dragon has crash-landed in my field!

A big bloody dragon! I run, and a profound fear floods through me. It's not feasible, it can't be him, it can't be. As I get closer, the dragon starts to shift.

"Aragon!" I scream, throwing myself down in the furrow his crash-landing has created. I land in the deep hole next to him.

Flakes of snow cover his beautiful face.

I brush the snow away gently, my hands trembling. He is freezing to my caress. I try not to panic as I think of a way to get him safely into the warmth of the house.

Why the fuck is he so enormous, he's so much bigger than I remembered. His heartbeat is slightly fast, but I can't see any wounds on his naked body. He must have healed when he shifted back. Tugging off my coat, I quickly cover him—not that my ankle-length coat covers much of him, bloody colossal bastard.

I send my flames out around him as close as I dare in an attempt to keep him warm. I know he's fireproof, but my coat isn't.

I jump up and scramble back up the farrow, trying not to let any of the snow and soil fall on him. I run as fast as I can towards my garden shed. I have a tarp in there that I can use to roll Aragon onto and drag him into the house.

It seems to take me forever. It's too cold and too far to drag him to the field gate, so I have to kick some of my wooden fence down to slide him underneath the rails. It's better to get him inside as quickly as I can.

I get him into the house, and somehow I manage to get him wrapped up and into bed—I am so glad that I am strong. With relief, I slump against the bedroom wall.

Shit, he is still unconscious.

I have no idea where he came from and why he ended up in my field or who hurt him. I hope to hell that he wasn't struck by lightning.

I shuffle across the wall towards the door. I need to leave the room and gather things Aragon will need when he awakens. I magically stoke the fire, and I use my warrior markings to enforce and strengthen the ward around the house as a precaution.

I can't believe he's here in my home—wow, this is surreal. I rub my face. My hands are shaking and I feel dizzy. I need to keep myself busy to prevent myself from sitting and staring at the naked dragon in my bed.

Or even worse...I have a little episode where my imagination goes positively nuts. I urm, see myself grab some hot soapy water and some tiny handcloths and I carefully wash Aragon's body, with bow-chicka-wow-wow dodgy music playing in my head. Shit.

I go back outside. The thunderstorm has moved on, although it's still snowing. I check on my solar power and switch it onto the battery-only option; the lights in the house come back on. Sticking my head into the cottage, I turn on my outside lights, grab my hammer from the shed, and then hammer the shit out of the fence while putting the rails back on. I might as well do it now, while I am freaking out. If I don't, Lucifer will just wander off and get lost, and even in wolf form, I don't want to track him in the snow.

It's freezing, and my hands are blue, but I can't go back in as there's a bloody gorgeous naked dragon in my bed!

Lucifer watches me; he isn't bothered about the snow. He rolls onto his back ,wiggling. In the winter he prefers to sleep in the cooler utility room. Most nights, I have to drag him inside; he much prefers being outside on guard.

When I have no more excuses I go back into the house. I shed my layers of outside clothing, prod the fire again, and put another log on. I don't need the wood, but I love the smell. My hands sting with the heat. I poke my nose into my bedroom, and Aragon is still out. I decide that he might be hungry when he awakens, so I set to making chicken noodle soup.

When I have finished the broth and I just need to heat the noodles in the microwave, I have a thought: what if Aragon needs healing? Oh my God, I have just left him in my bed, unconscious, for the past hour and he might need help! Yes, he's all-powerful and probably the strongest shifter I will ever meet, but that doesn't mean he doesn't need my help. I feel like a total idiot.

I creep into the bedroom. Aragon is still unconscious, his breathing and heart rate steady. I pull the cover away from his naked chest and lean over. My warrior mark glows. I'm just about to place my fingertips on his chest when Aragon suddenly moves, and one moment I am leaning above him and the next I am on my back with him lying on top of me. I let out a whine of shock. One massive hand is entirely wrapped around my throat, and the other is gripping my arm so hard that I can feel the bones grind together. I yelp with pain and Aragon slowly blinks at me.

His beautiful eyes widen in horror, and he lets go. I roll out from underneath him and crash to the floor. *Oomph.* Well, that wasn't quite the greeting I'd imagined in my head.

My heart hurts a little. I get up, using the wall to guide myself. I nod at the clothing I had left on the bedside table and point towards the bathroom.

Then I hurry out of the room and go back into the kitchen. I brace my hands on the counter and try my hardest not to cry. I know the dragon got startled when I leaned over him, it was probably just an instinctive reaction. He wasn't trying to hurt me deliberately.

I rub my wrist, and my lips wobble.

The shower in the bathroom goes on, and then not even ten minutes later, Aragon comes into the kitchen, dressed in the standard warrior-recruit jogging bottoms and t-shirt that I had knocking about in my car. The whole outfit looks like, if Aragon breathed wrong, it would burst open like the Incredible Hulk's from all his muscles.

"I am sorry I hurt you, Forrest—I didn't mean to grab you." Instead of sitting, Aragon prowls towards me and stands in front of me.

I hide my sore arm behind my back and shrug. I can quickly shift to heal, so it's not an issue.

I stare at his chest, feeling awkward. What do you say to the guy you are still madly in love with, and who has just found out that you faked your own death? Should I shout "Surprise!" while waving jazz hands?

Aragon puts his hand underneath my chin to lift my head so I will meet his eyes. My head lifts, and his concerned, beautiful silver eyes meet mine.

"Hi, Nutty. I am sorry I crashed back into your life—that wasn't my intent." God, he is beautiful. My stomach goes all swirly. He gently reaches for the limb that's hidden behind my back and inspects it. He shocks the shit out of me when he brings my arm to his mouth and softly kisses my wrist in what I can only think is an apology. I shiver.

"Are you okay?" I squeak out.

If this is a dream, I so do not want to wake up. I cannot take my eyes off him. I greedily take him in.

I thought my memory of him was detailed, that I recalled everything about him, from the exact colour of his silver hair and skin, to the shade of his beautiful eyes. The Aragon in front of me...my memories did not do him justice. It is as if I had remembered him in black and white, and now he is standing before me in full HD colour.

Aragon's chiselled face is a masterpiece of masculine beauty. My eyes drop to his full lips, with the bottom one slightly fuller than the top. I stare at him in awe, and shockingly he is looking at me in the same way. Like I'm the most beautiful thing he has ever seen. He must have hit his head.

"I am okay… I miscalculated the storm."

My eyes widen, and I ask incredulously, "You got struck by lightning?"

"I got struck by lightning."

I giggle. Aragon smiles, ruefully rubbing the bridge of his nose, the movement stretching the t-shirt to its limits. I gulp. Every lump and bump of his chest is defined.

"Are you hungry?" I ask, licking my lips.

"I could eat."

I nod and disappointedly move away from him. It's for the best, as I have the almost uncontrollable urge to lick him, then shout at the top of my voice: *I licked it, so it's mine!*

Aragon sits at the island and watches me as I throw the noodles into the microwave. His presence and substantial size take over the whole kitchen. I huff in his smoky scent and feel safe for the first time in years.

I pop the noodles into the bowl, pour in the chicken broth, and hunt down some extra chicken that's hiding at the bottom of the pan to add to his bowl. I smugly put the bowl in front of him, *look what I made* written proudly all over my face.

I have had yet to cook for another person, so it's nice to show off. *Look at me, I can make food, I am adulting perfectly, hear me roar.*

Roar.

Aragon scrutinises his bowl with a smile; a chicken bone is floating at the top. I know the noodles are slightly stuck together and the broth is a tad salty, but it's perfect comfort food. The pink pieces of chicken are delicious, and the black bits make them crunchy. He looks up at me, his eyes sparkling, and I give him an encouraging smile. He coughs into his fist and takes hold of his spoon.

After we have finished eating, it seems that Aragon wasn't that hungry after all. My curiosity has been building to an epic level. "So how did you end up here?" I ask.

"Forrest." Aragon taps the counter. With a sigh, he ducks his head and peers up at me from under his brow. "Since fate has forced my hand, I won't lie to you." His tone drops and his eyes are imploring, "I have known where you have been this whole time. I tracked you down the night you left, but I arrived too late to divert you from your plan," he says in an almost-whisper. "I would never have stood in your way. Your friend Ava? She was going to send you to America. But I changed her mind. This is one of my safe-houses." He taps the countertop again.

Huh, Aragon doesn't shout, "Surprise!" or do jazz hands either.

CHAPTER FORTY

I blink at him, think for a few seconds, and then nod. "Okay."

"What?" Aragon says in a strained voice. "That's it? 'Okay'? You're not angry" He searches my gaze.

I shrug. "How can I be mad when you have helped me? I ran away, faked my death...yet you let me go and continued to help me. I should also be saying, "Thank you.""

"I have been visiting you a couple of times—"

"—A month?" I interrupt with glee, bouncing on my seat. Aragon shakes his head, a self-amused smile of mirth on his face.

"No, a day," he says, rubbing the bridge of his nose. He visits me a couple of times a day? Wow. I can't believe I convinced myself that he wouldn't care if I was out of his life. The sneaky dragon has been watching me.

I emit a strangled cough and mumble under my breath, "Stalker."

"Absolutely." He huffs out a laugh.

"Did you ask Madán to give me my job?" I reach over and squeeze his forearm, dreading the answer. I like my job, and it's important to me. I want to make the world a better place. I know it sounds so damn idealistic and naïve. But honestly, I am proud to be a warrior. If I can stop one child from having a childhood like mine, if I can take down the bad guys...it might not be world-saving, but each person I help is one more life living safer in the world. Aragon flips his arm over and takes hold of my hand.

"Forrest, no, you got your job on your own merit. Madán is extremely impressed with you. I certainly would not have picked such a dangerous career for you." He grunts. "Over the past few years, I have had the honour of not only watching you grow, but of seeing how strong, compassionate"—he grunts again—"and brutal you can be." He shakes his head. A proud smile flashes across his plump lips.

That smile makes my insides mushy.

Something clicks in my head, and I know before I have even asked the question. "Madán gave you access to the footage from the magic cameras." Aragon nods.

He rubs his chin in preparation for telling me something else.

"I do have one last thing I need to confess. You were alone, unable to shift, and sleeping a lot. I was concerned—" I narrow my eyes at him—"so I found the best guard-dog breed, and I made sure you would find him." Guard dog…Lucifer? Aragon bought me my dog! Lucifer is mine to keep, forever!

I burst into tears, big embarrassing sobs. I can't help it—I bloody love my dog. I ignore Aragon's horrified face as I lunge from my stool and throw myself into his arms. I pull Aragon down towards me. I kiss my amazing, incredible, thoughtful dragon all over his handsome face.

He gave me my dog, 'cause he wanted me to have a friend and something to care for.

"Thank you, thank you so very much. I love him. I am so happy that he is mine and no one is going to take him from me." Well, that was what I was attempting to say—it sort of came out a bit mumbled, what with all the snot and tears. Aragon nods...I think he got all that. He gently takes my head in his big hands and thumbs the tears from my cheeks.

"You're more than welcome," Aragon says roughly. He coughs to clear his throat. "There will never be another person like you, Forrest Hesketh. You are so unique. I want you to know that I never acted out of duty when it came to you. It was always personal. That first day in my office, you lit up my world as if everything before you was just darkness. You have taught me the meaning of loneliness because when I don't see you, I feel alone, and missing you is like physical pain." He rubs his chest with his other hand, over his heart. "Losing you because I misjudged a situation was the worst moment of my life. Knowing I had to let you go and not knowing if you would come back to me…" Aragon closes his eyes; he leans forward. His forehead brushes mine. "I should have talked to you. Told you my plans. I lost you because of my arrogance. You were hurt…" Aragon growls, still stroking my cheek. "Forgive me?" he begs.

"Okay," I whisper in shock.

His beautiful eyes meet mine.

"You are it for me, Forrest. I waited lifetimes so we could meet." I blink at him. That lightning has seriously messed him up. "I understand if this has come out of the blue. I know you will need time to process—" Fuck it. I grossly use my sleeve to clean my nose quickly and then I kiss his beautiful mouth to shut him up before he talks himself out of whatever is happening here. Oh my God, Aragon likes me!

"I love you, you crazy dragon," I mumble. I move away and peek up at him, checking to see that I haven't made a stupid mistake.

Aragon doesn't run away screaming. Instead, he stands, and his arms circle me. He lifts me onto the counter. I suck in a ragged breath, my heart pounding in my ears. Butterflies explode in my tummy as he stands between my legs and pulls me in close.

He growls. I bite down on my lip in response. One of Aragon's big hands wraps around my waist. The other goes to the back of my neck.

Aragon leans forward, curling around me, crushing my body against his muscley hard chest. Oh my God. My heart jumps, missing a beat, and my tummy flips with more dancing butterflies. We are so close together that his face blurs. I close my eyes. I can feel his breath on my lips. I lick my lips, trying to get any trace of his taste that might be left on them. As I do, my tongue catches his mouth. I hum with appreciation. Aragon closes the tiny gap between us and kisses me, his full lips surprisingly spongy.

The kiss at first is gentle, then with swift graduation more intense, harder, deeper. I gasp. Aragon's tongue, as if it has been waiting for an invitation, slips into my mouth and tangles with mine.

I cling to his forearms, the only things keeping me stable in my dizzy, swaying world. The stubble on his face rubs my skin, but I don't care. I groan into his mouth. He pulls his lips slightly away and whispers, "Breathe, Forrest…" I gasp in a shaky breath, belatedly realising I had neglected to breathe. Oxygen is so overrated. How can anyone kiss and breathe at the same time?

I inhale his smoky dragon scent. I want to breathe him, lick him, and eat him up.

I've had a taste, and unequivocally I realise it will never be enough.

Aragon gently kisses my gasping lips and pulls away from me.

I slowly open my eyes and blink up at him; my lips are tingling in the best way. I give him a bright smile and with a grin say, "That was my first kiss, and I am so glad it was with you." I bite my lip and bounce with excitement. "Could we please do that again? I will get better if we practice." I stop bouncing and meet his heavy-lidded eyes. "Will you teach me, Aragon?" Aragon groans. Shit, that is an incredible sound.

I stare at my knees, feeling a little shy; I am twenty-seven, for God's sake. I needed to get this whole thing down.

"Practice?" Aragon's voice is deep and smoky, "I would love nothing more than to practice *everything* with you."

Yay. I nod. I refrain from doing a fist-pump.

I give him a beaming smile, grab his hand, jump off the counter, and attempt to tug him towards the bedroom.

Do I just take my clothes off?

Or is it better if Aragon removes them?

I worry a little. Hopefully Aragon knows what he is doing. I tug, but Aragon doesn't move; instead, he reels me back into his arms.

"But we're going to go slow, Nutty. So that's enough for tonight."

What! What? Noooo. After that speech, that epic kiss—what? Well, that's disappointing. I huff, I even stomp my foot.

"Spoilsport," I mutter under my breath. We go into the living room, and I throw myself down on the sofa.

I am not sulking.

What is it about Aragon that brings out my immaturity?

Aragon shakes his head at me, his eyes dancing. He sits elegantly beside me as if he has a suit on and not the borrowed jogging bottoms and t-shirt. He takes hold of my hand and plays with my little finger.

"May I stay over? To sleep? I would feel uncomfortable leaving you, what with the storm." I grin at him and nod like crazy. Do I want the handsome dragon whom I have just kissed to stay the night? Do I want to wake up with his arms around me and the smell of him filling my nose? I am not daft—no way I'm going to say bloody no.

I jump up with a squeal and run towards my bedroom to get ready for bed.

THE SILVER DRAGON

That was the best sleep that I have had in years. It is unbelievable, how much I missed him, and since he has come back crashing into my life, I feel so grateful. I have at least a week off work, and I can spend it getting to know Aragon again.

I so need to work on this practising kissing and stuff, to add to my adulting portfolio. I admitted I was in love with him. He didn't say it back, but that's okay. I will make Aragon love me.

"What are you thinking so hard about?" Aragon says below me. I am lying on top of him, all snug in his arms, back to being the little puzzle piece that fits so perfectly with him. I feel his words rumble through his chest. I shouldn't be worrying; Aragon is here with me in my bed and for the first time in a long time, I feel safe and complete. He cuddles me to him and kisses my forehead.

"Nothing," I mumble.

"Liar," Aragon says gruffly, "I can feel that brain of yours going crazy. What has you worried?" he whispers into my ear. Aragon gently rubs the back of my neck—seemingly unconcerned about the horrible bite mark. I tip my head and look at him. He brushes the hair from my face.

"Do… do you… Aragon, do you love me?"

Aragon's whole face softens as he meets my eyes, and I see the truth shining in them.

"I love you more than anything in this world. You are my treasure. I will spend the rest of this life with you, if you will do me the honour. When we're no longer on this earth, I will spend my new existence searching for you. You are the other half of my soul, and I am only ever complete if you are in my arms."

My eyes widen with shock. I huff out a breath and blink at him. *Tell me how you really feel.* Wow. Phew, that makes me feel better.

In comparison to Aragon's words, my snotty "I love you" seem kind of shit.

"Oh, urm, okay thanks…" I whisper.

"In my office, I was in total awe of you. You were so endearing, with the dress and the antics with the water glass."

Aragon chuffs and takes the rogue hand in question and kisses it. "When I read the report delving into your life, knowing what you had to endure...it was distressing. I was devastated. I wanted to make things easier for you. I have been alive for a long time, and you hadn't had any chance to live."

Aragon sits up, and with his hands on my hips he lifts me, turning me around to face him. My legs drop either side of him—he is so wide that they don't touch the bed. He tucks my hair behind my ear and cups the back of my head, meeting my eyes.

His eyes hold conviction.

I bite my lip to hold in a moan. *Oh, this is nice.* Warmth pools deep in my stomach.

"Able to partial-shift at twenty-three, and when you used your fire magic, I was so damn proud of you. It also frightened me to death. How the hell was I going to keep you safe? You'd already dealt with so many men trying to control you. You had just shifted to human it would have been inappropriate. I couldn't throw myself into the mix." He places my hand on his chest and traces my warrior mark. "You would have run a mile. So I thought if I could be your guardian, I could officially protect you, and you could get to know me and trust me. Then we could build from that. I wanted to give you what you needed at the time, and it certainly wasn't a foolish dragon."

I lean forward and kiss his chest. "You're not a foolish dragon. You might be old, ancient even. I love you for you anyway. It is more about your soul than the body that houses it, and my soul is ancient too."

Aragon moves quickly, and he flips me over onto my back. I let out a shriek of surprise. He rests his forearms on either side of my head, holding his weight above me.

"Who are you calling 'ancient'?" Aragon leans down and runs his nose across my jaw, blowing his breath gently across my skin, making me all goosey. I wiggle away, and he follows me, blowing gently into my ear. I half-giggle and half-groan.

"Now stop worrying, I have spent over four years without you. I am never letting you go." Aragon kisses my nose. I beam a smile at him; he groans deep in the back of his throat. His chest rumbles above me, vibrating in almost a purr. "Would you like to practice this morning?" Aragon, coos at me. I giggle, and then I smack my lips to his in answer.

* * *

"I have to go and handle a few things; I might not be back until tomorrow morning. Please try to keep out of trouble until I get back." Aragon gently kisses my swollen lips.

Lucifer grumbles at him. My dog isn't impressed with the new man in my life. He has been grumpy all day and will not do anything that he's told.

"No problem."

"I'll come back with a car." I laugh, imagining Aragon with his knees to his chin as he squishes himself into my tiny blue Citroen. Honestly, the car isn't that small, Aragon is just that big.

He goes to pull off his top...oh my God!

I realise he's going to shift and I am getting a show. The t-shirt slowly rises and an eight-pack appears...I know conventional shifters do this all the time. But as I have already established, I am not normal, and I have never seen a man undress.

"Fuck, seriously. It's like you're photoshopped." Bow-chicka-wow-wow dodgy music plays in my head as I ogle his beautiful body. He is seriously cut; the man is that perfect, he doesn't look real. I refrain from the urge to give him a poke. Aragon hooks his thumbs into the waistband of the jogging bottoms, and he slowly reveals his lower half. I almost swallow my tongue. I gulp, I blink, and I stare at his toes.

He has excellent feet.

Okay, okay! I don't get a good look at his penis.

I'm purposefully avoiding it; penises freak me out. I have never seen a live one before, in the flesh. And Aragon's penis? Gulp. It doesn't take a genius to understand that his monster penis will be proportional to the rest of him...oh my fucking God I'm freaking the fuck out!

I think I need a paper bag.

"Coward," Aragon says with a deep throaty chuckle as he prowls past me. I get a lovely view of his bottom.

His bottom is total perfection; I follow him, trying to keep my tongue in my mouth. I have a massive urge to run at him and bite his bum.

When we're outside, Aragon gently grips my chin between his thumb and forefinger and gives me a sweet kiss with his squidgy lips.

"I love you; I will not be long." He then vaults over my fence, into the field in which he crash-landed just last night, and he shifts.

His dragon is incredible.

He must be the most exquisite creature I have ever seen. Just like Aragon in his human form, Aragon's dragon is silver. He is way bigger than our house; he's breathtaking.

Aragon's elegant head is long and flat with a rounded nose, and several impressive sharp silver teeth poke out from the side of his mouth. I can see my faint reflection in each and every one of them. He has four horns, two at the front of his head and two at the rear facing backwards. A lean neck runs down into a solid muscular body covered in silver scales that catch the light and reflect it. It's the perfect camouflage; you would never see him in the sky unless you knew where to look. The skin underneath him is slightly darker. He has four strong limbs that allow him to stand, sturdy and intimidating. Each leg has five digits, each of which ends in a pointy, curved silver claw.

Aragon's giant wings start from his shoulders, and he is holding them behind him and slightly away. The wings are bat like. The membrane of the skin is thick, and I can see the flexible bone structure through the wing. At the top of the curve of each wing is a curved silver claw. His tail, from what I can see, is substantial, muscular, and covered in the same silver scales, and it's tipped with what looks like a silver blade.

Aragon watches me as I take him in, and I realise with delight that he has been posing his various body parts for my inspection. I can feel the slight tremor of the ground when he moves. I find that I am leaning entirely over the fence. I hold my hand out, palm up, wanting to stroke him. His big head ducks and he slowly—being mindful of the fence—lets me run my hand across his nose. Wow, his head is the size of my car.

Aragon's scales are soft, like silk to my touch; for some reason, I imagined he would feel hard like he was armoured, or like metal.

"You are so beautiful," I whisper, the awe evident in my tone. He puffs out a breath that blows my hair back. I can't help but giggle. I lean forward and kiss his soft nose.

"Fly safe, Aragon, and I will see you soon. Drive carefully on the road coming back as well; the roads will be icy. Oh, and message me when you get home, so I know you're safe." Aragon huffs out another breath, and I think if he could, he would roll his eyes. But instead, he backs away and gives me a nod.

Aragon moves to a safe distance and then goes from standing to launching himself into the air with such agility, it's as if he weighs nothing. The way he moves is with such grace. I watch him go until I can't see him anymore.

I shake my head; it's inconceivable that I am telling another person that I love him and asking him to be safe. It sounds silly out loud, saying "please be careful" to a humungous dragon. But Aragon is mine.

He loves me; no one has chosen to love me before. I have decided that there's no going back for me.

These scary feelings I have...I am going to embrace the shit out of them.

The wind picks up, and I grumble as I totter my freezing self back into the house. Aragon's naked bottom has made me neglect to put on a coat.

CHAPTER FORTY-TWO

"Forrest, wake up." I feel the whisper of my mum's lips on my cheek. I groan. My eyes are heavy-lidded with sleep.

"Mum, what's happening," I rasp.

Awareness creeps through me. I'm alone in my room, it's the middle of the night, and my phone is ringing.

Wow, that was freaky.

Another moment in time comes back to me, when my mum did a similar wake-up in the middle of the night. That moment changed my life forever. I lost my pack and my childhood as a result.

I roll onto my side and slap the bedside table in search of the handset. After a few seconds of fumbling, my fingertips knock the phone, and I grasp the bloody thing. I wince at the bright screen—the mobile is doing its best to sear my eyeballs. I close one eye and squint with the other. The blurry name comes slowly into focus. *Huh, Ava.* Something must be wrong if she's calling so late. I rub my eyes and answer.

"Hi Ava," I say curiously, trying not to yawn.

"Hi, Forrest. Are you okay to talk?"

"Yes, what do you need?"

"I didn't want to ring you, but unfortunately I've not got a choice. The case with this serial killer and the girls...it got picked up by international news. Unfortunately, it will be all over the UK media by the morning. They've named you, Forrest, and now the shifters know that you're alive." Ava sighs down the phone. I groan. My heart misses a beat, and my tummy cramps with worry. *Oh, for fuck's sake.* "I'm so sorry to be the bearer of bad news. Daniel knows that you're alive and he's on the warpath." Ahh, shit. Now I feel fully awake. My nerves are buzzing, and the excess adrenalin sloshes through my system, making me tremble. Any second now, I'm going to freak out and drop the phone, so I switch the handset to loudspeaker. Okay, this doesn't sound good.

What is it about me and my talent to tempt fate? Fate, the fickle bitch, is getting involved again big-time. I know I said I wanted to deal with Daniel when I was in that bloody basement, but come on, I wanted it for once to be on my terms, not his. That fucking wanker is never going to leave me alone.

"Forrest, Daniel's financials have lit up like crazy." Ava continues, "Over the last twenty-four hours, he has been hiring mercenaries, and paying good money, too. I wanted to let you know that Daniel is coming, and he's going to find you, Forrest. He's going to find you fast."

"Ava, how long do I have?"

"Hours…if you're lucky. The information currently shows that Daniel has at least thirty guys. Of those men, at least a dozen are well-trained mercenary shifters; the rest are paid thugs. I will send you everything I have on them and keep you updated. I can track them anywhere there's tech."

Hours. I cringe.

"Thank you so much, Ava," I say. "I am sorry I did a shit job of keeping my head down."

"I'm sorry that I am not giving you enough time to prepare. It's been four years, and I have so many people to monitor and protect—"

"No, please don't. Ava, I royally fucked up—this whole damn mess is my fault. I should have kept my head down better." I rub my face in frustration. "I didn't think that my name would go international with the media. Hindsight is a great thing. I feel like such a fool...I told the girls my name like an idiot, a proper idiot.

"Would you please keep me updated?" I ask, my voice a rasp.

"No problem. Good luck. Let me know if you need anything."

"Thank you. Bye." I sit on the edge of the bed and put my head between my knees. After a few minutes, I dial Aragon.

"Nutty, are you all right?" His deep chocolatey voice rumbles.

"Ava called. Aragon, I've fucked up…" I explain what has happened.

"You have alerts around the house and a strong ward in place. We will know if anyone comes within miles of you. I won't let him touch you." He growls.

"Aragon, I am so sorry." My voice breaks. "I have been selfish. I should have dealt with Daniel when I had the chance, but I chose to run away from my problem. I should have stayed and fought him. I should have spoken to you. I should have done so many different things. I'm a bloody coward, and I feel so ashamed." My eyes fill with tears.

"Hey, you are not a coward. Everything happens for a reason, Forrest. The journey you have been on, becoming a warrior? That's important. You have saved so many lives, and you have grown. You did what you needed to do at the time, and remember, I chose to help you leave. It was the best thing to do for you at that time, the safest thing. The only person that's responsible for this mess is Daniel. You cannot control everything or plan for every outcome. What's done is done. If you need somebody to blame? Blame me; I left Daniel alive. When Madán broke your bond, I should have hunted him down. At the time I wanted vengeance, and killing him wasn't enough for me—I wanted to make him suffer. You think with age you gain more wisdom. That is true...but even ancient dragons get it wrong. None of us is infallible. We all make mistakes, and now, Nutty, we're going to fix this mistake together. I'm on my way."

That scary part inside of me chuckles—it's glad that piece-of-shit Daniel is coming for me. I am not the same scared girl I was when we had last met. I am now a different creature, and my magic is stronger. I am a fucking warrior, and this time I have my dragon at my back.

Urm...or not. As soon as those thoughts clear my head, my warrior mark tingles, indicating I have unwelcome company. Whoever it is has just passed my warning ward. For fuck's sake!

I dress quickly, putting on various layers consisting of my thermals and my dark combat clothing. The snow has gone—it doesn't last long in Sligo, and according to the weather reports, the temperature is going to be milder for the next few days. I plan on hunting these fuckers, and I need to be comfortable while doing so. I pull my hair into a tight plait and secure the end by threading it through the base of the plait and securing it with grips so it can't be grabbed.

I methodically go through my kit, putting different spells in different areas of my combat gear. I attach various blades in their holders, and my black Wakizashi Japanese short sword I secure on my left hip. My disassembled bow and a dozen potion-tipped arrows I carry in a padded bag on my back. My scent masker is on my ankle. Unfortunately, my fire magic isn't sneaky enough, so traditional weapons and potions are my go-to alternatives. Hopefully I won't need to use them, as I have enough sleeping spells to knock out half of my local town.

As I leave, I send a quick text to Madán out of courtesy. I leave the phone that will not shift with me behind. Daniel has that much front and so much false confidence in his abilities; it beggars belief that he thinks he can bring a bunch of mercenaries into Ireland with no reprisals, no repercussions, ignoring a thousand-year-old treaty that bans shifters from coming into the country—unless you are a dragon given lifetime amnesty or a member of a Fae court. He can't pop into Ireland and kidnap a serving Fae warrior. Madán will be furious.

Daniel's strange obsession with me, his creepy instalove, has never made much sense. He must be coming for revenge—that's the only logical explanation I can think of.

I step outside into the winter night. The cold wind whips my hair and bites at my face. I pull my balaclava over my head. Lucifer snuffles underneath the door, not liking that I've left him locked in the house. "I'm sorry, Luca. Be a good boy. I will be back soon."

I have a plan that isn't motivated by the need to run. An offensive plan. I silently turn; let's see what these idiots are up to.

I shift into my wolf, and as I do, I pull on the power of my warrior mark. When my paws land onto the stone driveway, I'm wisps of shadow. I have to fight the urge to lift my head and howl.

In this shadow form, I can cover the distance required in a fraction of time. I follow the sound of intruders. My proximity to danger sharpens my senses, and the closer I get, the more often I pause. Listening. I'm the hunter, they're the prey. About four kilometres from the cottage, I find six vehicles and a group of twenty-eight men.

I settle against a hedge to watch. Angry. My eyes flick to each man, calculating and assessing. A few of the men, a dozen or so, move like they're trained. Professionally they check their gear and murmur to each other. The rest are messing about, laughing and joking.

Daniel is nowhere to be seen.

A bald guy steps up and claps his hands to gain everyone's attention.

"Fall in on me," he yells. Oh hello, look who it is: Meathead One, with his shiny bald head, sans goatee. I growl in my mind. "You nine with me—we go right. You nine take the left, and you nine take the rear. We're here as a support team. Back-up only. The boss is taking the front at dawn. Rules of engagement—this is capture, not kill. That doesn't mean it has to be a clean capture."

"We fuck her up then, yeah?" says a grinning fool. Meathead One smirks at the guy.

"Keep out of sight. If she rabbits, restrain her. Do not let this bitch escape. This will be easy money. Observe radio silence. Any questions?" A few shake their heads. "Don't fuck up. Let's go."

Meathead's group has all the best mercenaries. I want to smack my forehead in disgust as they move off with deadly grace, disappearing into the night. What is he thinking, putting all the best-trained guys in his group—why not use them to direct the other teams? I watch the others bumble about as they shrug, point, and argue with each other. One of them drags his gear behind him on the floor.

I might as well take out Meathead's group of ten first. I know with slight trepidation that I'll have to shift back to use my sleep potions.

I move ahead and find a place to wait.

Opportunity comes when they fan out away from each other. Dropping into mostly prone positions, they settle, chests to the ground, eyes on my dark cottage. With no one watching their backs, it's apparent that they aren't expecting company. I grin and shift back. With a handful of sleeping potion balls, I set to work.

CHAPTER FORTY-THREE

I never thought I'd be at home, hunting bad guys in my woods. I feel a little like John Rambo; this is kind of surreal.

I'm in the forest that sits at the bottom of our house. Tall pine trees surround me, and I am currently hiding up in an old sycamore tree nestled within the pines. With the snow and the heavy rain, the ground is saturated. The pines were initially planted on bogland, and no matter how you enter the woods, there's only one clear access trail through. The way of going naturally herds people underneath the tree that I'm currently hiding in. If they don't come through this way, someone will have to fish them out of the deadly bog later.

I wait for the chance to pick off my last quota of the bad guys.

Nineteen guys are already tucked away in bushes and dykes, sleeping. I haven't even broken a sweat. I'm after the last group of nine that have planned to reach the house from the woods, then come up through the field to gain access to the back of the cottage. Unfortunately for them, that isn't going to happen.

Once this is completed, I can check on Aragon and Madán while waiting for Daniel to arrive. With their strict radio-silence, Daniel will never suspect his backup is snoozing.

There's movement. The group has split further, and it looks like they're now in groups of three. The three guys heading my way are not stealthy. I'm a little embarrassed on their behalf. These men are supposed to be shifters, yet here they are, crashing through the forest. They are not ninjas.

Noisy creatures.

Now if there's a smart person in the group of nine, I'd presume that they had sent the three noisy ones out as bait and then follow stealthily to sniff out any traps. I doubt it, but I'm not going to give away my position by being silly.

I wait for them to move on, and when they're almost out of my line of sight, I use my bow. The arrows strike each guy quietly in quick succession. The arrows land cleanly, and I aim for their legs in case they're wearing any body armour. Thanks to countless hours of practice, I am a good shot, even in the darkness of the woods. I smirk as two of the guys get an arrow to the bottom. All three of them go down quickly, within seconds, the sleeping potion doing its job and working immediately.

I appear from behind the pines like a ghost and grab hold of two of the guys' legs and pull both of them into the undergrowth, followed swiftly by the third. Within seconds all three men have entirely disappeared. I am feeling a little smug.

I swing back into my tree and quietly wait for the next guys. It doesn't take long until another three thugs trample past. These shifters are quieter, but not by much. I shoot them quickly. Unfortunately, one of them lets out a small cry before he goes unconscious.

For fuck's sake. I sit and wait for sixty seconds to make sure that I won't have any further company. I need to move the bodies; everything seems clear. I drop lightly onto my feet. I listen, and I hear nothing. I make my way to the three sleeping thugs and drag them into the trees.

Luckily there's a handy trench behind a row of pines. It's wet, but still a perfect area for storing the bodies out of sight. I snort as I see my growing bad-guy pile. I arrange my guys carefully—I don't want them to drown—and just as I am about to make my way back to my tree, there's a slight movement to my right. I freeze. I bring my prepared bow up in preparation to loose an arrow.

There's a sound behind me, and before I can check it out, I'm grabbed from behind. The guy pulls me into his body. His hand goes up between my breasts and wraps around my throat, pinning me to his chest. His other hand pulls the balaclava from my head, pulling out some of my hair in the process.

I keep my hands slightly out by my sides. I am still holding my bow. My other hand surreptitiously reaches for a blade strapped to my thigh; I cup the small knife in my palm.

The movement that I spotted? A decoy. I feel stupid that I fell for it, but what's done is done. The guy behind me stinks. I wrinkle my nose; I think he's a hyena shifter. He squeezes my throat and runs his other hand down my body. He spends way too much time on my boobs; he has neglected to notice the weapons in my hands. I barely refrain from rolling my eyes.

"What have we got here, lads—look at this tasty morsel. I'm up for a bit—she's fucking tiny." He breathes me in. "Can't smell your fear—fucking magic." His breath smells of beer, garlic, and lust. He whispers in my ear the filthy things he wants to do to me and grinds himself against my back.

"Do you mind? I can feel the tip," I say with poorly veiled disgust. I breathe through my nose and out through my mouth. I force myself to remain calm and relaxed in his grip; I'm going to kill this rapist fucker.

He is going to die horribly.

He hasn't worked it out yet.

I'm no one's prey.

Surprisingly one of the guys looks incredibly uncomfortable. He is younger than the other two, and he glances about with fright, his scent distressed. The other guy is smirking, nodding and rubbing his hands together as if he's a kid on Christmas morning, about to open a present.

Nodding Smirking Guy glares at the younger guy when he starts to beg, "Barry, mate, come on, let the girl go—that kind of shit isn't right. We're here to do a job, not hurt girls. I won't let you do it—just let her go." The young guy steps forward as if to intervene.

"You're just going to have to watch then, aren't you, lad. Not my fault you're gay and you don't want to get your dick wet." The hyena shifter undoes the button of my combats, his focus entirely on unzipping my pants. His lack of focus means I can now react.

I bury my knife in his inner thigh. I pull out the blade, twist around on my toes, and put the blade through the side of his neck. It effectively keeps him quiet. I step to the side to make sure none of his blood spray gets onto my clothing.

The rapist bastard gurgles, and I smile as he falls to the floor. This is all done in a matter of seconds. I re-button my combats.

"Stay," I say as I step towards the smirking guy. I keep the young guy in my peripheral vision. He gives me a nod and then opens his arms wide, puts them behind his head, and kneels. Without overthinking and without breaking my stride, I loose an arrow into his chest. I drop the bow on the floor as the young guy falls unconscious.

My total focus is now on the smirking guy. My wakizashi short sword comes out of the *saya* with a hiss. Smirking Guy pulls his shocked eyes from the other two men on the floor and meets my cold gaze. His breath catches and he shudders and vomits. He holds up his shaking hands in a placating gesture.

"I wasn't gonna do anything, lass," he pleads. I have zero sympathy; if given a chance, he was going to rape me.

I prowl towards him. I grip the sword in my right hand and keep it pointed in the shifter's direction. At the last moment, I jump to the side but forward, dealing a swinging cut that makes the air sing. I step and half-turn, the blade drawing a fan of black blood droplets in its wake. The shifter's head topples to the floor.

I turn back to the rapist hyena shifter. I tilt my head to the side as I listen to him gurgle. Black blood seeps through his lips. "Are you not going to scream for me, Barry?" I say, kicking him in the ribs so he is flat on his back. "What a pity. Oh, look at that—least you managed to get your dick *wet*," I whisper, pointing out unnecessarily that he has pissed himself. I grind my boot between his legs. "Guess what, Barry lad, you smell of piss, blood, and fear." His eyes are wide and rolling. "I was going to cut your cock off and feed it to you. But you're not going to live long enough, I'm afraid, which is a real shame." I draw my short sword over my shoulder and bring it down, severing his head. I kick the head into the hole where the other bad guys are sleeping.

I stand in the darkness of the wood, forcing myself to take a few slow, deep breaths. My white breath fills the air, announcing my presence and frantic state. My body is singing with the need for more violence. My mind is more than on board with that. I'm twice as deadly when my back is against the wall.

If I've learned one thing, I do not want to be the judge and executioner of others—that path only leads to bad decisions and self-destruction. But today with these two guys I'm willing to make an exception. I will take the hit on my soul, knowing that other women are safer.

I clear up the two dead bodies and put the unconscious young guy in the hole with the others. I'm still feeling a tad homicidal.

Aragon appears in front of me silently. A muscle twitches in his jaw as he stares at me intently; for once, he's unable to conceal his rage. Even in the darkness of the pines with almost zero light, he spots the redness on my neck. His nostrils flare as he also scents the hyena shifter and blood.

"Are you hurt?" I shake my head no. Aragon growls and pulls me towards him. I squeak as he lifts me into his arms. I instinctively wrap my legs around him as he looks deep into my eyes as if trying to read the truth on my very soul. Aragon grunts, then smashes his lips on mine. *Oh my.* The kiss is rough, passionate, full of anger, fear, and relief.

"What happened?" he asks when he finally pulls away and swipes a gentle finger across my throat. My lips are tingling, and I feel a little dizzy from his kiss. He allows me to drop back to my feet. I wobble a little.

I nibble on my lip and shrug my shoulders. Now isn't the time. Aragon puffs out a frustrated breath. "How many?" His voice is dark and dangerous.

"Back-up guys, twenty-eight. Twenty-six I took out with sleeping potions. Two fatalities." My eyes flick to the hole, and he strides over and takes a look at the dead bodies. "Daniel is supposedly on his way."

He growls and prowls back towards me. Leaning close, he cradles my face in his big hands. "I am sorry I left you. I am sorry you had to do that. Where is your warrior team?" he says, rubbing his thumbs across my cheekbones. I look down, and he growls again.

"I texted Madán."

"Madán is an old Fae. He doesn't do text messages." I was aware of that, that's why I did it. I shrug.

"I dealt with them. I'm not sorry that I didn't get others involved. It was nothing I couldn't handle." He kisses my forehead, and I take hold of one of his hands and squeeze it.

"Daniel is twenty minutes out," he says quietly. "I flew over the cars." I nod; we'd better get moving. I planned to meet him at the house. I want Daniel to think he has surprised me and taken me unaware. Aragon pulls me towards him. "I can get us back faster." He then shocks the shit out of me and does a partial shift. Beautiful silver dragon wings appear on his back.

I gape at him. "When did you... how... I don't..." Aragon kisses my forehead again and lifts me back into his arms. I wrap my legs around him again. He folds his arms around me, one arm underneath my bottom to support my weight and the other in my hair, holding my head against his shoulder. I put my arms around his neck.

Aragon prowls away from the trees, and as soon as he clears the canopy, we're flying. He takes off with elegance.

I bury my head in his chest and close my eyes tightly. I dare not move in case I throw him off balance and we end up crashing. Which is daft, as in Aragon's arms I am in the safest place I'll ever be. Within minutes we're back at the house. We land safely.

Once inside, I stumble when I catch sight of Owen, who is sitting on my sofa. Lucifer is sitting on the floor beside him with a big doggy grin. Owen is running his big hands through his fur. My dog, who doesn't like anyone, seems to love Owen.

"Owen…" I whisper in a shaky voice, "how did you get here? What are you doing here?" Owen stands and smiles at me. I throw myself at him. Aragon grunts.

"Your dog is amazing. I got a lift." Owen nods towards a scowling Aragon. *He got a lift…but Aragon flew in as a dragon…oh, wow.* "Oh, you know. Seeing as you aren't publicly dead anymore, I thought I might come and lend a hand. Chop-chop—Daniel will be here soon. Before I forget, first dibs on Daniel." Owen waves his hand in the air as if he has asked for the front seat. "I've wanted to beat the shit out of him for years."

I huff out a laugh and give his solid middle an extra squeeze. "Fine by me; I don't want to touch him. Go for it, Nanny Hound. I better get ready." I reluctantly let go of Owen, and I'm halfway across the room when he booms, "Oy, you've been boasting about your cooking, so you can feed me later as a thank-you."

I turn back and catch Aragon vigorously shaking his head, his silver eyes wide. I frown. What's up with him? "Or we can go out for a full Irish breakfast…" Owen's voice trails off as he smirks knowingly at Aragon.

"That sounds like a splendid idea," Aragon replies as he gently nudges me towards the bedroom.

I remove my clothes and weapons, shift to remove all traces of forest, the scent of the hyena shifter, and blood. I quickly change into my regular leggings and a jumper.

After we go over the plan, I use my warrior mark to make the ward impenetrable to anyone except us. Aragon and Owen disappear outside into the garden after using a few potions, including one to link our minds.

I make myself a cup of tea while I'm waiting. I've just removed the teabag when I hear the cars pull up outside the house and the *clunk clunk clunk* of the car doors as they open and slam close.

Finally, the wolf is at the door. There's no running away this time. I take a shaky breath in. Well, here we go. It's showtime.

CHAPTER FORTY-FOUR

"Forrest, come out, come out, wherever you are. Forrest, come out to play, your mate is here for you," Daniel shouts. I roll my eyes. What a dickhead.

Aragon growls in my head, not impressed at all with Daniel's mate comment. I take my time and slip on my combat boots. I grab my big warm coat, stuffed full of sleep potions. I open the door, take a deep breath, and make my way to the front of the house.

I crunch across the stone driveway and appraise my unwelcome visitors, who stand on the other side of the garden wall. I stand with my back to the house, holding my tea in both hands. The sun has risen. I look up at the sky with a relaxed smile, pleased to see that it isn't raining. The weatherman did promise it would be mild.

"Ah, there she is. Hello, little wolf. Nice to see that you're not dead. Are you surprised to see me?" Daniel smiles, showing his teeth, and a familiar greedy hunger fills his gaze as he looks me up and down. He is wearing his custom black suit and a crisp white shirt. The men scattered on the lane around him are wearing black fatigues. Daniel slowly claps his hands. "I do have to say, bravo on your fake suicide; it was extremely realistic. You had me fooled. Was it your dead mummy's suicide that gave you the idea? I know you failed to kill yourself the first time around." Daniel smiles brightly; he makes a show of miming putting something in his mouth and then dropping it. I lock the rage I feel inside. I don't respond; it takes everything I have to look back at him blankly. He frowns at my lack of response and then chuckles. "I've come to bring you back to England, where you belong. Have you forgotten that you're mine? Now come quietly, or these gentlemen will make you." Daniel waves his arm around, indicating his men.

Within the group of ten men stand Jason and a struggling Harry. It looks like Daniel has been very busy collecting my stepbrothers—God, we just need John now for the full set. I'm glad to see that my hellhound brother isn't among them.

I pull my attention back to Daniel and make eye contact. I tilt my head slightly to the side as I study his face. I can't help the smug smile that I give him. I'm amused to see a flash of anger as I continue to stare at him—his ruined face. Daniel is missing his left eye. Thick white scars crisscross the whole left side of his face in a mass of scar tissue. By stark contrast, the right side of his face is still perfectly handsome. I take a sip of tea, showing him I'm completely unaffected and unconcerned by his presence.

If it was anyone other than Daniel, I'd never in a million years say what I am about to: "Daniel, have you got something on your face? It's just there?" I point out helpfully, making a circular motion with my finger and pointing at the left side of my face.

As predicted, Daniel goes nuts. He roars, runs at me, and bounces off my bad-guy impenetrable and invisible ward. It's my turn to chuckle. I shake my head. "Oops, are you okay? That must have hurt. I hope you guys are getting a lot of money to work with this idiot, " I say condescendingly to the men at his back.

"I want that ward down now, get that fucking ward down now!" Daniel screams. "You think it's going to stop me? You stupid bitch. You won't be laughing or making smart comments when I've got hold of you. I've got such plans. Your life is going to be a living hell." Daniel slams his palm against the ward. Aah, now there he is, the real Daniel.

I catch movement out of the corner of my eye. The passenger door of the leading vehicle opens. A foot encased in a blue high heel and the hem of a blue dress appears. I am stunned to see who steps out of the car.

Like the proverbial bad penny: Liz Richardson.

I huff and my eyes go wide: a heavily pregnant Liz. Wow, Harry has been busy.

Wearing a tight blue dress that emphasises her tummy, Liz waddles towards Daniel and takes hold of his elbow and tugs at it. "I don't know what we're doing here. We should be at home with our two boys. I can't believe that I've been forced to follow you. Just kill her so we can go home, darling, I just want to go home," Liz whines. I scan them both, and I raise my eyebrows.

I take another sip of tea to hide my confusion. I puff out my cheeks. Wow, Harry hasn't been busy at all. I blink at the pair of them. I guess Harry has had a lucky escape? My perusal of Liz makes me shudder—that could have easily been my alternative fate. I can't help worrying. I hope that their relationship is consensual—if Liz chose Daniel, that is karma at its finest. She must be an absolute pain in his ass. But Liz ending up with a monster like Daniel? I really couldn't have predicted this outcome: with all her manipulations, she ended up with a bigger monster than herself.

"Wow, Liz, you —"

"I'm not fat; I'm pregnant, you stupid cow. Why hasn't somebody killed her already!" Liz snarls.

"Wow, okay. I was going to say, 'scraped the bottom of the barrel' in regard to being with Daniel, not that..." My voice drifts away as I pull a face and indicate her tummy with a floppy hand.

"Why didn't you stay dead? Daniel, mate, kill the bitch so we can go home," Liz whines. Daniel attempts to pull his arm from Liz's grasp, but she hangs on. Her nails dig into his suit-clad arm.

"I'm a little confused. Didn't you say that I'm still your mate?" I point at my chest, widening my eyes. "I didn't know that you could have two mates at the same time…that is a little greedy, Daniel. Hey, I don't mind stepping aside," I say with a wave and smile. A few of the shifters shuffle. I bet they don't like Daniel claiming two females either.

"Dog, what are you talking about? I am his mate he's just coming here for justice. Who would want to be your mate?" Liz sneers, looking me up and down with disgust, as if I am covered head-to-toe in dog poop.

Daniel shakes Liz off his arm and shoves her none-too-gently back towards the vehicle. She stumbles. "Get back in the car. This has nothing to do with you. We're not mates; there's no bond between us, you stupid cow. I've come here for my real mate, my true mate. Who was made for me! She is going to give me daughters. Three children, three useless boys...you are incompetent. Get in the car." My mouth pops open in shock. I can't believe he just came out with it like that. The mother of his children, and calling his kids useless.

What. A. Dick.

Liz turns her attention back to me and screeches her rage. "This is all your fault." I can't help rolling my eyes. She thrusts her arm out, and a sharp nail points at me. "We wouldn't be here if it weren't for you. We're happy. Why do you always want to take what's mine?"

"I don't want Daniel. Please keep him." I shrug—my bad. I can understand where she is coming from, I guess, but that has never been my intention. I only tried to stop her from hurting Harry. I never set out to hurt Liz. Even after she kicked me and continually encouraged others to kill me and she stabbed me with fucking silver. Yet I'm the problem? She's such a psycho.

"Don't blame my true mate. It was never about you—you approached me, remember? Do yourself a favour and shut the fuck up," Daniel snarls. "Once that kid drops, I'm selling you to a hyena shifter. He knows just how to deal with women like you. He will have you trained. I might have your tongue cut out. It would be so much better if you couldn't speak. I quite like that in my women." Daniel grabs Liz roughly by her shoulders and shakes her. I watch him with growing horror. The men around him don't bat an eye.

"Hey, dickhead let her go!" I shout. Out of the corner of my eye, I can see Harry going nuts. Usually I wouldn't be bothered, but if she is that pregnant that she waddles, Liz must be almost ready to pop.

"You were always only going to be the second choice—hell, you'll always be the last choice. I wouldn't have touched you if I wasn't grieving. I always planned to sell you. I'm not crazy enough to want you around forever. Put her in the car."

Liz screams. She tries to scratch Daniel's remaining eye with her nails. He grabs hold of her wrists to stop her. Two of Daniel's men rush forward and force a growling, spitting Liz back into the front of the vehicle. One man stands guard against the car door.

I wonder if that's the same dead hyena shifter, Barry, that lost his head in the woods? If it isn't, I will be hunting him down.

"Now the ward. I wanted that ward removed ten minutes ago!"

A guy moves into Daniel's view; he shifts from foot-to-foot anxiously. "Sir, the, urm…the ward is Fae magic, sir, I won't be able to remove it," he says, wringing his hands, his body visibly shaking.

"You're all useless," Daniel mutters. "Well, Forrest, I'm glad I brought your beloved brother with me. Liz told me about how much you care for and love dear Harry. I wanted to give you a pack reunion." Daniel waves his hand to indicate my old pack. Jason steps forward, pushing Harry. At least that explains the mystery of why Harry's here. *Nice one, Liz.*

I turn my full attention to my two stepbrothers. Jason looks at me with pure hatred. It's rare for the puppet to show emotion. I give him a small wave. *Yeah, that makes two of us, buddy—you're a dead man walking, and you don't even know it.* I frown at Harry. He is bleeding, bruised, and his left arm hangs at his side, broken. I can't do anything for him yet, but I will.

"So you have a choice, little wolf. Come out from behind your ward and come with me, or I'm going to kill

Harry here." Daniel grabs hold of Harry by his hair, and one of his men hands him a silver blade.

"Hey, little sister." I want to roll my eyes at the term, but now isn't the time. "Don't you be going anywhere with these bastards—stay where you are. Better yet, go into the house, lock the door, and call for help—" Daniel wallops Harry in the face with the handle of the knife, cutting off his words. Harry groans. I cringe.

Jason continues to stare at me with dead eyes full of hatred, not sparing one glance at his younger brother. "You always were a selfish bitch. Nothing is going to happen to Harry unless you don't leave with Daniel," Jason says in a high, nasal voice. The normally stoic shifter is usually not one for talking—no wonder; his voice is worse than mine. "Do as you're told for once in your life—save Harry. Sacrifice yourself. God, it won't cost you anything apart from opening your legs, and that's all you are good for anyway." I think this is the most words the quiet, creepy shifter has ever said; it's like Vincent is speaking through him. I can't help my shiver. "I've seen you on the news playing the warrior—the Fae token shifter. You're no hero. You're a coward. Still the same feral dirty wolf that we had to lock up in a cage for years."

I ignore Jason's rant. I yawn; I couldn't care less what he thinks. Why everybody thinks that I'm responsible for everyone else's actions is beyond me. Yet it's always my fault.

I'm done giving a shit.

"What did you mean when you said I was made for you?" I ask Daniel instead.

Daniel smiles. The softness that floods his blue eye is disconcerting. He enjoys my attention. "Little wolf, you were made for me, my true mate. Everything was designed by magic to be perfect." Daniel waves his silver knife in the air. "For me. For my needs. You are my fated mate.

"I wanted the best. Faster, stronger, smarter, and look at you…forged in fire. Made of steel." Daniel pushes Harry's face against the ward and traces my outline along its surface with the tip of the blade. A strange, manic smile plasters his face; the creepy smile is slightly lopsided due to the scars on his face. "Little wolf, haven't you worked it out yet? I paid that demon to take you when you were a child."

CHAPTER FORTY-FIVE

I wobble on my feet. I feel a little shell-shocked as I stare at Daniel's now-delighted, smug smile.

Daniel put my pack on that demon's radar. He caused the events of that day to unfold; it was him.

Bloody hell.

Shit, I can't believe I hadn't put it all together.

I rub my temple, and a hazy memory comes back to me: the demon in the car saying something about a council member buying me. What was it? I take a mental peek inside that box:

"Unfortunately I am the middleman for this transaction—you have been sold to a council member for an extortionate

price. When you're more mature, once your body changes, you will drive him wild. Now that I have seen you…well, I have such a desire to keep you for myself." The demon bops me on the nose. I blink at him. "I would have thoroughly enjoyed parading you in front of all the shifters. So exciting that a council member has bought you. Who knows your fate? I have a feeling you will be in my care for some time. Then your owner will come in on a proverbial white horse and rescue you—that's why all this is just so much fun." He taps his fingers on the seat between us.

"I made a bargain to collect you. Your owner said nothing about keeping our bargain a secret." The demon chuckles; he winks at me. "I might not be able to keep you, but I can sure mess things up a little bit. I do so hate happy ever-afters. So you will remember, young Forrest, that everything from now on is your owner's fault and nothing to do with me. Don't be taken in by his handsome face, that's a good girl."

Fucking hell.

Daniel starts to rant. "The demon took everything too far. He made a deal with your stepfather, greedy Dave, behind my back. His instructions were simple: to take you. One missing little shifter girl, I could have covered up. Not the death of a whole fucking pack. Your mother should have handed you over. I paid a hell of a lot of money to get hold of you. After a while, I realised if I wanted the job done correctly, I would have to do it myself." He stops talking and gives me that crazy, bright smile again.

"Oh, and the reason you were stuck in wolf form? Jason here kept slipping you rare, untraceable magic that stopped you from shifting back." Daniel chuckles and keeps on smiling, his silver blade tap-tapping on the ward. "I wanted you to gain access to your innate magic quicker. But to do that you had to suffer. You had to struggle. The more you struggled, the stronger your magic would eventually become. I also wanted you pliable and grateful." Daniel shakes his head, and his lips twitch into a snarl. "I was days away from rescuing you. I had everything in place. I had Jason reduce the dosage to almost nothing. Then, little wolf, you just had to go and try to help this idiot." Daniel smacks Harry's head on the ward. "You saved yourself. Thanks to that stupid bitch ruining my plans." He glances at Liz in the car with another snarl. "Little wolf, you will always be mine. I made you. I made you the only female hellhound in existence. Your fire magic, your ability to partial-shift? That is all down to me. I paid for you. Now I've come to collect." My eyes flick to Jason; his dead eyes don't show any emotion. But his lips curl up in a smug, satisfied smile. I take that as confirmation.

I blink back at Daniel.

What the hell? This is getting to be a little bit too much. I expected a hint of "muahaha," but not this!

Instead of rage or horror, the relief I feel is peculiar.

I knew I was different. Hell, stuck in my wolf form, I blamed myself. The partial shifts, my fire magic, the warrior markings. I was so worried, frightened about being a freak. But now it all makes a strange type of sense. For the first time, I know deep down that I'm going to be okay. It wasn't me, and I was never broken. It was Daniel all along.

It's all been the fault of the delusional wanker standing in front of me.

I give myself a little mental shake. I have to get back on track and wrap up Daniel's weird villain speech.

"Don't look so worried, little wolf, you're one-hundred-percent perfect. The magic inside you was left to build and is now giving you the most potent traits. You are unique. Our daughters will be incredible," Daniel continues smugly. "I'm days away from taking over the assembly—your time in Ireland is coming to an end anyway. So whether I take you today or next week, it's still going to happen." Daniel pokes his blade at Harry's neck. "The only difference is, Harry will be alive today, but he will be in the ground next week. Choose wisely, little wolf."

I tap my fingers on my cup as if I am thinking. Then I nod and say with a smile, "I think I'm going to choose option B." The chatter in my head lets me know we're a go on my signal.

"Option B...what the fuck are you going on about?" Daniel asks. He doesn't like my smile or my answer.

Aragon appears behind me. I hand him my cup and he kindly takes it out of my hand. "Thank you," I say with a small smile.

"What the fuck—" Daniel says.

"Now," I say out loud, and all hell breaks loose.

I hear the *thud thud thud* of falling bodies as the surrounding bad guys are taken out with my sleep potions. Three down, seven to go. At the same time, Owen, who is in wolf form, pops out of thin air and bites Daniel's calf.

God, I love magic.

Daniel drops his hold on Harry, and he tries to slash Owen with the knife that's still in his hand. Owen grabs hold of that arm and bites, effectively stopping his strike. Daniel shifts into a brown wolf. His clothing flutters to the floor, and they start fighting.

I call my flaming sword, and I leave the ward by vaulting over the gate.

I pull Harry to his feet and stand in front of him, then shuffle us both backwards. I back Harry up towards the wall and the safety of the ward. I twirl my sword, protecting us from anybody that's trying to get close.

"Forrest...where the hell did the fancy sword come from? You need to get to safety, Forrest..." Harry mumbles. Aragon unceremoniously grabs Harry by the back of the neck and plucks him over the wall.

"Get down on the ground," I shout. The anxious man who was supposed to deal with the ward drops to his knees and puts his hands behind his head, Six. I flick a potion at him.

"Where the fuck is our backup?" Jason screams, mashing his phone with his fingers.

"Are you talking about the twenty-eight guys who were

surrounding the house?" I answer helpfully. "Yeah, they are not coming." I shrug, twirling my sword. "I dealt with them ages ago. Not bad for the Faes' token shifter," I say snidely. "You've got no backup. Do yourself a favour and get on your fucking knees and put your hands behind your head." The remaining four shifters look at each other, then completely ignore me. They start pulling out weapons.

Hello, flaming sword here! I huff. Sometimes I wish I looked scarier. Aragon clears the wall and joins me—*oh hello, handsome*. He is partly shifted, with his wings, fifteen-inch silver claws, and an impressive set of chompers on full display.

"I am getting impatient!" Aragon warns with a low growl. Smoke escapes his mouth in an intimidating fashion. The four remaining shifters immediately drop to their knees and prostrate themselves in submission.

I growl and raise an eyebrow at my dragon. Aragon shrugs and gives me a wink.

I hit them all with potion balls. I keep a careful eye on Jason, who's still standing—if you can call leaning against one of the cars and shaking like a leaf "standing." His wide eyes are fixed on Aragon. Owen and Daniel are still fighting, but Owen looks like he has the upper hand and he's just playing with Daniel.

Jason, seeing an opportunity, charges at me with desperation, a silver knife clutched in his hand. Aragon steps in front of me. His claws pierce Jason's chest.

I peek around Aragon's bulk and watch as the light

CURSED WOLF

leaves Jason's eyes. "Rot in hell, you evil bastard." I can't help the smile of satisfaction. God, I'm getting to be a bad person. "I had him, Aragon," I whine. "I could have done that myself." Aragon shifts back to fully human and leans down and kisses me gently on my lips.

"Nutty, I didn't want you to have to kill your old pack," Aragon says earnestly.

Jason was never my pack. He was just the guard to my cell. Jason had it coming, and it was only a matter of time before I hunted him down. I wasn't going to leave him alive after what he did to me. He would have always been a threat.

The black wolf that is Owen is standing over a prone wolf-Daniel. He has his jaws wrapped around Daniel's throat. Daniel whimpers his surrender. Owen backs away and shifts. Daniel also shifts back into his naked human form. He stands, glaring at Owen. There's a click of a car door opening, and Liz steps out of the car. Tears are running down her face.

She holds something in her right hand, cradling it between her breasts. Daniel has his back to her. Liz moves the object, and with a war cry, thrusts it into Daniel's back.

I realise too late that it's a silver blade. Liz has done what she does best: she has stabbed her supposed mate in the back. Liz pulls out the knife. Daniel makes a choking sound, and he turns to face Liz, a look of incredulity on his face.

"You can't sell me if you're dead, you bastard. I could have mated anybody, anybody! Yet I chose you. You with your deformed face! You lost power, money! Yet I stood by you. You couldn't help yourself from going after that whore, and for what? The possibility of a daughter? You are an idiot!" She ends her rant with a scream. The knife that is still in her hand goes back into Daniel, into his chest. She impales him another three times, following him down as he falls to the ground. Daniel's blood splatters across her face and neck.

The words *poetic justice* come to mind as I stand with my lips parted as Liz goes all-out slasher. Liz is also a victim of Daniel's. No, not a victim—I shake my head at that thought—a *survivor*.

Owen and Mac wrestle with her, trying to get the knife from her hand without hurting her. I give Mac a wave. I didn't know he'd arrived.

Madán strolls up, late to the party. Casually looking around, he raises an eyebrow at the manic woman. He gives me a smile and Aragon a nod.

"Status report, any casualties?" Madán asks.

"No casualties on our side, sir," Owen replies, having won and gained control of the blood-covered Liz. "But three fatalities—" he glances at Daniel—"four fatalities, thirty-six captured, plus this lady." Owen points his thumb at Liz.

"Good job. I will get them collected and handed over to the Hunters Guild for processing," Madán says with a nod. "Oh, Forrest, I have had a transfer request—a shifter called Owen? He named you as a reference? I guess that will be you…" Madán says, lifting an eyebrow at Owen. I beam a smile at him and Owen. Nanny Hound!

"Oh my God, yes, he's my friend! You'd be nuts not to take him. Please say you will? I am so excit—" I squeak in fright. Aragon picks me up and moves me away from a bloody hand that is stretching out towards me. Fuck me, that is some creepy shit. Daniel has managed to pull himself across the floor towards us, towards me.

A trail of blood follows behind him on the floor.

"You will always be mine. I've owned you since you were a child. I am your destiny, I made you." Daniel holds out his hand, and on what must be his last breath, he says, "Little wolf…"

His hand drops.

We all gawk at the now-dead Daniel on the ground—although I am kind of waiting for that classic final horror moment where he jumps up and tries to kill me. I shiver. Aragon pulls me tighter to him.

I can hear Liz telling Owen and Mac, "I'm not a bad person. You do realise this is all due to pregnancy hormones. I had no idea what that man was up to. So that you know, I've got two young babies at home to look after—they need me. Plus one on the way. I am heavily pregnant, don't you know." I can't help feeling sorry for her and I'm worried about her kids. What's going to happen to her children?

"Why does that dog get away scot-free?" she whines. Honestly, she just can't help herself.

"'Dog'? If you are talking about Warrior Hesketh, the warrior is doing her job, protecting the innocent. Now shut up." Mac growls, "The Hunters Guild will want to speak to you."

Liz shrugs at the news. "I'm a pureblood shifter. The only place I will be going is to the next male. There's a new law that will protect me. 'Forrest's law'…" I can't help my rueful grin. The new law protects shifter women impartially, even if the woman is a horrible person. I have a feeling Liz is going to be okay. I watch as Liz is bundled into the back of a car. Mac slaps an anti-magic band onto her wrist.

I really hope I don't see her again.

Harry is crouching over Jason. Harry reaches down, and using two fingers, closes Jason's eyes. He stands and makes his way towards us. He holds his hand out to Aragon to shake, and after a pause, Harry drops his hand. Aragon grunts. I don't think Aragon likes Harry.

"May I?" Aragon narrows his eyes, then grudgingly nods. Harry pulls me into a hug. "Thank you for saving my life." I huff. Harry runs his hand through his blond hair. I glance up at Aragon, and he is glaring at Harry as if he is contemplating ripping his head off.

"Harry, Harry, I need you!" wails Liz from inside the car, tapping the window with her nails. Harry gives me a small smile and scurries away. *Bye then.*

I take a moment to think, and I feel…lighter. Vindicated. Many of the imaginary boxes in my mind have disintegrated, the memories losing the power to hurt me.

Aragon leans down and kisses me on the top of the head.

Everybody clears out. Owen goes inside to get changed. Madán gives us a nod. "Statement tomorrow, Warrior Hesketh. I will sort out the paperwork for your friend. The sleeping and dead bodies scattered around will be dealt with," he says as he leaves. Yay!

"Is it over?" I ask, leaning into Aragon's warmth.

"Yes, Nutty, it is over." He kisses my cheek.

"Can we go back to the glass house?" I like this little cottage, but I miss my first real home. I will also feel safer behind Aragon's ward. I miss our runs, plus Owen needs somewhere to live, and he'll love living in this cottage.

"Anything that you want, Nutty."

"Oh, can we get cake?"

"We will always get cake," Aragon answers.

THE END

Dear Reader,

First of all, I'd like to *thank you* for taking a chance on my book. My very first book! I hope you enjoyed it! If you did, and if you have time, I would be *very* grateful if you could write a review. Every review makes a *huge* difference to an author—especially me as a brand-new shiny one—and your review might help other readers discover my book. I would appreciate it so much, and it might help me keep writing.

Thanks a million!

Oh, and there is a chance that I might even choose your review to feature in my marketing campaign. Could you imagine? So exciting!

Love,

Brogan x

P.S. DON'T FORGET! Sign up on my VIP email list! You will get early access to all sorts of goodies, including signed copies, private giveaways, and advance notice of future projects and free stuff at www.broganthomas.com

Your email will be kept 100% private, and you can unsubscribe at any time, zero spam.

P.P.S. I would love to hear from you, so come and say hello on Facebook: www.facebook.com/ BroganThomasBooks

I try to respond to all messages, so don't hesitate to drop me a line at: Brogan@broganthomas.com

ABOUT THE AUTHOR

Brogan lives in Ireland with her husband and their eleven furry children: five furry minions of darkness (aka the cats), four hellhounds (the dogs), and two traditional unicorns (fat, hairy Irish cobs).

In 2019 she decided to embrace her craziness by writing about the imaginary people that live in her head. Her first love is her ~~husband~~ number-one favourite furry child Bob the cob, then reading. When not reading or writing, she can be found knee-deep in horse poo and fur while blissfully ignoring all adult responsibilities.